> Andrew said to Him,
> "There is a boy
> here who has five
> barley loaves and
> two fishes; but
> what is that among
> so many?"
>
> John 6:9

a boy
& his lunch

KENNETH G. OLD

TATE PUBLISHING & *Enterprises*

Tate Publishing
& Enterprises

The recent stories told in this book are as true as fallible memory permits. Where possible and appropriate, they have been checked with individuals involved in them. Names of people and places have sometimes been changed. Immaterial details of the stories themselves have also sometimes been altered.

Where material written by others has been quoted, it also may have been slightly changed, but the basic content and meaning have been retained.

Royalties from the sale of this book are dedicated to the education of poor Punjabi children

Dedicated to

All of us who feel
we are too small
to make a difference

The Ant and the Elephant

The ant said to the elephant:
I'll push too, every little helps
- And the tree fell over!

Only the elephant was surprised.

Table of Contents

a boy & his lunch

Map of Central Asia

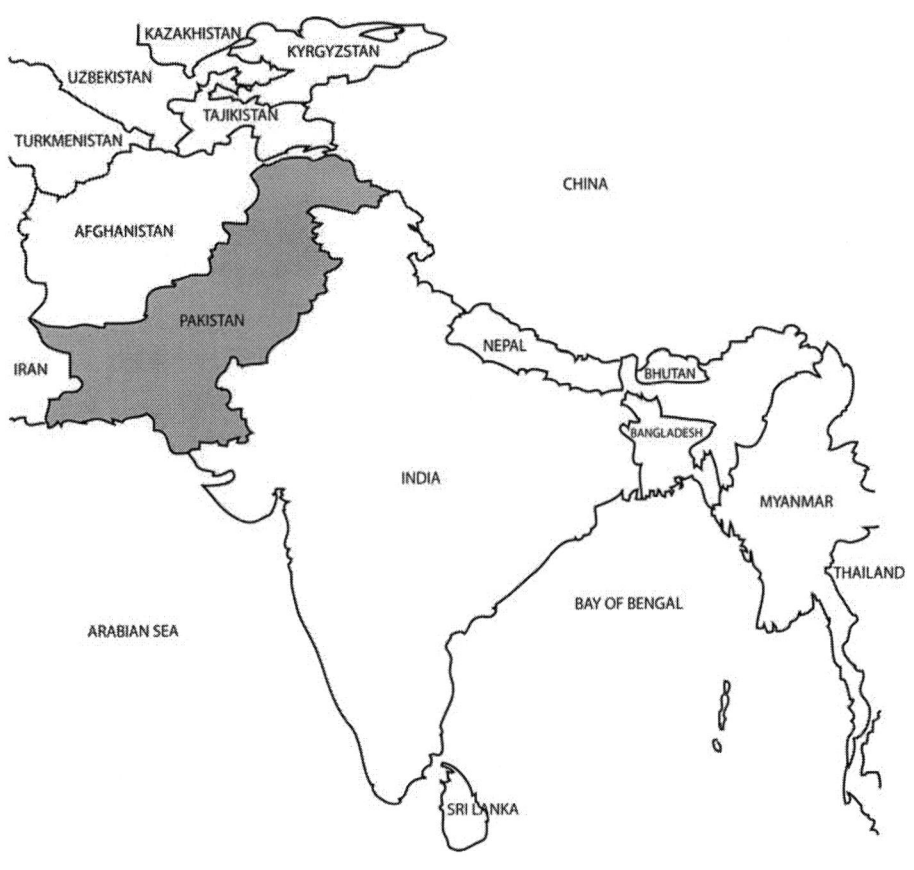

Many of the stories that follow are set in Pakistan. This country, separated from India in 1947 and broken into two parts by internal division in 1971, is an Islamic state. In it, along with a smaller Hindu minority, the two communities, Muslim and Christian, live together, sometimes—but not always—uneasily. Christians make up two to three percent of the population. The population of Pakistan is now about 150 million.

This book is a miscellany of reflections and recollections. Some are just stories that I deem worth the telling. The various tales that follow are not always in chronological order, and some reach back a long way. They are framed, however, within a basic assumption that God is at work in the twenty-first century as much as He ever was in the first century, whether we see it or not. Whatever we as individuals can contribute in changing our world for the better in our own time helps. After all, it is His Kingdom we want to come on earth, or so we pray.

A man I know locally lives by the LIBTYFI principle: "Leave it better than you found it." When he goes for a walk, he takes a plastic bag into which he places garbage carelessly thrown by others; he takes hedge clippers to cut away brambles encroaching on footpaths, and in other quiet and unobtrusive ways seeks to leave the world a little bit better than before he made today's journey. It's hardly earth shattering, but it's a small step in the right direction. It doesn't take money, just being sensitive and responsive to the world around us. The very little that we can offer God from our own resources of character and courage and innovation and invention and interaction and passion and personality and possessions, He can take and use and even perhaps turn into a modern-day miracle.

This book is not about divinely ordered congruencies helping organize our scattered goodness. It is more about interesting people met on the way as we travel together. It tells how He uses people to accomplish His purposes, and it follows some of their journeys.

I wonder if Mrs. Patras ever stopped you in your tracks as you were hurrying across the terminal building in one of many airports between Lahore and San Francisco. You are racing for your departure gate when an elderly woman in simple, Asian garb thrusts towards you a letter she has been holding in her hand.

Mrs. Patras is the very Punjabi wife of our storekeeper at the Technical Training Centre in Gujranwala in Pakistan. I can't understand her Urdu very well, and her Punjabi leaves me no wiser than before. I doubt if she has traveled more than a few miles from the most direct route between her village and Gujranwala. Of all the staff wives, she is far and away the most Punjabi.

One day she and her family come to me. They have solved all the problems relating to the journey they've planned for her, and now they merely want to know how Momma is to travel safely to San Francisco to visit her son there. He has been ill. She will be traveling alone. They show me her passport and the visa and the airline ticket from Lahore to San Francisco. There are changes of plane in Europe and New York. Her son will meet her at the airport in California in a few days time. What do I need to do to make sure she arrives safely?

Their complete confidence that I can somehow arrange this is almost unnerving.

They wait patiently while I type a letter something along the following lines on the school letterhead paper:

Dear Friend,

> *This woman, who has accosted you with this letter, has chosen you to help her. She speaks not a word of your language, but she needs your help and thinks you will further her on her way.*
>
> *She is joining a son who is sick in San Francisco, and she leaves Lahore in Pakistan alone and trusting to God that strangers along the way like yourself will bring her to her destination.*
>
> *You will be busy and in a hurry. Nevertheless, please take a few moments to look at her tickets, see where next she needs to go along her journey and help her along the way in the place where you now are. You may have to take her by the hand.*
>
> *May God bless you for this act of kindness to a stranger.*

After anxious days, Mr. Patras reports to me that his wife has arrived safely in San Francisco. There have been no problems anywhere along the way.

She stays in San Francisco many months.

When next I see her, years later, she comes for a replacement letter. I take the original letter from her. It is grubby and is coming apart at the seams. She has clearly used it for other journeys besides the one for which it has been written. For her, the key to getting from one place to another is that letter. That she has her passport, the visa and the airline tickets is scarcely relevant. It is the letter that matters. It never failed.

Hurrying passersby would stop in the airport concourse, turn in their tracks, tuck their briefcases under their arms and take her luggage in their hands instead, take her other bemused hand gently and lead her where she

a boy and his lunch

needed to go. There they would pass her on to someone else who knew what she should next do.

I make her a fresh copy with the same wording and keep the grubby original as a keepsake and a reminder of the genuine human gentleness within a world that is usually far too busy to show it possesses it. The thought of that letter brings tears to my eyes. It was a passport into the genuine human love and kindness within our common humanity, and it was God, using perhaps you—and you without knowing—to bring an old Punjabi stranger to her destination halfway across the world.

It is the way God works, using ordinary people like us to bring about good ends.

There is a little more to add. Most of the stories that follow are stories of a holy tenderness moderating our self-centeredness and working as a leaven within our modern world, that of

an uncommon love
cutting its gentle way
through the wilderness
of man's dark night.

These are stories of courage and often of the power of generous friendship. Hopefully you will occasionally glimpse back beyond the goodness that ordinary people, churchgoers or not, have and share. Hopefully, too, you will recognize the Author behind the concurrences and holy conspiracies that enrich our lives and the lives of those dear to us and perhaps even beyond to those we shall never hear about.

Life is a huge puzzle of the three linear dimensions and time falling like snow in a snowstorm, and all the flakes falling like solid multi-faceted puzzle pieces, each into its perfect designed place to make a composite whole where the purposes of an omniscient, omnipotent God finally are perfected. Somehow you, we, are involved in the process!

Jeanne Dillner of the SIGN organization writes on her return from helping the earthquake victims in Pakistan:

Once you get involved in a project like this your faith is tested and becomes very real. You begin to see just how much God is in control, how He brings the right people to you just when you need it . . . and that you can let Him create the flow.

Yes, that's just it! It is like getting a new pair of spectacles after years of near-sightedness. Suddenly you are seeing things as they really are, not as you thought they were.

This book is intended to encourage you along your own way as you seek more and more to blend it with the way that He would desire you to take.

Introduction

All the words which the Lord hath said we will do. Exodus 24:3

God is the great communicator. He speaks, and, if we are listening carefully, we hear and respond. Just as Moses started out from Midian back to Egypt with the only resources to make a difference lying within himself and his relationship to God, so it is with us in the twenty-first century. The intended consequence of our Christian faith is that we become God's handiwork—changed, charged and enabled to accomplish the *"good deeds for which He has designed us."* We are not our own nor are we on our own. Each and every day is charged with expectancy. God's reliability and purpose translates itself through us into human action in insignificant ways often brought to completion in an awesome surprise.

Once we accept this premise and the challenge that goes with it, we acquire a different perspective on life. We look around, prepared to be surprised. Things around us fall into place in a different way. Emphases and priorities change. There are times to engage, and also times to disengage, even from apparently fruitful activity.

Interventions appear out of nowhere that cause us to deviate from our course and bring unexpected results. Coincidences become divinely planned events (sometimes, not always). Short-term encounters bear fruit decades later. Casual, apparently insignificant conversations acquire, for some, life changing significance. Congruencies between events, geography and people wandering their apparent random way through life become something more, a network linked by an intervening and interconnecting holiness.

We recognize divine directions and also, to our surprise, that we ourselves are walking on a footpath to the Infinite more clearly marked than we had earlier dared suppose or hope.

God, if we accept that He exists, sees and knows our potential long before we ourselves are awake to the possibilities within us. He doesn't give up on us when we fail to make the grade but continues alongside us, suiting His counsel to our changing circumstances. He has the patience of eternity, and He knows us better than we know ourselves.

It goes without saying that He communicates with us in a variety of ways.

He communicates with us most visibly perhaps when we are in a group or a congregation worshipping and praising Him. He communicates with us when we are experiencing calamities common to man and in other shared experiences.

He also communicates with us as individuals, one-to-one, as though we, just the two of us, are sitting together on a lonely park bench. This is the thrilling encounter that sets us jumping to our feet and searching in our minds where we have never searched before.

God speaks to us for many different reasons. He may want to send us on an errand. He may want to stop us in our tracks. He may want to admonish and correct us. He may want to encourage us. He may want to forbid us to take a certain step or challenge us about one we contemplate. Again He may want us merely to take the next step forward in a successive line of actions and consequences that will bring us to where He wants us to be.

Whatever the reason, He wants to guide our steps into harmony with His own purposes for us. There is not one of us to whom He is not saying, "Come up higher!"

He also speaks to us in different ways. He speaks to us directly and He speaks to us indirectly.

When He speaks to us directly, it is not necessarily with an audible voice picked up, apparently, by our ears, although that sometimes happens. More often, He speaks to us within prayer, in the silences when we are listening for responses, and during the times when our hearts are engaged in the study of Scripture or in similar pursuits focused upon Him and not upon ourselves. He often speaks to us through the nature around us.

At other times, God speaks to us through intermediaries, heavenly or human, that He chooses to use. Some of them are unlikely messengers. They may have no idea of the divine connection. Often it is only hindsight that reveals how they have been used in the furtherance of divine purposes. Words spoken well and wisely and in "due season" have an uncommon reaching and lasting power.

It is likely that God has spoken to you both directly and indirectly, and equally likely that, perhaps to your surprise, you have been the intermediary between Him and others. When you begin to suspect that any of these events has happened, continue to explore how and what happened. You are on the verge of a leap forward in your understanding of the way He works and one more step on the journey moving from receiving the word of God for yourself to communicating it to others as a co-communicator with God.

The lesson for all of us is simple. If we want to hear God more than we have been hearing thus far, then we should put ourselves, and keep putting ourselves, where we are most likely to hear Him, and then listen carefully. Too often we cannot hear what He is saying because there is too much noise right where we are. It helps if we are on our toes. We can live expectantly at all times, recognizing there may well be an unseen hand guiding our feet, even down cul-de-sacs.

If you're really anxious to know
What your God has to say to you
You may have to slip from the flow
Of your friends who haven't a clue
And find some other place to go,
Even, perhaps, to a church pew.

There is a compelling aspect to the way God works in our own day and age and in some kind of mysterious cooperation with us. He has His purposes for others besides ourselves, and, if we are compliant and willing, He will use us to help effect them. Sometimes He will send us on apparently useless and abortive journeys to bring about some unrecognized consequence. Something we say or do may be a critical factor in someone else's journey, although it may never be known or recognized by us. Sometimes we find out our part in the story only years later. It's the way He works.

Prologue

Almost sixty years ago, I made my first trip to India, on a troopship at the expense of the British army. We landed in Bombay, spent some time in Poona, and traveled to Rawalpindi in the northwest. Eventually, I, a young engineer officer, received orders to go to South Waziristan, a part of the North-West Frontier Province. This was not far from the border with Afghanistan. I loved the country, and I loved the people. I had found a place that rivaled Cornwall as a place to call home.

Later, at the close of 1949, a voice in the night gave a message to a civil engineering student in Plymouth, Devon.

It was probably about 2:30 am. I was suddenly awake, alertly awake. I listened intently. What had wakened me?

I could see the moonlight coming through the window, but my portion of the room was in shadow. Someone, someone unseen, was standing at the right hand side of my bed, two or three feet away. I could see nothing of or about the visitor. I just knew he was there.

A voice spoke, a man's voice, a normal voice, no dialect to notice but positive and firm in tone. Loud enough to hear easily. It was a statement, not a question.

"Ken, God has a purpose for your life. He is going to put you to work in a land that is not your own land, amongst people of a different color and race and culture and creed, and He is going to put you to work amongst boys and He is going to bring it to pass."

In 1953, I returned again to the sub-continent as a civil engineer with an indigenous engineering company. My three-year contract turned into a period of thirty-seven years.

During this time, I met Marie, an American missionary nurse who had recently lost her beloved Mac to a sudden and unexpected illness. A year later, Marie and I married and shortly thereafter adopted two sons. For much of the time, we lived in the Punjab as missionaries of a fellowship known as the Sialkot Mission.

This missionary society was established in northern India a couple of years before what is known as the Indian mutiny of 1857. Its principal area of work was the Punjab, the land of the five rivers, the fertile plains where the waters of the rivers issuing from the Himalayas were set to work.

My initial journey to and within Pakistan took twenty years. It culminated in a reluctant appointment to a boys' technical school in the Punjab province, where we served a further twenty years until retirement.

Some of the stories that follow are set within the framework of life as a missionary. This book is, however, only incidentally a story about missions.

The word "missionary" is taken to imply spiritual division and an attempt at reconciliation—Christians bringing their particular understanding of God into an alien situation and attempting, with the aid of the Holy Spirit, to bring others of different faith and behavior into harmony with their own.

In practice, it's not like that. We are strangers meeting; listening; accepting that truth flows both ways, not just one way; learning from each other, not condemning; seeking to understand; asking and responding; and, on both sides, letting our faith live and speak for itself.

Just to be there, being ourselves—that is enough. Truth has its own way of speaking, and example is a wonderful teacher.

We spent the last years in a town called Gujranwala in the Punjab of Pakistan, forty odd miles from Lahore. It has about a million people and one traffic light, which most of the time seems not to work. We were involved in community development and in the education of boys in craft skills at the Christian Technical Training Centre.

Our home church was initially the United Presbyterian Church of North America, but this merged into and became part of the Presbyterian Church USA.

We retired in 1990; Marie was 75 and had been in Pakistan 43 years. Three years later, her breast cancer returned, and in 1997 she died.

We had loved each other very much, and I felt that before I followed her, my work, too, was done; I should try to record something of her life. I applied myself to writing her—our—story and, over time, completed the task.

However, my own journey was, to my surprise, not yet done, and as I write, eight years after her death, the pace of the journey seems to be accelerating rather than slowing.

My thoughts are not your thoughts,
neither are your ways my ways,
saith the Lord.
For as the heavens are higher than the earth,
so are my ways higher than your ways,
and my thoughts than your thoughts.
For as the rain cometh down, and the snow from heaven,
and returneth not thither, but watereth the earth,
. . . so shall my word be that goeth forth out of my mouth:
it shall not return unto me void,
but it shall accomplish that which I please,
and it shall prosper in the thing whereto I sent it.

Isaiah 55: 8–11

Although I lived in England in a lovely old Tudor farmhouse in Kent, with no intention of ever again venturing beyond the nearest town, I had a whirlwind courtship in November of 1998 connecting two other continents. It took all of twelve days. You will read about it. As though this had all been worked out long beforehand, my new wife then took a leading role in creating from my rough work the books that were to follow.

In *Walking The Way* I tried to describe some experiences Marie and I had shared together and, in the process, what we had learned about God and the way He works.

Since then several other books have evolved, and I have also discovered I have an illness that will undoubtedly limit my days.

There is inevitably an increasing urgency to complete unfinished work.

This morning, while drinking tea in bed and discussing the amazing ways of God, both Patty and I realized there is yet another book to be written—about how patiently He works through the tiny and insignificant and through little and ordinary people to achieve good and sometimes great things.

The journey that *Walking The Way* described did not end with the conclusion of that book. There is not only a sequence yet to complete, but there are spaces of life in Pakistan left to fill in more adequately. This companion volume, which seeks to fill some of the gaps as well as extend the story, we decided to call *A Boy and His Lunch*. Read on.

Gibbins Brook Farm, September 2005

A Whisper in the Wind

Hold on!
Keep holding on!
He knows what is to come
And intervenes
Beyond the reach of dreams.
Beyond the Plan He has for you,

Further far than you can see
He sings His future song.

Demands compliance with His Holy Will.
Commands the massing clouds be gone
The future winds be still.

Beyond your grasp or deepest sense
All things random and by chance
He captures into congruence.

While trickles back so far behind
To the Now wherein you stand
Only a whisper in the wind
To say the Years are in His hand

And He is not asleep!

a boy and his lunch

A Choice to Make

Fall 1997, Sellindge, Kent

Less than two weeks ago, Joseph Lall wrote to me from Taxila Hospital in Pakistan, which lies between Islamabad, the capital, and the Indus River to the west in the northern Punjab. Joseph and his three brothers have been good friends over many years. He invited me to return to Taxila to supervise the installation of a water reclamation scheme.

I am a civil engineer. I have worked in Taxila and its adjacent city of Wah on and off over the past forty years. I love Taxila. Mac is buried there. Marie and I were married there. Our boys, Tim and Colin, spent early years there. I know that I would be happy there.

And yet!

Up till Jo's letter, I had no thought of returning to Pakistan. I know that this Taxila task would lead to others, and I could see out my days there, and see them out in useful service.

But there is another factor. Twenty-five years ago, God delightfully gave Marie and me one of His surprises—a wonderful, fifteenth century, half-timbered farmhouse in the English countryside, isolated at the end of a path across the common. Lonely we were, yet at the same time we were surrounded by other family members in a warm and loving community. We returned to Gibbins Brook from the United States in 1993 as soon as Marie's diagnosis was confirmed. Strangely, even with the constant awareness and effects of the encroaching cancer, our happiness deepened and our joy, not only in each other, increased. Neither Marie nor I wanted any other place to live for the rest of our lives.

Now that Marie is gone, I have been asking for clear guidance on how to respond to Jo.

It seems to have come in distinct steps.

The first was an absolute, although reluctant, readiness to give up the loveliness of the farm and return to Pakistan. I have been getting my passport renewed and working out the earliest date I could leave. Tim and Colin have both affirmed I should go back. Pakistan is not only my home, it is theirs as well, and they have warned me to expect them to visit.

My scripture readings this morning have emphasized this message: *Go in the strength of the Lord; He will not leave you nor forsake you.*

However, from conversations, from Scripture and other readings and from prayer, I have been realizing that we look back even as we prepare to go forward. Jesus said: *"No man, having put his hand to the plough, and looking back, is fit for the kingdom of God."* Then, before we put our hand to the plough, it behooves us to look around well, including behind us.

It is in looking back that I have been discovering something: that the major activities that occupied our missionary days in Pakistan were probably less significant on the divine canvas than some of the minor, incidental, extracurricular activities that seemed to slip across our paths almost unnoticeably.

Marie's most significant single action during her life over forty-three years in Pakistan was, I think, sending a little girl of about twelve years of age—the child of a servant—to boarding school. That little girl's name was Zeb Zaman.

Mine was, I think, urging a woman who lived in Wah Cottage a few miles along the road from Taxila to keep a spiritual journal that later became the foundation of the book *I Dared to Call Him Father*.

It became increasingly clear that for me, too, there was a book to be written, and it should not wait. Whatever might then follow, this should have first claim upon my time.

Later

I have enjoyed the discipline of recollection and the refreshment of recaptured memories. The need to verify what I remembered has renewed lapsed contacts with friends in several countries. The book I visualized has become, in the process of writing, more than a single volume. Alongside these gathered memories is an almost incidental collection of stories with the same setting but less personal in nature. We called this book *So Great A Cloud*.

A Boy and His Lunch

First amongst the stories I tell is one of long ago, about a little boy and his lunch. It is quite a long story, somewhat like a poem, so put your feet up.

Right from the start,
  From the very beginning,
    It was an unusual morning,
      From the moment he opened his eyes
      The morning was sparkling
      And smelt of adventure
        And off-on-your-own kind of things
          That somehow smelt different and better
          'Cos, just for this time,
          Your grownups aren't along
          Ready to raise a song
          If things go wrong—
          It was that kind of a morning to wake up in.

He didn't have to be wakened up,
                not today
Do you ever wake up like that?
  Saturday, no school. Yippee,
    The sun shines and says, "Howjado
      Come on out," instead of,
        "Hey, Giddup, you'll be late for school."

Boy had a string of names,
  He was the only one,
    The only son and likely no other
      So they strung him a line of names
        As long as your arm might be
        But no matter, no one used them
          He was just Boy—"Hey Boy," "Slowdown, Boy,"
          "Whereyuhoffto Boy?"

Up the hill from the lake,
On the west side of the lake he dwelt,
And on this beautiful morning

As he pulled on his clothes without any urging
And his dog crept under his bed
Because of the haste
And the scrambling around him,
Boy could see through the window
The crowd of folks gathering way below,
Way way below on the quayside,
Where the boats were moored.

Behind them, on blue water,
 White clouds are reflecting,
  Having a sports day
   Playing and jumping,
    Tumbling their high jinks
     And tag games way off
      In the blue sky
       Above the brown mountains.

"Now, Boy, you can't go until ..."
- Hear mother chatter on
- You know the list, it's ...
"Do up your shoe lace,
   Pull up your socks,
     Wash your face
       Comb your hair
         Don't gallop your food
           Where's your hanky
             Don't sniffle your nose
               Don't forget your lunch
                 Be polite to your elders
                   Be home by dark
                     Your buttons are crooked!"
                                    Parents! Honestly

But at last all is done
 And like a dutiful son
   Boy kisses his mother
     And hears not a word
       Of the warnings she utters
         Of water and strangers and ...
             But no matter, he's not hearing it anyway.

a boy and his lunch

And Dad, who loved Boy
More than he ever could
Put into words
Just patted his boy's head,
And his eyes filled with tears
Of loving, it hurt so,
Loving this boy, his heart and his hope,
As out through the door
And down the rough hillside
The boy like a whirlwind was off
Chasing his dog way ahead.

Boy scampered on, but not far
For he heard the yell his Dad uttered
Turned round on a penny
Or perhaps two or three
While ahead his dog skidded on four paws
Splayed out wide.
Mother in the doorway
Waves his lunch bag, almost left it behind,
And a towel to dry himself with
In case he falls in
As boys are like enough to do.

                                   Boys, honestly.

Off again now,
 Arms, legs, head, shoulders
  All moving disjointedly
   The way boys do when they come running
                            And waving
                            And yelling
                            And shouting
                            And jumping ditches
                            And climbing fences
                                  Older and wiser legs would
                                  have avoided.

At last on the quay-side
Where the boats have a meeting
And the crowd is still gathering
To hear the young preacher
From over the hill.

Oh how he goes on and oh
The brouhaha oh haha
As he tells them of marriage feasts
                    And marketplaces
                    And mustard seeds
                    And moneylenders
                    And mending garments
                    And mercies and blessings
                    For those who believe
Oh, the crowd loves him so
 As he goes on and on so.
  And they all laugh with him
   And weep with him
    They won't rest him or leave him
                    Till at last he says he must go,
                    Much though he'd like to stay
                    And drops himself down to a boat
                    That's just pulled alongside the quay.

And as the boat pulls away
He waves his farewell
And the sails fill out
As he moves from the lea
Of the quay
Crowded with people,
And, among them, a boy and his dog.

                    But still they'll not leave him go
                    And, guessing he'll make for the far shore
                    They run north round the lake to hear more

On foot and on asses and horses
While others more wealthy
Or more slow and laggardly
(Or more sized like a boy)
Importune boatmen and fishermen
To cast off without waiting for others.

                    A fleet of boats follows now—
                    The one far ahead of them,
                    Each other deep to the gunnels with people
                    Watching the sails filling out

a boy and his lunch

Leaning back now and relaxing
And way up in one of them,
Right up in the bow
The place God made for boys in boats,
Boy perches twixt others
The size of himself
With his dog twixt his feet
Sniffing the air and scuffing his paws
Trying to say by his look oh so knowing
He knows like the others just where they are going.

And now the lovely long pull 'cross the lake
With the wind abeam
In the sail's fullest reaching.
There are other boys, too,
With fathers alongside
And occasional mothers and sisters
Mixed in.
As the rippling of water
Laps farther and faster
Out come the lunch bags of those who remembered
But Boy pays no attention to hunger—
He's fishing.

Under the lea of the hills at last
Pace slows, the breeze softens.
Down lake, boats are tacking to come up toward them
But they are on course
To ground on the beach
Where the people have gathered.

Not from boats only
But from both sides,
At the foot of the hills,
Converge groups of people,
Scores of them, nay hundreds
Nay, even more than that, thousands—
Families, friends or just-met-today groups of people
All come together
For one special reason
Like a huge picnic (without any food)
Or a convention for electing a president

Or a '76 celebration
Way off below the hills,
Flanking the lakeside,
Roughing it kind of.

And now they have gathered
And continue to gather
In the lap of the hills,
Hills like great thighs resting each side of them
Sitting in rows where the stewards have placed them
On grass that has thickened greenly and softly
From the last recent raining.
And in there amongst them
Up in the front row in fact
Has wriggled our boy, perspiring and happy
And with him a scruffy, old, know-all brown mongrel.

And now comes the moment
That in the Book we have read about
And in our hearts we have thought about
And wondered just how about,
If it's all true like it says,
It all came about.
Now listen!

'Twas Andrew the brother of Peter, we know him,
Who came to Boy first as he sat
With the others just waiting
For things to get moving
The way kids always have to wait
When grownups are organizing
Anything, just anything.
Kids can do things so much faster
If only grownups would let them!

There always has to be lots of waiting
So to use up time, you make eyes at others
And strange faces
And see if you can wiggle your ears
And scribble short notes
And make paper darts
And wriggle and fidget

a boy and his lunch

Or untie knots in your fishing line.

There must be an evil spirit in string sometimes
The way it knots up and tangles
And tightens till teeth cannot loosen it
And the way it wraps itself round towels
And wrapped barley cakes
And two little fishes
Re-netted and throttled by string.

So Boy had everything out on his lap,
Blind to all going on around him
When Andrew, quite worried, goes by, looks down,
Sees what is there and grins,
Remembering when he, too, was a boy,
And goes and talks to the Preacher nearby
Who says, "Fine, tell them all to sit down
I reckon 'tis time we are going to dine."

'Twas late when Boy
Reached back to his home
The moon swung its light
O'er the lake like a lantern
As the boats one by one
Crept back to the quay
And nestled up close.
And the moon lit the way
For a small boy to clamber
Uphill with his dog
With a wet towel on his shoulder
And his shoes and his line in his bag.

"Well, what happened then?"
It's mother who questions.
Tho' tis late she can't wait
Till the morning to ask.
Dad sits in his seat
By the window,
Looking out over the lake,
Where he's been
The last couple of hours, looking,
But the cock of his head

KENNETH G. OLD   35

Shows he's catching
Every word the boy utters.

And Boy answers now
Like a kid might do
Unveiling surprises galore
As gifts from his store
For small brothers and sisters
Around him at Christmas time.

"Then Jesus walked over to where I was sitting
And looked down at my line
All tangled and twisted
And the barley cakes you'd baked
Just yesterday, Mom,
And the fishes
And said in a nice kind of way
'Boy, will you help me, no, don't rise,
The folk all are hungry
Can you share your bread with us, please?'

"Gee, Mom, guess that, he wanted your bread
The bread you baked yesterday
So I gave him the bread,
Yes, all of it, and the two fishes, too
And he said 'Thank you, Boy'
(Do you think he knew my name, Mom?)
And gave them to the man with the platter beside him
And patted my head
And 'God bless you,' he said."

"And what then?"
"Patience, wife, let the boy drink,
He's parched.
Take your time, Boy,
Just don't miss out a thing."
Both of them, loving so much this small lad,
Wrapt in his tale,
Unfolding its grandeur
Caught up in wonder
And wondering quite who

a boy and his lunch

This Jesus might be.
And Boy, refreshed, carries on:
"And then Jesus, he raised up his hands
And a hush seemed to fall
On the people, the children and all
And the talking all stopped
And those who were moving
On paths at the back paused
And he took back the platter
From the man that was holding it
And gave thanks for the food
Just like we do here at home
Except that he spoke to Jehovah
In a strange and wonderful way
As though Jehovah was father-
Like you, Dad, to me—
And His Father was here
Amongst us today.

"And then he divided the loaves and the fishes
And shared them among the men
Who seemed to be with him
Standing around, just waiting
To know what to do
And they broke off pieces of bread
And shared them amongst the people,
Amongst the men and the women and children.

"They went down the rows,
Breaking off bits of the bread and the fishes
Sharing them row by row
Right to the back
Till everybody had some
And Mom, Dad, I don't know how it happened
And p'raps you won't believe me
But really and truly it's true
There was enough for everyone sitting
And even for them
Who were standing behind us
And lots left over besides
Baskets and baskets left over
And everybody was full.

KENNETH G. OLD

37

I had all that I could eat
And so did everyone else.
　　　　"And then … and then
　　　　　When the people saw what had happened
　　　　　　Out of the fishes and the bread that you made, Mom,
　　　　Before he had chance to start speaking, they began
　Like the sound
　　As the breeze rustles
　　　The leaves of the trees,
　　　　Gathering strength for a storm
　　　　　Coming up off the lake,
　　　　　So they began
　　　　　　Whispering and murmuring, then talking
　　　　　And calling and shouting and jumping
　　　　　　That this was a miracle
　　　　　　　　　　And Jesus was a prophet
　　　　　　　　　　And He was a King
　　　　　　　　　　And—"

"That's enough for now, Boy"
Mother cut in to stay the lad
Bright-eyed and excited.
"It's late and you're tired
The day has been long
The rest can wait for tomorrow
There's time enough then.
Off to bed, sleepyhead."

　　　　　　　　　And as the boy, sleepy-eyed
　　　　　　　　　With the song in his heart
　　　　　　　　　Slowing to a lullaby
　　　　　　　　　Climbed off to bed
　　　　　　　　　She murmured to his father,
　　　　　　　　　Soft in her tone,
　　　　　　　　　"He's been gone too long,
　　　　　　　　　Been out all day
　　　　　　　　　It's a touch of the sun."
　　　　　　　　　And she was right in her way

It was a touch,
A touch of the Son, not the sun.

　　　　　　　　　　　　　　　　　a boy and his lunch

Offer What You Have

And you will wonder about this story you have just read and why I tell it
    About a boy so long ago.
        We don't even know his name
            But he has something to show us
As one morning he opened his eyes to a new day
    And went out to a new place
        Full of opportunities and uncertainties
         And temptations
           And crowded with people,
                Many of them—most of them—strangers.

For this story is an encouragement to us who can do or can give only little to Him who guides us all or to others in the company traveling with us along the Way:
    Let's look a little closer at him
        As he crosses our path for a fraction of time.
           We have hardly even noticed him before,
               For he is overshadowed by events around
               him.

Notice these things about him:

He went out from a loving home, from parents who cared for and loved him and hedged him in until he was strong enough to stand the wind by himself.

He went out prepared. Others didn't.

He took with him solid food, food with goodness in it. He had no idea how much he would be able to nourish others just by being where he was that day.

He went out full of expectation and found even more than he expected.

He found Jesus not in the solitude that dreamers crave but in the middle of a crowd of people needing help.

He avoided the temptations and distractions along the way . . . Come on Boy - let's go fishing! He wanted to get as close as he could to Jesus.

He was in the right place at the right time.

He was there when he was needed and held nothing back to nourish his own hunger. He handed over his need as well as his food. And Jesus didn't forget him and met his need, too.

He gave an immediate response, didn't vacillate or temporize as we adults are prone to do.

Jesus didn't ask for more than he had to give, but He did ask for all that he had.

Jesus took the little from a boy and made it a feast for thousands.

What a way to startle the day!

There are many lessons this boy can teach us as we reflect upon this story.

We each carry into our encounters with God things He can transform if we will just give them to Him to use. Our gifts, whatever they are—tangible or intangible, physical, moral and spiritual—are brought into interaction with the needs of others. Sometimes even miracles are born.

He challenges us to be vulnerable, yet doesn't forget our own needs when we make ourselves vulnerable for His sake.

He doesn't ask for more than we have, but He does ask whether we are willing to give all that we have.

Faced by difficult choices, we may look back later saying, "If only I had" or "If only I were" or "If only I could." But Christ doesn't want to hear "If only I . . ." He asks us to give whatever we have, asks for it right now and then puts it to work.

There are these points, too, from the story:

1. The story is simple, uncomplicated. Whatever convolutions in faith we may have followed in our own journey, this story is simple. Jesus asked. The boy gave. A miracle resulted.

2. The hungry crowd is a microcosm of a world in need, the crucible of the Kingdom. Jesus takes another micro—the boy's lunch—and feeds everyone there full and running over.

a boy and his lunch

Everyone in the crowd had a need. Jesus knew that and was able to meet each need.

Are the needs and burdens that we are carrying or facing any bigger than the need on that hillside that day?

3. Every day, if we have eyes to see, we are seeing small people giving small gifts to God and God taking them and enlarging them and turning them into good, like the gifts of individual skills and compassion and active concern given by ordinary people made and being made extraordinary. People like Albert Schweitzer in Lambarene and Mother Teresa in Calcutta and George Verwer and Loren Cunningham and Cameron Townsend and Paul Brand and Norval Christy and Pramila Lall and Lew Zirkle and Phill Shorter and a hundred scattered others. Among this list your name could be and perhaps is.

Jesus takes the boy's bread, and it becomes the intercession between Him and his Father; and then the bread itself becomes the response of God between Him and the people.

He didn't lift up empty hands. He needed the seed of a miracle, and the boy provided it to him.

Lew and His Nails

Richland, Washington 2005

Lew Zirkle is a kindly, enthusiastic man in a local setting, and he is in a hurry. I guess he is in his late fifties or early sixties. I can't see the word retirement ever fitting this human dynamo.

There are not enough hours in his day. I met him first at West Side Church, which we visited on furlough, and then we spent three years there immediately after retirement. Our friendship with and appreciation for this remarkable man grew with longer acquaintance. He has a passion to share Jesus Christ, he teaches a regular Bible class in church, and he has a passion to help people, particularly poor and needy people. The two passions are indistinguishable from each other.

Lew is a local doctor—an orthopedic surgeon—and he is loved and admired by the people amongst whom he lives and works. But his passion is for a different world, the whole world, a larger hurting world. And he is out to change it. It started almost forty years ago, and now the huge sphere on which we live is beginning to rock just a little.

It began when Lew was in the U.S. Army Medical Corps in Vietnam. His primary assignment was to treat the surgical needs of the military casualties. However, that still left him with occasional spare time, and this he put to good use treating civilian casualties of the bombing and fighting. Some superior officers were not happy with this diversion of military resources, but the commanding general overruled them. In fighting to win the minds of the people, Captain Zirkle was possibly doing more than the whole military machine was achieving. Let him continue what he is doing, and don't stand in his way.

Lew was dealing with bone fractures of every kind, from simple, clean, one-break fractures to trying to repair bones reduced to a multitude of shattered fragments. Under the pressure of his environment, his practical skills developed rapidly.

After the war ended, Lew didn't just settle back into developing his orthopedic practice. The pictures of Vietnam haunted him, and he shared his concerns with his wife, Sara. She also is a doctor. Was there anything they could do?

The wealthy could buy the treatment they needed. What about the poor? They could afford nothing, yet surely their need was greater. One breadwinner in a bicycle accident, out of action because of a broken leg, could mean starvation or near-starvation for a whole family.

During breaks away from his practice, Lew would return to Vietnam, to Ho Chi Minh City, and work in the hospitals there, training young doctors. They carried no resentment because he was an American but were only keen to learn all this kindly foreign man could teach them. Each time he went, he took equipment and supplies with him. He knew all the while he was only touching the fringe of a huge abyss of human need. But every little bit helps, and at least he was doing something.

The time required to permit such bone fractures to heal could run into months, even years. Many bones inadequately treated would heal out of alignment, leaving physical deformation for the remainder of a person's life. Lew was horrified to find, on one of his return trips to Indonesia, a man who had been lying in traction for three years because of lack of an implant to fix his fracture. Checking further, he found that the whole ward was filled with patients in traction with similar stories. The families of patients had to find the money to pay for the implants their relative needed, and often that money was not available.

If only there were a better way to ensure that broken bones healed in the correct alignment and that also, somehow, the weakness of a break could be bridged over during the long period of healing. That way, the limb could remain mobile and active and function almost normally. The breadwinner could resume work while the healing was still going on.

All the time his mind was active. There must be a better way. That better way was to be achieved not by a sudden, huge leap in knowledge in a startling breakthrough, but by a thousand little increments that extended the knowledge and experience that he already had.

Lew knew what he was after: a simpler method of fixing broken bones. He wasn't sure it was achievable, but he would do the best he could. What would be needed was a stainless steel rod ("nail") of the highest surgical quality and the minimum feasible diameter. When drilled near its ends with threaded holes, it could be implanted for life in the canal (marrow) of the broken bone. The IM (intramedullary) nail would need, if necessary, to be long enough to bridge across even a complicated multiple fracture from robust bone to robust bone. It would need, if it were a broken tibia (leg bone) or femur (hipbone), to be strong enough to carry the weight of the human body. The broken limb would be brought into correct alignment and the break brought as close as possible to zero. Then a pair of slender screws, painstakingly designed to extremely close tolerances to lock on final closure without needing a securing nut on the far side, would be tightened by the surgeon before closing up the open wound.

a boy and his lunch

Would it be possible to devise a system of placement that would not require the use of monitoring X-ray machines, which often were simply not available? Surely ingenuity could devise a way. It did. A very accurate measuring clamp fixed external to the limb guided the interlocking screws accurately into position to meet the prepared holes in the nail.

At the same time, the growth of the Internet was gathering force to help Lew achieve a product where use could be reported to and monitored on a worldwide database, enabling surgeons across the world to have entry into a shared project where everyone's experience could be valuable to others. Questions could be responded to immediately over e-mail.

There were various difficulties to adjust to. The human frame is not the same across the world. Bones are of different diameter and length. The bone canal varies in size. The bone canal positions for the nails and the geometry, such as shape and curvature, are distinctly different for the various ethnic groupings. This affected the design of the nails and the position and angle of curvature. Slowly, a broad database has been built up to facilitate the development of appropriate variations.

The implant nails were going to be installed for life. The best surgical steels were identified in Britain and then later in Japan.

In the next three decades, Lew made numerous trips to Vietnam and other developing countries. By the late 1980s, he had established four teaching centers for surgeons in Indonesia. The number of trained orthopedic surgeons in that huge nation grew from one to fifty. When he returned later, he found highly skilled men eager to learn new techniques. However, the implants and corresponding measuring instruments they needed to fix the fractures were not available.

Teaching alone was not enough. Together with continuing training in the techniques still being developed, there had to be a whole backup infrastructure of the materials these surgeons would need and a constant process of visitation ensuring surgeons everywhere maintained the highest current skills.

Lew was finding out many things as he went along. Most of the fractures are caused by traffic accidents, not war. This is the leading cause of death in young males and the fifth leading cause of death for women worldwide. There was an unlimited need for something better in the way of treating bone fractures; there was an immense amount of goodwill and encouragement among his fellow professional orthopedists, and others were willing to join in and help. He needed to find a way of multiplying himself. He did.

The result was SIGN—Surgical Implant Generation Network. It has its own website at www.sign-post.org. It was born in January 1999. Within six months, four cooperating projects had been started in public hospitals in

Vietnam, Thailand and Indonesia. At home in Richland, the first nails and screws were being manufactured by state-of-the-art machining equipment in SIGN's own modern factory. Because of the extremely narrow manufacturing tolerances, Lew decided he couldn't risk outsourcing this task to the developing countries themselves or even within his own country. Tight quality control would be essential, and the members of the staff with this responsibility are key employees within SIGN.

The products they manufacture were designed for an almost unlimited need, even though the customers largely lacked the capacity to pay what they would cost commercially.

About 80 percent of severe fractures occur in developing countries. SIGN donates without cost its systems of fracture care to help the poor in these countries and looks to the generous hearts of others worldwide to make and keep that possible. It is currently supplying over 10,000 implant nails a year, and the number steadily grows. More than 900 surgeons throughout the impoverished world operate and heal patients using Lew's nails. So far, the database reports 15,400 surgeries.

At this time of writing, SIGN has projects in operation around the world in 36 developing countries; besides the initial three, there are projects in India and Bangladesh, Nepal and Pakistan, Honduras, Guatemala and the Philippines. There are projects in Africa, Swaziland, Nigeria, Kenya and in Cambodia and Russia. More than one hundred hospitals across the world are involved. The list continues to grow.

The project that began with one man's desire to help the poor is now coming full circle. To establish the integrity of the SIGN nail to specialist surgeons worldwide with a stamp of quality and assurance, Lew went to his own country's regulatory body. The US Food and Drug Administration has approved the use of the SIGN methods in hospitals in the United States.

Let me give you an excerpt from a recent newsletter from a US army surgeon in Iraq.

> *I am working rather nonstop, with 2–5 hours of sleep a night. I thank God for the gift of not requiring much sleep. As the only orthopod, and over 250 cases in just over four months, I don't feel like there is much help out there. However your nail is a Godsend! I am very glad to hear of the wide femoral modification shortly available. The nail I did last weekend barely fitted (femur fx) and I did it completely without a C arm!!!! Unbelievable, I felt like Luke Skywalker, blindfolded, and "trusting the force."*

Lew, in a recent letter, comments:

> *In my walk, which I am not always sure if it is along the "way", I sense God's footsteps only as I look back. I see that many events through the years have come together in the creation of SIGN. They continue to come together as we grow.*
>
> *I don't remember words but rather reflections. The factors that come together probably started with the DNA I inherited.*
>
> *(Incidentally, I have observed along the way that religion is not the only influence on people's character.)*

Besides Lew, twenty US surgeons travel around the world to provide hands-on training to the local surgeons in surgical implant techniques.

It seems to me that Lew is rather like the boy with the lunchbox that we have been reading about, and that he is now in the process of distributing lunchboxes to others. He is helping show that with focused passion and purpose, it is possible to change the world or, put another way, for an ant to surprise an elephant!

He adds, as a footnote to this chapter, the thought:

> *There is an analogy of SIGN relating to ants. The ants in an ant colony all have specialized jobs. All are important for the welfare of the ant community. SIGN is like an army of ants moving through the world with many people helping as well as helping many people. For the SIGN equipment to function successfully in healing a hurting part of its community, it needs the help of fellow ants everywhere.*
>
> *Maybe for the earth to function in the way it was intended, we all need to take a lesson from the ants.*

Earthquake in Pakistan

October - November 2005

This morning, a surgeon specializing in treating facial injuries was reporting on the BBC World Service after his return home from Rawalpindi. Some of the facial injuries to children trapped under rubble need following up until the child reaches puberty. What is going to happen to the winsome youngsters he has operated on? Will they ever get the continuing care they will be needing? He does not know, but his heart is clearly grieving for these little strangers with smashed faces he will never see again. There are now more than 75,000 confirmed dead and about three million homeless.

Fred Stock, (you'll read more about him later) working in the earthquake area writes:

Sunday October 9th

There was a terrible 7.6 earthquake yesterday morning followed by numerous aftershocks. It was widespread from Afghanistan to India but the epicenter was the part of Kashmir under Pakistani rule. It seems to have followed a path through the foothills of the Himalayas, east-west, not north-south.

Monday October 24th

We are now helping at Bach Hospital run by TEAM Mission right in the midst of the earthquake area. We had four shakes of 5.1+ the first day we were here. The death toll is now over 54,000 and those injured and homeless are more than double that amount. Remote areas are still unreached with food supplies.

Quite a few former staff members have returned from Sweden, Finland, England, Germany and the USA to help in this crisis.

Earthquakes here are usually rolling but this time it seemed like the ground shot straight up bringing down roofs as it descended. It lasted over six minutes. Six mountain peaks fell producing landslides that buried whole villages, obliterated roads, changed the course of rivers and have greatly hindered rescue efforts. In some places they heard a loud noise and the air was so full of dust it seemed as dark as night for about an hour.

Thousands were crushed by the roofs of their homes, shops and schools. Those not killed sustained head wounds, broken bones and serious bruises which in some cases have caused dead tissue that has to be cut out. Freezing weather is now only days away.

Monday October 31st

There have been 880 aftershocks since the earthquake, some big enough to be counted as earthquakes in their own right.

Evert Lall, secretary of the Society for Community Development, living in Gujranwala, writes:

November 2

We are talking of a project proposal submitted for funding. It is to provide from Gujranwala in the Punjab Fitweld roofs for the victims of last month's disastrous earthquake in northern Pakistan.

Ken adds: This is a wonderful use of a design originally developed in 1987 for Afghan refugees and that has since been used for many churches. The corrugated sheet roofs, supported on braced 2.5" diameter steel water pipe columns sitting on small concrete foundations, are an ideal long-term solution as a response to the needs for shelter in the mountains. The sloping roofs can shed the snow. There can be Styrofoam insulation beneath the steel sheeting. The columns will keep the roof from collapsing on the people below in a future earthquake or tremor, even though the local walls of stone in mud mortar may crack or fall.

One of the small local trucks can carry the complete foundations, pipe columns and roof modules for a roof 26 feet by 20 feet and also the roofing sheets and door and windows that can shelter a family. The team of Khokherke boys at Gujranwala now has eighteen years of experience and should be able to deliver and erect such a framed roof in two days, at the most three. It shouldn't be hard to replicate that team or expand the production of modules and roofs even tenfold.

Ah! - I could wish I were twenty years younger!

Lew Zirkle writes:

November 2nd

As I traveled from Islamabad to Abbottabad I passed the sign towards Taxila. I visited Dr. Luke and his wife at Bach Christian Hospital at Qalandarabad and found them to be absolutely great people. I felt an immediate kinship with Luke. He is unassuming, works hard and has the best interests of his patients in mind. He works with a tough group of people who live up in the hills. He has established a rapport that was evident as we made rounds.

In the hospital where I have been working three hundred and thirty patients with fractures were admitted in the first ten days. Admittance means being placed in tents around the hospital. The SIGN nail is the only nail that can be used to treat many of these fractures because we do not need a C-arm. They have two C-arms in the hospital but both of them are broken. C-arms are ways you can take an x-ray and get an immediate reading to see if the nail is in the slot and the C-arm is also a mechanism to put the nail in the slot.

When I was in Pakistan I felt of all the places in the world that that was the place for me to be.

I must tell you a story that occurred as I was traveling from Abbottabad to Islamabad. I didn't have a way to get back to the capital because suddenly I was asked to go to Islamabad to operate on my last day so I operated Friday in Abbottabad and then left Friday night for Islamabad by car. I didn't know the driver and he spoke very little English but we had a communication. It is Ramadan so we stopped at the mosque and I sat in the car while he prayed. Some Muslim men had gotten out of a bus in front of us and had gathered around the car a little. As we traveled more we stopped at a fruit stand where he could get his figs and an apple and some grapes. At 5.20 we stopped the car because they must break their fast at 5.25. Before he ate his date he offered me one. At first I didn't want to take it, mainly because his hands were dirty but he was quite insistent so we ate dates and grapes together with the somewhat soiled apple pieces.

As we traveled along he told me the names of the towns and gestured and I could understand about 25%.

When we got to Islamabad I didn't know how I would find where I was going. I was going to stay at a house while I worked at PIMS which was also treating earthquake victims. We pulled up on the side of the road to figure out where we were and the car stalled. He took this opportunity to make a call to the home where I was supposed to stay and about 2 minutes later a man with a long beard opened the gate and came to the car. It turned out that we had stalled directly in front of the house that I was going to stay in that night in preparation for surgery the following day.

Best regards, Lew

PS: I feel the SIGN system is the only system that can be used to treat the victims of an earthquake because they do not have x-rays in the operating room and SIGN is the only system in the world that can be used without an x-ray. It was a great trip! I plan to return to Pakistan in late November, early December.

a boy and his lunch

I hope to have a conference on treating non-unions and infected non-unions which I think will be a big problem as time goes on. I intend to work on a new clamp to help with the difficult reduction that I have had on some of the patients when treating fractures that have begun to consolidate and shorten.

November 4th, Richland

I will be returning November 23rd. The SIGN staff is working on a new clamp that I requested. The fractured bones that I saw in Pakistan have begun to telescope where one bone goes back over the other bone and fuses, making the reduction very difficult. I don't want to shorten the bones so we are devising a clamp to distract the bone so that we can get a good reduction and place our nail down. I am absolutely humbled by the fact that the SIGN nail is the only IM nail being used because it can be used without a C-arm. Lew

Timekeeper

How many of your waking hours,
Count in minutes if you will,
Do you spend causing,
Not just allowing,
The love that is in you
To overflow into the lives
Of others who need it?
How do you rate?
Ninety makes a tithe.
At the end of your day
It is only these minutes that count.

Bryce and the Stranger

October 5th, 1998

Bryce, in his late forties, lives in Sellindge, our village in Kent, England. He has a local one-man business, but it is enough to give him a living. Things, though, have never been worse for him. It's not his work, which he enjoys; it is his life outside work, if you can call what he is experiencing life! His wife has recently left him, and his two children—full grown—are away from home and more in touch with their mother. They seem to have little in common with him. He doesn't wonder at it. He is not a man people light up about. Rather, quickly seeing through his facade of cheerfulness, they tend to leave the room or overhear and move to a conversation elsewhere.

He is getting to hate his empty house. If the drain isn't blocked, then they miss collecting his garbage. Just one never-ending thing after another. He is totally depressed. He feels like a zombie. Someone without a heart. Someone with body actions, little mind, and emotions only of anger and something akin to hate. He lives as though his life is already over. Just like the milk this morning, everything he touches seems to turn sour. He should have finished at the university; things might then have turned out differently. Too late now. More and more recently, his thoughts have turned to suicide. He recalls to his mind Hamlet's soliloquy he learned when a boy. Who cares about dreams?

Bryce leaves the dirty dishes in the sink, on top of the others. He has a business appointment in Wye in fifteen minutes and will need to hurry. The car is reluctant to start. He jiggles the sparking plug wires. Oh, for just one day when from dawn to dark, things go right! The engine fires, and he is exceeding the speed limit. After Brabourne, he slows down. Life like this is just hell!

Something snaps inside. It is as though a dam, filled to the top, is breaking under the pressure. He cries out into the empty car "Jesus, Come into my life!" His wife, not he, has been the churchgoer in the family. He is giving up the struggle and surrendering himself to an unknown Jesus, completely. "Do what you like with me, I can't handle it anymore."

And something happens, right then and there in the moving car approaching Wye! A transaction is completed, and the old Bryce is dead forever, and a new Bryce lives instead.

He tells with awe in his voice of what happened.

"It was as though I had been suddenly doused and washed clean in a spring of living water, my resentments and anger were washed away, my heart was beating madly with vitality and love. I knew I was alive, and I desperately wanted to live. I was translated from purposelessness to purpose. Suddenly I knew, with complete unquestioning certainty, that Jesus was, is, the Son of God. It's really true! I needed to share this with everybody I could, and I have been trying to do so ever since."

Whoever will trust himself
To the caring of His Father
For a moment absolutely
Shall devoted to His service
Anchor all his life thereafter
For that moment has he proven
How trustworthy is his Father.

Sunday, February 27th, 2005

Bryce attends a growing church in the center of Ashford graced with much vitality. The pastor has recognized in Bryce a kindred spirit; he has traveled a difficult journey himself. Under the nurture of the church, Bryce is continuing to grow spiritually, and his zeal does not diminish with time. He has been on a church mission trip to Guyana in South America. When he has spare time, he is usually involved in church matters or, on Thursdays, at the village Bible Study.

It is the Sunday evening service, and a young man, a stranger probably in his early thirties, sits next to him. Nothing particular to notice about him—the kind of person you'd pass in the street without a second glance. Just under six feet in height, neatly dressed, mousy hair.

His name is Cullum, and since we will follow his journey further, let us learn a little more about him. His sitting next to Bryce at a Sunday evening service is clearly not happenstance. There is some celestial weaving going on.

Cullum, although no longer living there, is a native of Ashford and attended the town's best boys school until he was eighteen, when he was through his A-levels. Cullum lives in Islington, central north London. He has returned to his hometown to visit his parents, although recent parental asso-

a boy and his lunch

ciations have not been particularly happy. Everything in his life is a mess. He has problems in his job. His engagement is broken. Unusual for someone as young as he, he is worried about what happens when people die—a great unholy void, pain and punishment or what?

He has felt the inner prompting today to attend a church, this particular church, which is a couple of miles away from his parent's home. His faith is nowhere. *"If there is a God somewhere out there then show yourself," he thinks.* Before the service, he has met, by chance in the central shopping area, one of Ashford's street people now re-established in faith and serving actively in the church and in ministries to others on the streets. This man has encouraged a visit to his own fellowship.

Vulnerable, searching and receptive, he makes his first visit to church in many years. The service is one tailor-made for Cullum's needs. The testimony shared is by a man with a journey much like his own. Emptiness and searching, and then a vivid, timeless moment when all doubts are swept away in a flood of new certainties. Cullum instead feels condemned for his sins.

Halfway through the service, he has had enough. This is not for him. He should never have come. He's off! But not far.

Bryce, his neighbor, suddenly hears a clear audible order thrust at him from somewhere outside himself. Go After Him! Responding without hesitation, he catches the stranger at the entrance door. Cullum is making a call on his mobile phone before leaving.

Bryce is urgent. This man is important to God. He can't just let him go back out into the street without appealing to him. God has brought him here. Words tumble over themselves.

" I don't know you, friend, but I can see you're troubled in your heart. This night you are keeping an appointment God has made for you. He loves you. You can't keep running away from Him, you know. You're the Prodigal Son. I was one once, too. The only way you should be running is back home to Him. Give God a chance."

The words are spilling out of Bryce. They have a searing urgency. He can't let this young man go. It's where he himself has been a few years previously. He has made the journey to faith, and this young man must do so, also.

His words hit home. The stranger puts his phone away. He turns earnestly to Bryce, and his words are anguished, his eyes hunted.

"I've got to talk to somebody, I need to talk to somebody."

"Listen, friend, you can talk to me for as long as you like. I'm here, and I'll listen, I promise. Right after the service. Come back in with me, and when the service is over, we can talk as long as you like. By the way, my name's Bryce."

Cullum introduces himself, and together they rejoin the worshiping congregation.

The service finishes at 8:15, and Bryce and Cullum are still talking, in a side room of the emptied church, two hours later. Bryce shares with the stranger a reading from Scripture that has spoken to his own heart and urges him to memorize it as he himself has done.

"For I know the plans
I have for you,"
declares the Lord,
"plans to prosper you
and not to harm you,
plans to give you hope
and a future.
Then you will call upon me
and come and pray to me,
and I will listen to you.
You will seek me and find me
when you seek me
with all your heart.
I will be found by you,"
declares the Lord,
"and will bring you back
from captivity."

Jeremiah 29:11–14a NIV

It has been an amazing two hours. Cullum has been prone on the floor torn by tears and repentance. He is talking to God, not to Bryce. He confesses his sins and sinfulness. He confesses to the problems in his job, the way he has hurt his fiancée, the problems with his father, his worries about death and what happens. He is a mess and he wants, needs, pleads to God to help him.

Bryce realizes that he is listening to a nervous wreck trying somehow or other to establish a new foundation for his life. Well, however long it takes, he's willing to be there.

When the transaction is completed and Bryce prays for Cullum with his arm around his shoulder, he prays, too, that God will use Cullum to reach others with the same good news they have both encountered and experienced.

As they part outside the church door, Bryce urges the stranger to seek and to find and continue in fellowship with a community of believers such as this one in Ashford once he has returned home. He'll try and identify one in Cullum's own community in north London. They exchange telephone numbers.

Bryce has not seen Cullum since that late night in February, but the story is by no means over.

The Weaver

Canopied by space,
Seated on the universe,
He weaves away.
His hands are deft
And swift to move.
All time is His.

Among the warp and weft
He stretches out His hand
And sets a thread in place
And yet another.
Colours blend in tune
To make a harmony.

One day at a time,
He weaves for each
Of us our sep'rate world,
The willing way that He
Would have us undertake
Were He, not we, to choose

All the time He hears
The urgent clamour
Rising heavenwards
From our distant star.
He never sleeps but
Often for us weeps.

How hard He has tried
To prepare for His Son
On earth a holy bride.
'Thy Kingdom come' alas,
Is a burp in the glass
Of a roisterer's tune

Wry His smile of love.
How much will it take
For our hearts to break?
He wonders sadly if
We'll ever come to see
The Man of Galilee was He?

KENNETH G. OLD

Cullum and the Bag Lady

Tuesday, March 1st, 2005

We will call her Anna. These are going to be the last few hours of her life. She lives on the streets of north near-central London with no fixed abode. All her possessions are in the large shopping bag that is inseparable from her. She wonders, in a detached way, what will happen to her things that are so precious and necessary to her. Probably the dump. Well, she won't be needing them any longer, that's for sure. She eats one of the two chocolate bars that she has been saving for supper. The last one she'll save till just before she goes to buy a Tube ticket to the next station on the line.

There are many others like her, sleeping sometimes in homeless shelters and sometimes in a shop doorway, huddled against the cold and hoping the hot exhaust air from the doorway floor grille will be on all night. Each of the bag ladies and the similar bag men—she knows many of the regulars—have staked out their particular sleeping patch and have established usage rights.

Anna has her favorite place, the doorway of a furniture store on the local High Street. She always moves away from her sleeping area before opening hours, she doesn't want to queer her pitch. She is not a Londoner; she came down from the north of the country years ago. She was younger then. Didn't know so much about the world as she does now. She's in her sixties. Life has been hard for her. She has been raped twice, but no one seemed to want to know. Her evidence, they told her, would never hold up under cross-examination. "Sorry. Try the Salvation Army."

She is going to end it all. This afternoon. Throw herself under the first Tube train that comes in. Before the rush hour starts. She is at peace about it. She doesn't want to cause more inconvenience than she has to. She'll buy her ticket at two o'clock and, by 2:30, it should be all over. They'll have her cleared away well before the traffic builds up for the evening. She wonders if the regulars who throw her a coin in passing will notice she's missing. Probably not. She sighs. Hers has been one wasted life.

Bryce is eating his lonely lunch in Sellindge before going back to work. He is thinking about the stranger he has met in church last Sunday night. His phone rings. It is Cullum. He is excited and his voice urgent and loud.

"Hey, Bryce, can you hear me. Do you have a spare moment or two? I want to tell you what has just happened. It happened this morning, on the Tube. I was sitting opposite a man on the train who was distressed and agitated. I wanted to help him, but there was no vacant seat beside him so that I could talk to him. I decided to copy out that passage from Jeremiah you gave me that I've memorized. However, as I was finishing doing so, the train stopped at the station, and the man got out, so I missed contacting him. And I don't know what happened to him.

"My own stop was the next one, but between stations, a voice spoke to me, out of the blue somewhere but very clearly. It was an order that would accept no excuse. "*Go and find the bag lady. Now!*"

"I didn't question the voice; it had authority, and I knew whom the voice meant, Anna. I passed her often in the course of my work journeys and would give her an occasional coin. I stayed on the train an extra stop. I hurried up the steps and out into the street. There she was, in her usual place. What's all the hurry about, I'm thinking.

"Are you still there, Bryce? I hurried up to her, relaxing with every step. Anna, sitting in her usual place on the pavement with her bag beside her, was surprised when I stopped to talk. 'Anna,' I began, 'I just want to give you this,' and I passed her the passage I had copied out for the man on the train. ' . . . And to tell you that God Loves You, and you are important to Him.'

"Anna took the paper and read what it said—my writing is not all that easy to read—and by the time she had finished reading it, great tears were rolling down her cheeks, and her face was twisting with deep emotion in the strangest way. I helped her to her feet, and she hugged and held on to me, weeping with great heaves as though her heart was breaking and that if I let her go she would collapse in a heap on the ground. She eventually settled down, and midst her sobs, she told me she had been planning to commit suicide today by throwing herself under a train. If God loved her enough to send me to tell her that He loved her, then she would put that out of her mind. There must be something more still ahead for her.

"Isn't He amazing, Bryce? I only met Him myself the day before yesterday, and now this."

An hour later, Cullum is again on the phone with Bryce.

" Bryce, do you have your Bible with you? Can you look up something for me? I was paying for my groceries in a supermarket. I looked across at the adjacent empty checkout position, and written on the back of a notice to customers, the clerk had written Luke 1:79. No, it's not Luke 1 7–9, it was clearly Luke 1:79."

Bryce is not sure Luke 1 has that many verses and is surprised to find that it does.

The reference is a prophecy of Isaiah reflected on by Zechariah unto his newborn son, John the Baptist. *"And you, my child, will be called a prophet of the Most High . . ."*

to shine on those living in darkness
and in the shadow of death,
to guide our feet into the path of peace.

Luke 1:79 NIV

Wednesday, December 7th, 2005

Over the months since March, Bryce has kept in touch with Cullum by occasional phone calls. It is clear that Cullum has sorted out some things but not others. Sorting out the twisted and damaged relationships of the past has not been easy. It is often the more difficult part of the faith journey.

He has sorted out things with his ex-fiancée, and they are now friends. However, his relationships with authority in his work and his father are still strained almost to breaking, and he has not found peace. In some areas of his relationships, he still has strong feelings of suspicion and persecution almost akin to paranoia.

Free as grace may be
It bears its penalty
Coming, cap in hand, behind
For we are constrained,
Once the gift is claimed,
To reach back to the past
We'd left behind to find
And set to rights
Our wrongs unrectified
And this can be

A heavy price to pay,
Even for peace!

Today Bryce calls to check up on him and to encourage him in his struggle. They haven't been in touch for a while. He finds a different Cullum. A man at peace with himself and with the world and with God. With great excitement, Cullum tells him how it has come about.

"Bryce, something wonderful has happened. It's taken a long time to get here, but it's okay with me at last. It's so strange, it's almost as though God planned the whole journey from start to finish. This is what has happened since I last spoke to you.

"I was in the High Street a few weeks ago and passed a woman—I suppose she is in about her mid-forties—looking out at the traffic while talking into her mobile phone. I caught a few of her words and swung to pretend to look in a shop window so that I could continue to hear what she was saying. I edged back a little nearer, but she paid no attention to me or the other pedestrians; she was intent on her conversation.

"She was offering Christian counsel to someone in deep trouble, almost as though she was speaking to me and all my problems over the phone. She finished off her conversation with a prayer for her listener, and before she could resume her journey, I took bold to speak to her. 'Ma'am, excuse me, I couldn't help but overhear your conversation. You seem to be a Christian. I'm in trouble, I believe in God but I still have no peace within myself. Would you please be good enough to pray for me?'

"We stood back out of the way of the foot traffic, and we talked a little more, and then she prayed with me. She asked if I often came this way. When she found it was close by my work, she suggested that maybe we could meet and have coffee somewhere nearby next week at the same time and check how things have been going. I was delighted that she was willing to waste time on a stranger like me and happily agreed. We have met for a half hour at lunchtime these last four Mondays. We talk over my questions, and she responds from her point of view. It's surprising how many of the answers are within myself and not due, as I'd been thinking, to what is happening around me.

"You were absolutely right, Bryce. I needed the support and the authority of a caring fellowship, and Angela has put me on to one where I feel completely at home and welcome. I wouldn't miss it for anything. I've changed my job, too. That's made a huge difference. I work for an Asian human rights organization. I actually count for something now. God is good, isn't He?"

a boy and his lunch

Yes, He is and so are the people like Bryce and Cullum and the unnamed member of the Ashford fellowship and the unknown checkout clerk who left a Bible reference on her counter and Angela and you that work with Him, knowingly or not, to effect His purposes. You are all part of a holy tapestry being woven in our present day. And who knows how far it extends?

What is Truth?

Easter 1965, Richland, Washington

This is simply a story of an enduring friendship between two people. It has its lessons for us. We may be empty-handed in terms of wealth, but the gift of friendship is always available for us to give away—and to receive. As you read, you will discover once again the way God weaves together people and events to work out His ultimate purposes.

In one of the three towns in southeast Washington State, north of the bend of the Columbia River where it turns west towards the sea, lives a family of husband and wife and five children, one a babe in arms. They are comfortably off. Both husband and wife work on the Hanford nuclear energy project. They are recent members of the West Side Church in Richland, and the children attend the youth programs at the church.

Pat works as a computer programmer at the Federal Building in the town.

One day, not long before the lunch break, one of her work colleagues, a Mormon, asks her a question. "Do you believe in Jesus?"

Her answer is instinctive and immediate, drawing on her foundations developed since childhood. "Of course! I've been taught to believe in Him since I was little and I do." Another question follows. "But how do you know that is the truth?"

"Well, what *is* truth? It's what you've been taught to believe," she replies without hesitation.

As Pat drives home during her lunch break to check up on her baby, she is reflecting on that question. "What is truth?" What really is the truth? Is what she's been taught to believe about Jesus true, or is it all a fairy tale? She has never ever considered such a thing before. It is as though the devil has thrown that question at her. It will not leave her. Is Jesus real? What is truth? She is questioning now all her old certainties. How does she know what is truth? Suppose her parents, her grandparents, or other faith mentors have been wrong. Is truth objective or subjective? Do we each believe to be truth that which we want to believe is truth? Better her friend has not asked her that question. Peace of heart and mind has been replaced by unease, deepening unease. "What if—" questions crowd her thoughts.

For three months this turmoil is going on inside. She does not share these intimate thoughts, doubts bordering on personal heresy, with her husband or children. Nor does she share them with her mother or even close friends. She does not take communion in church. It doesn't seem right to do so.

Finally, there is a turning point. Pastor Homer has preached his Good Friday sermon, affirming that whatever is to happen afterwards makes no difference to the completion and effectiveness of the work of grace that has occurred in the crucifixion of Jesus.

She is alone at home and in near desperation.

She has been reading in John. *Let not your heart be troubled, ye believe in God, believe also in me.* She realizes with a startling suddenness what he is saying. Jesus is speaking to her heart and to her need. He is answering her question, and it is all truth. She sinks to her knees and stretches for a lifeline.

"Jesus, you know I don't even know if you are real. If you are, take my life and do with it what you want. It doesn't belong to me, anyway. You paid for it on the cross. It's all done and dealt with."

As if she has turned on a light switch, the whole room is filled with a sense of warmth, peace and love, overwhelming love. Everything is permeated with this sense of holy presence. She is no longer alone. Someone Else is also here. She jumps to her feet shouting, "He's real! He's real!" She wants to stand on the roof and shout it out to the neighborhood. She is filled with joy and excitement. It is something new inside her that, once obtained, will never leave her. As her family returns to the house, she does not tell them what has happened, but they are soon noticing that something, something gentling, has changed her. And they like what they see. She is no longer her own and is living out in externals the change that has taken place within. The Bible has suddenly come to life for her. She has tried reading it before and found it plain, dull and boring. Now the words leap off the page, and she finds that indeed Jesus is the Way, the *Truth* and the Life!

I have been greatly invaded—
There's no other word I can say—
By a strange and mighty influx
From somewhere outside the day.

There was no sudden expulsion
Of the forces once in control
But moving silently inward
Something strange took over my soul.

a boy and his lunch

There was no sudden inrushing,
No flooding, no sharp night attack,
But now I find myself conquered
Not knowing what opened the crack.

The fear and worry have left me,
Perplexity flew through the door,
Life is a new way of living,
Tranquillity, peace and much more.

Whatever it is gives power,
Direction, vitality, life.
Gone are the problems of living,
An end to perpetual strife.

Life is joyous and radiant,
Now there's nothing I have to prove,
All I asked is inconsequent,
I know there is God by my love.

Who invaded came unexpected,
And now my concern is to see
The road is ever kept open
For whatever invaded me.

Richland, Late Spring 1972

Pat has had rheumatic fever before, when she was ten. It had brought her very low then, and now again it brings her low. She stays with her mother and father while Jim, her husband, copes with the children a few blocks away in the new home they have built to suit their family needs. While she is recovering, she has time to reflect on her life, and in the quiet times again she questions what the Lord would be having her do for Him.

The thought comes to her mind, almost like a command. "Visit the lost and the lonely."

With the thought is her response "And who are they, Lord?"

The next day, a charitable pamphlet in the mail comes heavily headlined to attract attention to its appeal for "The Lost and the Lonely." The pamphlet defines the lost as those in prison and the lonely as the sick and elderly. This is a confirmation to her.

Pat is appointed to the deacon's board of her church. After a long spell of absence from work for her illness, she is soon in harness and finding time to visit the sick and the elderly in her community.

But God's plans for her are not yet complete. The servant is being trained, but the task still lies ahead.

Pat is attending a meeting of the Richland chapter of Women Aglow, and she picks up from the table a single page pamphlet called "One to One." It is something given birth in Seattle, focusing on visiting lonely prisoners in jails in the community. The women think this is a role they, too, can play. Pat thinks about it and prays about it. There is no significant local jail in the Tri-Cities. The nearest is in Walla Walla, a men's prison sixty miles away. That could prove a bit difficult. It would mean involving Jim, yet as long as visiting isn't too often or onerous, even that could be possible. Her husband is agreeable. She writes off affirming her interest, and over the ensuing weeks, the various suitability checks of both Pat and Jim as prison visitors are made and assessed. There will be an attempt to match interests. She underlines that she will not want to be allocated to a person involved in the more violent of crimes and signs and sends the forms back to Seattle. Is she in for a surprise!

Then shall the King say
unto them on his right hand,
Come, ye blessed of my father,
inherit the kingdom prepared for you
from the foundation of the world:
For I was an hungred and ye gave me meat:
I was thirsty and ye gave me drink:
I was a stranger, and ye took me in;
Naked, and ye clothed me:
I was sick and ye visited me:
I was in prison, and ye came unto me.

Then shall the righteous answer him, saying,
Lord, when saw we thee an hungred, and fed thee?
Or thirsty, and gave thee drink?
When saw we thee a stranger and took thee in?
or naked and clothed thee?
Or when saw we thee sick,
or in prison, and came unto thee?

a boy and his lunch

And the King shall answer and say unto them,
Verily, I say unto you,
Inasmuch as ye have done it
unto one of the least of these my brethren,
ye have done it unto me.

Matthew 25:34–40

Bernie in Jail

February 23, 1973

Bernie, a strapping young twenty-four-year-old of sturdy, medium build, stands before the superior court judge in Seattle.

He vaguely remembers other people present—his mother weeping silently as she sees her child's life seemingly come to an end, the family of his victim, faces filled with satisfaction at justice being served, onlookers wallowing in his misery.

He has pleaded guilty to murder, though unable to remember much of what occurred. It has happened when he was drunk. The evidence is damning. The sentence is severe.

> *I knew what sentence I would receive; in my cell my bravado made light of it. The reality however, was a much more sobering experience—LIFE!*
>
> *I made a feeble effort at apologizing to my mother, the victim's family, anyone who might listen. How pitiful it seems now. How pitiful I seemed. How do you make up for a life undone? I was led away, back to my lonely cell, my life in ruins.*

This is a man you may as well forget.

March - April, 1973

> *I had been transferred to the receiving institution in Shelton, Washington where I underwent psychological testing, was prepared for receiving my minimum term from the Board of Prison Terms and Paroles, and then for transfer to my parent institution where I would serve out my time. The board set my minimum term at 35 years, over double the average. This means I will have to serve a minimum of twenty-three years and four months before I am eligible for parole. However, I might earn earlier release through good behavior.*

The jail in which he starts serving his sentence is in Walla Walla in southeast Washington, four hundred miles away from his home, across the Cascades.

Almost alone among the inmates, he receives little or no mail. He has no visitors. If he has family, they are too far away to visit, estranged and probably too ashamed to admit their relationship. For the next 23 years at least, this bottled up volcano is going to be a charge upon the taxpayer. He is left alone for the anger and bitterness within him to fester. He is not going to let this wound ever heal.

Late Spring 1975, Richland, Washington

The response from One-to-One comes by letter. Jim and Pat have been allocated a number and a name that will become familiar over the years — Bernard Pierce, an inmate of the Department of Corrections high security prison at Walla Walla. He has no apparent friends or visitors and rarely receives mail. He has previously served in the US Navy, so there is that link with Jim. Visiting hours are spread throughout the week, but because of their own work, only visits on Saturday or Sunday will be possible.

Pat's young son is now ten years of age and his two sisters still at home are old enough to keep a responsible eye on him while his parents are away.

The first visit is on a Saturday morning. The guard towers and the barbed wire atop the walls are threatening. The whole routine of prison visiting is strange to the couple. They present their letter at the reception. Into the visitors room they can only carry a key to the locker into which they have placed all their portable possessions. Their shoes are inspected by security guards, and they are patted around their bodies. Rules for visitors changed frequently. The doors clang ominously behind them; they are locked in.

Once within the visitors' room, they are watching the visits of others. Mostly, they seem to be wives visiting husbands. They are sitting on one of the sofas waiting for a stranger, and eventually a young man joins them and sits opposite. He is wearing regular clothes, not prison uniform. He smiles. "I'm Bernard Pierce, people call me Bernie," he says. They look each other over curiously. Do they have anything compatible between them other than Navy service? Bernie is guarded. He has told them his name but offers little more except his own questions. Why do they want to befriend him? He doesn't know them. What's in it for them? Why have they come sixty miles just to see him?

Pat laughs. They just want to be friends, if he is agreeable. And she wants to make it clear that they are not interested in what has happened in the past, just in starting from today and going forward. It will be several years before she discovers the reason he is in prison. She'd like to write to him each week, she hopes he'll write to them, too, and she and her husband will try to visit him every month. They have three children at home and two who have left the nest. Her oldest son is now in the Navy, and her husband has also been in the Navy. A brief discussion confirms they have both served in Bremerton; well, that's one touching point.

Jim is leaving the talking to Pat. She is always the more talkative of the couple, and this is Pat's initiative, anyway.

His wife is surprised at how hard it is to make conversation with someone with whom you have little in common and when questions are answered guardedly with single word responses. She senses he is a gulf away from where they are. He is bitter and angry and hurting. With the exception of a sister he sometimes hears from, his family doesn't seem to care. She drops her own questions of curiosity about him. They can come later. She tries to imagine herself in Bernie's world. She asks more general, less invasive questions. Does he get to read newspapers? Does he have access to a radio or to a television? Are there ever provisions for their entertainment? Does he ever see movies? Is he alone in his cell, or does he share it?

Single word responses. It is better, she decides, to forget trying to find out about Bernie; he is uneasy, and this present encounter is all new and fresh to him, too. She finds it easier to focus on sharing their own lives with him.

She is not a native Washingtonian but hails from Central City in Colorado. Has he ever been to Colorado?

Central City, to the west of Denver, is 8,000 feet above sea level and was once known as the richest square mile on earth. She has lived on East High, looking down on Gregory Gulch, where Gregory had first discovered gold in 1859 and set the local gold rush in motion. There had been a disastrous fire fifteen years later that had destroyed the town. By the time of her childhood, though, everything important has long been rebuilt. She loved playing in the hills and near the old mine workings with her brothers. The aspens in the fall are her favorite trees. The colors of leaves on the same branch are a profusion of gold, red, yellow, orange and brown. The mountains change color and mood in the fall.

Pat's enthusiasm for her hilly childhood home bubbles over. She talks with her fingers and hands as well as her mouth. Bernie is interested and asks questions to lead on to more spilling-over memories. Oh, yes, she lives in Richland now, but if she had her druthers, she'd be back in Central City, though the needs of her family and the good schools and work available make Richland a far better place to live.

By the time the first visit is over, Pat has been carrying the conversation for more than two hours, but they have made some progress. They are slowly beginning to know each other. Bernie still has reservations about whether this is more than a pebble in a pool, and he isn't committing to anything. He seems to trust nobody. However, the couple has found Bernie can actually smile, and they have made promises that Pat intends to keep. She is going to be somebody that this young man will find he can trust!

Monroe, Washington - October 31st, 1998

Although many things have changed over the past twenty-three years for Pat, the friendship with Bernie has persisted through all the ups and downs of her life.

Her mother and father have both died. All the children are out of the nest. Her marriage to Jim has ended in an amicable divorce, and he lives not far away in another of the Tri-Cities. She lives alone in a smaller, more suitable home and, after her retirement in 1995, is occupied with many volunteer activities. Her baby son has grown, married and has sons himself. He has migrated to Texas.

Pat has kept her promises. She writes to Bernie each week and he, as regularly and promptly, responds. His doubts about motive long ago disappeared. He had early on agreed with her that if she did not try to convert him, then he would not try to corrupt her. However, her continuing involvement in good works in her own community shines through in her conversation and correspondence. His understanding of her friendship is no longer questioning but of complete trust. This is probably the only person he knows who is transparent and real and just truly good. Her friendship to him is a gift, and he accepts it gratefully. She can't possibly understand how much he looks forward to the monthly visits or even to her letters, breaths of sanity in a mad world. Over the years, she has learned about his family and on one occasion her visit coincided with a visit from his sister. This is when she finds out why Bernie is in prison.

The other promise, to visit once a month, has sometimes been more difficult to keep. After Jim had his stroke in 1991, he no longer visited with her.

a boy and his lunch

As Bernie's own record within the prison system develops, he is down-graded from a high security prisoner to a medium and then a low security prisoner. This leads to his being transferred to jails further away from Richland.

Spokane, 130 miles away, is still near enough to visit and return home before dark most of the time. Clallum Bay, on the west side of the Olympic Peninsula 400 miles from home, is more difficult and takes an overnight stay somewhere. Nevertheless, even when as occasionally happens her birthday coincides with the day for a visit, Pat is there for the two or three hours he has been looking forward to. Bernie especially appreciates these visits, although he can't understand how she can give up celebrating her birthday with her family just to keep a promise and visit him.

As time passes, Bernie builds his own month around these visits; it is something as firmly fixed and inevitable as the new moon. He has a long memory. He can recall to her virtually all of the occasions over the years when she has failed to visit, even though he doesn't question the reasons, such as icy roads or family bereavements or her absence abroad on her volunteer visits to China or Estonia. He can also remember the time he wrote and told her not to visit, but she was there anyway, smiling and happy.

Last month, Pat had told him that she plans within the next month a visit to Africa with two of her retired friends to see the game reserves and some mission work that she is interested in. However she expects to be back to see him as usual at the end of October.

Although today is her birthday, she has driven 300 miles to Monroe from home to keep her rendezvous, and when the visit is over, she will make the return journey to be back home the same day. A long journey for two hours conversation, but a promise is a promise!

She shares the adventures of Kenya, the elephants walking just a few inches in front of the car, the giraffes, and the vast herds of wildebeest. It had been a wonderful time, and she does her best to communicate the space, the freedom and the beauty and wildness of nature and its forms to this man separated from it all.

She explains, as the visit comes to its end, she won't be here next month, probably even the next month and possibly the month after. She has journeys ahead in her mind that might even see her back in China before she is home again. She is starting off with Thanksgiving with James and his family in Texas, leaving in a week or so. Anyway, he can be sure he'll get her regular letters, she'll give him forwarding addresses for mail and she'll see him as soon as she can after she returns.

However, unseen ahead, in a dramatic twist of events before they meet again, a perceived breach of trust built up over two decades is going to cause Bernie to have Pat's name removed from his visitor's list!

What follows happened to a little eight-year-old girl, Patricia, when she was playing tag with her friends on the side of a mountain. She was scared her mother would be angry at her carelessness and told no one until much later in life.

Safe Hands

For he shall give his angels charge over thee,
to keep thee in all thy ways.
They shall bear thee up in their hands,
lest thou dash thy foot against a stone.

Psalm 91:11–12

Running, racing,
Laughing, hasting,
Jumping, playing,
Never a thought
Of the danger.

Deaf to the yell.
Over the edge
Falling headfirst.
No time to scream.
No time to think.

Gasp and a groan.
How shall they tell?
Run to the edge
Injured or dead?
How dare they look?

Standing erect,
Shaking her head,
Dusting her dress
Is the child; then,
Back she climbs slow.

a boy and his lunch

Awestruck she tells—
Headfirst she falls,
Terror at heart,
Arms spread out wide—
Would they were wings!

Of a sudden,
Blink of an eye,
Hands at her waist,
Certain and sure
Catch her mid-flight,

Flick her upright,
Midst of her fall
Slow her and then
Set her soft down
Onto the ground.

Whose hands?
Father's?
Son's?
Spirit's?
Or an angel
Watching o'er her?

KENNETH G. OLD

81

Patricia Louise

Patricia Louise was born in Colorado in 1931 and has spent most of her life in Washington State. She has five children and has recently been divorced from her husband. She has worked as a computer programmer with the Hanford Energy project. She is a petite 5'1" and her children have all left the nest. She has had a deep personal experience of Jesus Christ and has been both deacon and elder in the West Side Church in Richland in Washington State.

Let her speak for herself:

In early 1998, I was an active and, I thought, contented woman of 66 enjoying traveling and volunteer work of various types. I had no thought of getting married again. No thought, that is, until two elderly women in my church in Richland married for the second time and two elderly men did the same. It made me think about how I wanted to spend the declining years of my life. Perhaps it would be nice to have someone to share those days with, but the question was, "Who?" No prospects on the horizon that I could see.

Then the church asked for volunteers to help plant a memorial rose garden for Marie Old, who, with her husband, had served in the church for three years following retirement from the mission field in Pakistan. She and Ken then moved back to England from Richland in 1993, and over the next four years welcomed visitors from around the world.

In 1993, I was one of their guests when I stopped over on my way home from Estonia. In 1996, my daughter and I stopped by again on our way to Estonia, and later that same year, I took my daughter-in-law to experience their wonderful hospitality.

Each time they came back on furlough, Ken had told our church of their work in Pakistan. He was the one missionary who visited our church who seemed actually enthused about the work he was doing. Others could be inspiring, but all seemed to be wearied by their long service abroad and to lack the enthusiasm that exuded from Ken. He had that same vitality in showing visitors the English countryside. He enjoyed life. So when I went to help with the memorial rose garden for Marie, I realized that Ken was the kind of man I was looking for. Full of energy and joy and, most importantly, a man who loved the Lord with his whole heart.

In October, I was planning a trip to Kenya with two friends and told Ken I wanted to come down from London for the day to check on him. The people at West Side Church were all wondering how he was managing since

Marie's death. He said "Oh, no! You must come and stay." So we arranged to arrive on a Saturday and leave on a Tuesday.

On Sunday he took us to a church service in a neighboring village. The church was built in 633 as an abbey by the daughter of the king of Kent. The eight bells in the church tower are rung for half an hour before the service by a team of local bell ringers. It was during the service that I felt something I have never felt before or since—a remarkable flow of warmth from him to me like a strong electric current, but he had taken no notice.

I really wanted to stay on and not continue my trip to Kenya, but of course it was impossible to cancel it.

We had another two days in London before going to Kenya. I sent him a card saying I feared I had left my heart at Gibbins Brook Farm. He just thought I really liked the place!

From Kenya, I wrote another letter telling of my fresh experiences in Kenya but saying all my thoughts had been of him. Not sure if I should mail it, it seemed to jump out of my hand into the letterbox. During our change of planes in London on our return home almost two weeks later, I called him to say I thought I might come visit at Christmas. He was non-committal. Whatever I wanted to do was fine with him. There was no mention of my letter.

A week later, at home in Richland, I was preparing to go visit my son in Texas for Thanksgiving when I got an e-mail from Ken saying he had received my "love" letter. I had not used that word, but he recognized the letter for what it was. He wasn't sure how he could respond because the house was so full of memories of the lovely woman he had been married to for over forty years. But . . . he said it would make our time at Christmas more interesting!

When I arrived in Dallas on Saturday, he had already sent two more e-mails. Then on Monday I received an intriguing message saying he had written me a letter and I should wait until it arrived and then let him know what I thought. Not being a patient person over such a critical matter, I was not going to wait a week for a letter from England! Even though he feels the telephone an invasion of privacy, I called him the next day.

As soon as he heard my voice he exclaimed, "Oh! I am so glad you called. You must get over here right away. We're going to be married." I made him repeat it but still did not tell my daughters until I had called again the next day and heard the same message. I had planned to spend five weeks in Dallas. I left after the fifth day without ever having received the letter.

Grinning from ear to ear all the way across the Atlantic, I was trying to figure out what the six little words might be that Ken had said he would say to me when I arrived. "Will you marry me" was only four. "Will you marry me Darling?" was still only five. "Will you *please* marry me Darling" made six. That must be what he planned to say.

What I got was "What took you so long, Darling?"

We drove into Ashford early Monday morning to see about getting married. On the way to the registry office, we passed through more than a dozen stoplights. Every single one was green! Ken exclaimed, "That's a sign! We are meant to be getting married." Ken asked how quickly our wedding could take place. After some hesitation the lady said, "Well . . . we could do it Thursday." Ken insisted, "That's not soon enough. You must have something earlier." A quizzical expression passed over her face; she smiled and turned the page back. "We *could* do it Wednesday *morning?*" "That's fine."

And so it was arranged for the civil ceremony to take place then. The girls in the registry office were amused to find these two elderly people so anxious to tie the knot.

On the way home, most of the traffic lights were red, and we took the opportunity at each stop to snatch a quick kiss in celebration.

Before receiving my letter, Ken had no thought of marrying again. Yet just twelve days from the Friday morning it arrived, we were man and wife. Later we had a religious ceremony at the farm so our families could share our joy. It was only when that ceremony was over that Ken finally proposed. I teased he had just informed me we were to be married and never actually proposed. He dropped to his knee immediately and asked, "Will you marry me?" I told him it was too late—I already had.

Ken continues . . .

Gibbins Brook Farm, Kent England August 1999

What made me so certain that marriage to Patty, not quite but almost a stranger, was so right and so urgent?

As I have told elsewhere, my marriage to Marie followed a fleece that I had put out at Taxila one afternoon.

That afternoon I knelt down in my room at the Browns on my own and talked to God about the strange thing that was happening to me. I needed to get it straight. "God, I don't know what's happening. All I know is that I have promised You can have the rest of my life. I meant that. I mean it still; the rest of my life is Yours. If it fits within Your

*will for me that I ask Marie to marry me I want You to stop
the car tonight just in front of the shisham tree that's thirty
yards short of Gilani's garage so that I'll know. I need to
know for sure, God. Amen."*

*If Gideon could put out a fleece on the threshing floor
beneath the oak tree at Ophrah in order to make sure he
understood God's will, then I could put out my fleece at the
shisham tree in Taxila.*

At least with Marie I had realized I was falling in love with her. With
Patricia Louise, that was far too early an emotion, and there was no time
at all to put out a fleece. She was a nice, friendly woman, but I knew many
nice, friendly women. However, someone up or out there was not wasting
any time, or allowing me to waste it, either.

After Sunday church two days after her letter arrived, I was carrying a saucepan across from the stove to the kitchen sink when something
happened. It is easier to call it a thunderous voice, because that's what its
effect was, but it was really as though I had been hit hard, very hard, on the
head with the saucepan I was carrying. Imprinted indelibly on my mind was
the clarion message: "Patty *must not delay,* she must get here *right away,*
she *will* get here right away!" I swayed against the table, recognized that
wherever this had come from, it had not originated in *my* mind, and I wrote
it down on a scrap pad to prove it to myself later. Someone else was giving
some clear counsel about this. God's hand was in this marriage no less surely
than in my earlier one, and I should waste no time making it happen. So I
didn't!

Bernie Finds His Father

December 2005, Monroe, Washington

Bernie is still in jail in Monroe. It is now well over thirty years since he was sentenced, and over the years, he has changed and mellowed. It could hardly be otherwise.

In 1985, twenty years ago, Bernie, pleading for release from jail by any means possible—even supernatural intervention—offered himself exclusively to Satan if he would bring that miracle about. It didn't happen.

Through all the interminable years, Bernie's appreciation of Pat's undemanding friendship is growing. To please her, but without any persuading from her, Bernie decides to become a Christian. It will make her happy.

Bernie buys himself a Bible and starts reading at the beginning. By the time he is through the first two books, he has decided, if he were God, he would have wiped every last Israelite off the face of the earth and started again with someone else. Nevertheless, at one of the prison chapel services at that time, Bernie professes Jesus as his Lord. This is twelve years ago, in 1993.

> *I faithfully read my new Bible every day and studied the devotional pages Patty sent to me each week. I did this for three months, but nothing seemed to stick, and I felt no change in my life.*
>
> *I remembered a conversation with Patty in 1985 or 1986. I asked her the standard non-believer question, "Why does God let innocent people suffer through war, famine, disease, crime and so forth?" Patty's response was, "God doesn't interfere in the affairs of men." I decided that if He wasn't going to interfere in my life to make it better, why should I bother?*
>
> *I also came to the conclusion that I could not have "blind" faith in what I could not see, hear or touch. I put my Bible in a drawer, and there it stayed for the next six years.*
>
> *At this same time, I received my first time extension from the parole board. I was still too dangerous to be at large.*

Pat observes and rejoices in the change in her friend as he begins to study the Bible. He is full of questions but, unlike previously, less out of aggressive disbelief than from curiosity, seeking to understand why God, if He indeed is, acts like He does. This is, as so frequently happens, no sudden overwhelming of God taking over in Bernie's life, but an opening of the doors of his mind to higher things than the world around him. He accepts an opportunity to work in the chaplain's office, and an unseen work of preparation of the ground for spiritual change begins to gather momentum.

Then, in November 1998, Pat lets him down. She abandons him without ever telling him what has been developing in her own life. He has seen her just two weeks previously. Now she writes a brief happy note from Dallas saying that she is off to England on Friday to marry someone he's never heard of and will be settling there.

The only friend he thought he could trust! All this has been going on behind his back with never a hint! And it has obviously been going on a long time. He is angry at her failure to confide in him. He cuts off her visiting rights, and, within two months, as though one event has necessarily to precede the other, he has met someone else who will change his life forever.

He writes to Ken later:

> *I know that I have been a trial to Patty over the years, and as God stayed faithful to the Hebrews, she remained faithful to me. No matter how much I grieved her, she waited me out until I had gotten over my snit. No matter how hard I pushed, she is the only person in my life that has refused to abandon me. There truly is a special place for her near God's throne. I must admit that when she ran off to marry you, I felt that she had abandoned me because I did not wait for an explanation. My lack of faith in her commitment to me still shames me.*

The cancellation of visiting rights had a mandatory minimum effect of six months. Although the explanations of an unplanned whirlwind marriage set everything back as it used to be in their relationship (and gave him another close friend) Pat was unable to visit Bernie as she wished when she returned to Washington in the spring.

Meanwhile, however, something wonderful has happened to Bernie. He has finally found, and been found by, His Father.

He reviews his conversations with Patty about God's Will.

> *Reflecting back upon my question to Patty about why God allows bad things to happen to good people, I realize the truth of her answer. He doesn't interfere in our lives to the point of taking away our free will to do evil if we choose. However, He most certainly will interfere in our lives to answer our prayers to do good!*

a boy and his lunch

I also now realize that Christians don't have "blind" faith. We have faith, but it is far from blind. We only need look around us at His creation and look within our own hearts to find His presence. I also know why He did not destroy the early Israelites: He bestowed on them the love, grace, mercy, compassion, and forgiveness that can only come from a God Who is love.

His relationship with Pat has soon been healed and restored, but as the year turns, there is a serious vacuum in his life, for she will no longer be visiting, and her letters will have longer intervals between them. He finds himself praying—and is answered by an overwhelming flood of certainty.

He writes:

Unlike many people I have heard, I cannot even tell you the exact day God touched me. I've heard people cite time, place, activity; all I know was that it was sometime between February 5–10, 1999.

For more than six years now, Bernie has been a prisoner in jail but free in his heart. He is in jail because God has work for him to do there, and in God's good timing, and not a second earlier, he is going to be set free. And God's timing is *always* perfect, never just 99 percent right.

His letters to Pat are full of this freedom. His anger has been sublimated by an understanding of God's love for him working its way out and through him in the way he lives his life among those in jail with him. Life has certainly not, in these recent years, been without its trials and disappointments. Hopes have been dashed time and again. No matter. God is good!

He has written his first book, laboring through the Bible, selecting and studying all the "I Am" passages and writing explanations of their context and meaning. He is working on a revised Harmony of the Gospels. He had been (with permission) using the chaplain's computer in these studies but felt convicted he was not to be using Government property for personal matters, so he hammers his text out on a typewriter. After all, he has the time.

He writes:

To date I have received five time extensions from the parole board totaling twenty years. I know that God has forgiven my sins but I still struggle with forgiving myself. Nevertheless I know that my life is in God's hands to do with as He will. Whether in prison or out, it is God's will that I will.

Whispers

There's a whisper in the marshland
Of a kingdom fairer by far
And it's blown across the dune sand
From over the distant star.

There's a call that travellers hear
That once was uttered aloud
Of living rich beyond measure
For those who jump over the cloud.

There's on the wind as it passes
A cry that's low to the ground
And a shiver in the grasses
Of silence the center of sound.

There's a stirring and a rising
And a song that sets man aflame
Of joy and hope for the striving
And wings for the limping and lame.

There's a whisper finds an echo
In the core of everyman's soul
Calling wanderers from the wasteland
To a love that makes them whole.

a boy and his lunch

Grandpa and Cassie

This is a story of a man who shares with others not material things as Lew does with his nails, but who shares, from the stripped-bare inner resources of his being, both faith and hope of such high degree that not one of us can fail to be uplifted by his struggle.

Marie has a first cousin in the United States with whom she feels very close. He is one of the Swedish Johnsons, and he has moved from Spokane in mainland Washington State to Whidbey Island. Whidbey Island is the longest island in the Puget Sound to the west of Seattle, aligned roughly north-south. Carl is a butcher in Coupeville, and on our furloughs we try to visit him and enjoy his company and also the sea views on both sides of the island. We meet and get to know his friends.

Carl is very lonely after his lovely wife dies, but he is supported and encouraged by his Tuesday evening Bible study group led by Stu Corey. It is Stu who visits him in a care facility in the town, and it is Stu who eventually lets us know of Carl's demise.

We keep in touch with Stu and his wife Laraine, but for the last couple of years have seemed to lose track of them. Since this story is about them, let us learn a little about who they are.

Stuart Corey, born and raised in Washington State, is a pilot before he is a licensed driver. His love of flying takes him into the U.S. Navy, where he becomes a fighter pilot. While stationed on the East coast, he meets Laraine and marries her in 1956. In 1960, they adopt their son Nathan. Becky (Rebecca) is adopted in 1963, and finally they complete their family with the adoption of Mary Beth in 1965.

His early years in the navy are spent as a naval aviator making many take-offs and landings from aircraft carriers. He serves in the Korean and Vietnam wars. As he advances through the Naval ranks, he becomes Air Boss on the flight bridge of a carrier. Needless to say, these are exciting and sometimes dangerous times, but for him, none is as exciting as the time when he first meets Jesus Christ as his personal Savior. He has many stories relating to what God does through various circumstances that he finds himself in while in the services. His final location, towards the north of Whidbey Island, is as the executive officer for the naval air station at Oak Harbor, with the rank of captain.

Following his retirement, Stu and Laraine purchase a local oil and gasoline distribution company in Coupeville and settle nearby. In 1984, Stu becomes an ordained minister, although he never pastors a church congregation.

He loves the island and its people and establishes a non-denominational organization called Island Ministries to reach out to the local communities in counseling and other areas of need.

However, there are storm clouds ahead that will test every quality Stu and Laraine have.

Sept. 1st 2003 Whistler, British Columbia, Canada

Stuart is riding a bicycle along a sloping gravel path near his daughter's home. Becky and her husband, Dave, cycling ahead, are with him at the time and have stopped at the bottom of a small hill to wait. As he is freewheeling down the hill, he calls out "Dave" as if there is something wrong, and then his bike goes off the side into a ditch. Stu flies over the handlebars of the bike and hits his head on either a rock or a log. When Becky and Dave reach him (within seconds) he has no pulse and is not breathing.

They pull him out of the ditch to get him onto a flatter surface and immediately begin CPR. About five minutes after starting, a doctor comes and helps monitor Stuart's blood pressure as they struggle to get air into his lungs. There seems to be some blockage that makes it difficult. As people pass by, some jump in to help blow air into his mouth. Mobile phones calling for help are busy.

The CPR continues for 25 minutes until the emergency team arrives. He is rushed to the Whistler Emergency Clinic and later flown out to Vancouver, b.c. At the hospital, it is discovered after tests that Stuart has a previously undiscovered degenerating disk problem in his neck.

Becky is thinking she knows what has happened. It is the only answer that makes sense. While riding, Stuart has been complaining of his neck hurting because he has to lean forward on the bike. As her father is coming down that bumpy hill, something has happened in his neck that makes him unable to respond by slowing down or jumping off the bike. There is no evidence of a stroke or heart attack, and she assumes that the paralysis probably occurred prior to the bike going into the ditch. Her father would surely have bailed off the bike if possible, for he has always had quick reflexes.

Stuart has broken the C1 and C2 vertebrae in his neck and severely injured his spinal cord. The doctors say his injuries are similar to those experienced by the actor Christopher Reeves after a fall from a horse. He cannot

a boy and his lunch

move, except to nod his head and shrug his shoulders. His lungs are unable to operate on their own, so he is on a ventilator.

Slowly, over the months, he learns how to speak once again.

The year 2005 is a year of significant progress.

Towards the middle of the year, Stuart becomes aware of a medical study group being established roughly 2,500 miles to the east, in Cleveland. This is tailored for him, he decides, and he needs to be part of it. It is a group working toward getting ventilator patients off the machine for significant intervals of time. His initial application is refused by the University of Cleveland Medical Center. He is too old. He does not agree and convinces them of his excellent physical condition despite being a quadriplegic and that the study needs at least one senior person to validate it. The decision is reversed, and he is accepted to come to Cleveland to possibly undergo a Diaphragm Pacemaker Implant.

Stuart, Laraine, Cassie (granddaughter/caregiver), and caregiver Tami head to Seattle airport on the journey to Cleveland. At the airport, *crisis!* The ventilator stops working!

Cassie and Tami grab the plastic bag that attaches to Stuarts tracheotomy and start squeezing to keep him alive. It is decision time—whether to call 911 Emergency or head to Cleveland. Laraine and the caregivers yield to Stuart's enthusiasm and set aside their commonsense. Head to Cleveland, come-what-may! While his caregivers squeeze the plastic bag to keep Stuart breathing, the Continental Airlines crew (totally oblivious to the desperation of what is going on) proceeds to load the party onto the aircraft, no small undertaking. For the next six hours, Cassie and Tami take turns squeezing the plastic-bag (for an estimated 12,840 squeezes) until with relief the girls plug the portable ventilator into the wall at their accommodation in Cleveland. So far, so good, even if it was a close run.

After two weeks at the Cleveland University Hospital and an implant successfully inserted, they return home without incident.

The diaphragm pacemaker is intended to enable Stuart to breathe with the aid of that implant rather than the external ventilator. Initially, Stu can manage no more than a couple minutes off the ventilator at a time. The diaphragm and the lungs are simply not strong enough to sustain successful breathing. With lots of work and practice, this can only improve. Stuart is also trying to learn to talk while he is on the pacemaker. The pacemaker functions are quite pronounced, interrupting him with each respiration. This is another challenge for him.

Let Stu bring us up to date, this Christmas of 2005, and share the story, his story, which he tells on his website at www.stuartcorey.com.

It is almost two years after the accident when the story resumes.

8/10/2005

Dear followers of my website,
I want to update you on 2 subjects.

1) Cassie's wedding last Saturday 8–6-05 couldn't have been more perfect for an outdoor wedding with the lagoon, Cascades and Mt. Baker as a backdrop. There were approximately 80 plus guests and the bride and groom were stunning.

I had had some concern as to whether I would be able to successfully officiate at the service.

a. Could I physically be up to the task and

b. Could I project my voice so everyone could hear?

Neither turned out to be a concern. We have thought that perhaps we set a Guinness record in that it is highly unlikely that another Granddaughter whose Grandpa is a quadriplegic has officiated at her wedding while also having the bride's sister as Grandpa's attendant caring for him.

2) Praise with the diaphragm pacemaker which allows me time off of the ventilator. I have reached 20 minute increments off the ventilator which is repeated 5 times a day and so totals 2 hours each day.

I think the one thing that has excited me most is that for the first time since my injury I can blow out a candle and blow my nose (with Kleenex help of course).

It will still be a very long haul before I will be free of the ventilator but what a wonderful goal to aim for.

Once again thank you for your continued support and prayers, Stu

God is Good - all the time

Whidbey Island 9/7/2005

Dear Website followers,

Just a word to update you on my breathing pacemaker. I am currently doing 8 or 9 twenty-minute sessions a day off the ventilator for a total of about 3 hours. I am quite pleased with the progress and the evident strengthening of my diaphragm and lungs.

One thing that I am not sure about at this point is that I am now talking quite clearly while I am on the ventilator. The same is not the case when I am operating off the ventilator. Then, my talking is quite stilted as I have to interrupt it each time my diaphragm expands to take air in. I have not yet discussed this with the experts. I do know that prior to my surgical implant I talked to a couple of patients who have had the implant and were off the ventilator and their speech sounded quite normal. More information to follow.

I am scheduled to be back in the VA hospital (Seattle) the early part of October. We have had some bad experience with the electrical wheel chair the university gave me after I left the hospital. The VA hospital has evaluated whether to try to improve my original wheelchair or to have a brand new one manufactured for me. They have decided on the latter and hope to have it ready for me when I return to the VA hospital in October. We are anticipating a significantly improved wheelchair which will be a blessing to me, my caregivers, and the patrons at the Walmart whom I periodically terrorize.

Life continues to be far greater than anything that I could have expected. God brings people into my life nearly on a daily basis who are a blessing beyond measure. It can all be summarized in three words, God is Good!

Last week I celebrated my second anniversary - two years since having my life spared! I celebrated by having *my first cup of coffee in years and it was terrible!!! Once again, God is Good!*

Thanks again for your part in all of this. I pray his richest blessing upon each of you. Stuart

9/27/2005

Dear Friends,

All is well here. I will be at the local VA Hospital for a few weeks starting Oct. 3rd. I will be getting my new wheelchair set up while I am there. My breathing pacemaker program has been going well. I was up to about a total of 4 hours a day off the ventilator until I got a head cold which set me back a bit.

Thanks for your prayers, Stuart

P.S. My daughter Mary Beth provided the above information. She refused to provide the following. I am looking for someone who has expertise in patients with spinal cord injuries. My problem is when I have a head cold I have no way of forcing air from my nose. How do I get rid of that stuff that none of us wants?

10/23/2005

Dear Friends,

My three weeks at the Seattle VA Hospital have been completed and I can verify that there is no place like home. Everything that I went to the hospital for was successfully complete. This included the destruction of a bladder stone, the servicing and refilling my Baclofen pump which controls my spasms by feeding liquid Baclofen directly to my spinal chord, and the fitting for my new electric wheelchair.

This new high tech electric wheelchair goes faster and further than the earlier model.

I am back on schedule for extending time off the ventilator by utilizing my diaphragm pacemaker. I am recognized by my medical team to be one of the world's truly bionic men.

With that distinction I am now half seriously thinking about what is being done in Korea, China, Portugal, and Israel in the area of stem cell implant. This is only a bit of a dream at this point but I would surely be willing to make myself available if the opportunity and finances became available.

Incidentally I appreciate some of your unique responses to my request on how does a paralyzed person blow his nose. I have decided not to gross you all out with the input that I received.

I am amazed that God continually provides new opportunities for me to tell this story of how He is bringing fulfillment into my life beyond measure.

A small example is that tomorrow I will be making a video tape for a large reunion of Naval Aviators in Corpus Christi, Texas next month and also a video for a church anniversary coming up soon. The videos are because I still am unable to travel these long distances in person to share what God has done.

Another terrific illustration of this particular opportunity was given to me last night by a friend in Boonville, Missouri. He has told me that he is going to share a video I made with 100 prisoners that are part of the organization Prison Fellowship in Boonville Prison.

Local opportunities continue to present themselves on a frequent basis and I am so grateful that God has given me not only a miraculous story but also many opportunities to share it with others.

Thank you again for those of you all over the world who continue to love and support me in so many ways.
Stuart Corey

To all of you who have not yet given up on me, greetings:

My chief caregiver and bride of 50 years, from whom I have not dared be separated for more than two years, is in Iowa for a week. She left Saturday just in time to find out that a good portion of her hometown, Stratford, had just been wiped out by a tornado. All of her many relatives are safe and she is enjoying a long overdue visit with many of them for the next few days in the town of Boone. I am still in the good hands of a wonderful team of round the clock caregivers.

The most current achievement in the diaphragm pacemaker program came a couple of evenings ago when we shut off the ventilator for a full period of four hours. It was going so well that I believe I could have spent the rest of the night free of the ventilator, but figured I had better try and get a little sleep. My medical team has seemed duly impressed with the accomplishment. Stay tuned.

A plaque that I recently received from long time friends in Florida reads: "God is good all the time" and that says it all. Best wishes and God's richest blessing to you all. Stuart Corey

Hello to all my friends,

I am enclosing the letter I sent to my physician regarding my breathing pacemaker.

"Pacing 10 hours from 7 p.m. to 5 a.m. continuously off the ventilator on a regular basis. I have so much to be thankful for this Thanksgiving - a wonderful family, a remarkable medical team, fantastic medical technology and a Great God!"

Hope all of you have a warm Thanksgiving! With much love, Stuart

I have just completed 24 hours on my diaphragm pace-maker completely independent of the ventilator. That may be a record for a 72-year-old geezer. Should be back on the tennis court by the time I'm 75 unless God ordains sooner. A very Merry Christmas and a blessed New Year to all of you. - Stu Corey

Christmas has come and gone and I trust yours was as blessed as mine. I had a couple of unexpected gifts that made my Christmas just outstanding.

The Veterans Administration sent an engineer to voice activate my room. I can now order the TV to do anything I want. And I can answer the telephone, make telephone calls and hang up—all hands off. I can order the lamp and the fan to turn on or turn off, and I will soon be able to tell my hospital bed what to do. This is real cool stuff and you could not believe the thrill that this newfound independence gives to me.

Secondly, my diaphragm pacemaker surgeon flew all the way from Cleveland Ohio to pay me a house call. He was greatly impressed with the progress I have made in being able to free myself for longer and longer periods of time from the ventilator. He fully expects that with the deter-mination he has seen, I should someday be totally free from the ventilator. He really stroked my ego and I received every word of it.

I've said it ten thousand times, God is good! And I'll say it again, God is good all the time. - Stu Corey

Let me now tell you some stories of my pre-missionary life in Pakistan.

Building a Cement Factory

1954–1955, Hyderabad, Sindh

There is nothing very romantic about building a cement factory, and this topic hardly seems pertinent to a story of missionaries in Pakistan. However my work there gives me an unusual qualification. There will not have been many missionaries who in their unrepentant past have been treasurers of a mosque and have raised funds for it.

I am introduced to nautch girls and hermaphrodite dancers at the farewell party for my predecessor. This is clearly not my style, but the following day, the dust settles, he leaves, and I move from the hotel in the desert town of Hyderabad to the two-room shack he vacates on the site that is to be my home (and later Stuart's also) for the next sixteen months.

Hyderabad is the hardest, most demanding job I have had. There are twenty-seven different construction contracts running. The whole task has fallen sharply behind, and we are facing huge penalties for delayed performance. This is not helped when, as soon as I arrive, I receive a delegation from the labor force we already have on site. There are roughly equal numbers of Sindhis and Pathans. They want an immediate doubling of their wages before they will start work. I wonder whether this has been orchestrated by my predecessor and respond by dismissing all four hundred of them on the spot.

This leaves me with the three men who have traveled down with me and some administrative staff. Wooden bolt boxes have not been withdrawn from the fresh concrete in time and have become concreted in. They will have to be chipped out splinter by splinter before the work can get moving again.

It is too hot during the day to work; the steel burns and blisters the hands. We have pressure kerosene lanterns. When the sun goes down we get onto our knees to try to remove from the concrete foundations the solid blocks eight inches square and up to eight feet in length. The bolts to hold down the long rotating kiln have to go into those holes, and there is no alternative location. We hammer away all night with chisels and hammers and rest during the day. Progress is slow, and there are scores of boltholes to be cleared. We don't dare burn them out for fear of cracking the concrete.

The site has an eerie silence. Occasionally the labor jemadars wander over to see how we are getting on. The laborers themselves remain in our labor camp, resting wherever they can find shade from the sun almost directly overhead. Several nights follow the same pattern. During the days, there is no work except for lethargic excavation by the Baluchis who, with their donkeys, are on contract.

Pete, the big Dane who is Resident Consultant Engineer, inquires anxiously what is happening. I tell him and the jemadars that I have sent telegrams north for Sah'b Gul and Mubarak to come with their gangs of labor, as many as possible, as soon as they can. They are back in their villages recruiting all the able-bodied. They will be here within a week, and then I will have the nucleus of a loyal and expanding labor force.

The fifth day is payday, but there is little pay for the men to send home to their families. The jemadars come to see me. They will bring all the labor back tomorrow to work. I say, "No, they will remain sacked." I am not going to be troubled by labor that has no loyalty. They would as likely go on strike again the following week.

I walk over to the labor camp that evening when the cool breeze off the sea fifty miles away begins to make the temperature bearable. The jemadars call the men over. I speak in Urdu, and others translate into Sindhi and Pushtu.

I will treat them fairly, but I will not be dictated to. They will find I am hard—and fair. I expect them to be loyal. I will do my best to ensure they are paid adequately and regularly, and I will pay each man myself so that no subordinate might cream commission off their pay. There is at least two years work here for them. I will need many more Pathan laborers. I am a Pathan myself, from Waziristan. They can send for their relatives and I will employ them as soon as they arrive. I do not want blind men or cripples. Any men who go on strike will be dismissed immediately, without discussion.

Next morning, everybody is back at work. Much to Pete's relief, momentum begins to pick up. Not difficult since it has been zero.

The office staff are few, but Zaidi, the head clerk, and Mehtabuddin, the quantity surveyor, are both good, competent men. Mehtab is a keen member of Jama'at-i-Islami and looks the part; Zaidi is a middle-of-the-road Sunni Muslim. I tell Zaidi we will start paying the men at four o'clock. We pay every two weeks. We have muster rolls. Even the donkeys are on muster rolls. I grab the proffered left thumb, press it onto an ink pad and then on to the muster roll, tell the man what his pay is and then personally count out the money to him. We already have an enlarged labor force, for both Sah'b Gul and Mubarak have brought more than a hundred men apiece.

Zaidi and Mehtab come in to see me together. There is no mosque, and they have no maulvi. The men cannot—should not—go two years without a place of worship and a priest to care for their spiritual needs. I concur. They go on. If we deduct only one rupee from each man's pay, that will give well

a boy and his lunch

over a thousand rupees each month. We can build and maintain a mosque and employ a maulvi and have a fund to help men with problems.

No deal! We are not deducting anything from anybody. They have earned every rupee by the sweat of their brow. Each man will receive every anna and paisa of what is due to him. We will place a basin on the wage table. Whatever any man chooses to give, he can give, and if he chooses to give nothing, that is okay, too. Mehtab and Zaidi don't think that is a good alternative, but before we start paying out, I explain to the men what the basin is for. The news passes down the line as the men come through. When the payment is finished, I am gratified with how much in coins and rupee notes has been given.

I push the basin over to Zaidi and Mehtab. They recoil in horror. "What's wrong? Here's the money, take it and count it, and then go and spend it." They look at each other in consternation. Neither is going to touch it.

"We can't touch this, Mr. Old, it's more than our lives are worth! The Pathans have given this. What do you think will happen to us when they suspect we are stealing from it?"

They both move urgently towards the door, leaving the basin on the table.

"There's only one person on this site who can dare touch this money, it's you!"

"This is nonsense. I'm a Christian. This is Muslim money, for your mosque. Here, take it. Both of you count it together, and I'll countersign it."

They are having none of it. They have families and dependents. They excuse themselves hurriedly and are gone. Slowly, I begin to count the money. I have just been appointed Treasurer of the Mosque.

The arrangement works well. The men continue to give generously, and throughout, there are never any questions raised about the accounts.

For a temporary building site, we build a rather attractive mosque. We keep it in good repair. We employ a maulvi and buy him a sewing machine so that he can supplement his pay by working as a tailor. I inspect the mosque whenever I inspect the labor quarters and supervise repairs and improvements. We distribute any spare money to the sick and needy.

Pervez and Pir Gul

Hyderabad, Sindh

At the labor camp, Pervez and Ghulam, two brothers, Sindhis, run a grocery store for the laborers. They have the usual things—peppers, rice, tea, spices, cigarettes, flour, sugar and ghee (clarified butter).

Mehtab reports there are no donkeys at work. The donkey walas are on strike. I find some of them over in the labor colony. Yes, they are on strike. They don't want to be on strike, but Pir Gul is in jail in Hyderabad City, and they can't work without his instructions. Pir Gul is their leader. He could have starred in a role as a mountain brigand. He is about 6'6" with a broad frame to match. He wears a purple velvet waistcoat, baggy trousers and has large twirling mustachios. He speaks Brahui but has enough Urdu so that we can converse intelligently. He is always more than one step ahead in cheating on the measurements of the excavations.

Why is he in jail?

Pervez, the shopkeeper, has reported him for assault. I go over to the shop. Ghulam is there.

Yes, Pervez is in the hospital in the city. Last evening, when Pervez has been in the shop by himself, the store has suddenly been burst into by a mob of frenzied Baluchi donkey-walas led by Pir Gul, who proceed, literally, to de-hair Pervez. They pull out his hair, his beard, his mustache, every single hair they can seize hold of and have done the job better than a barber can have done. They have left him almost dead and then gone back cheerfully to the labor camp.

Ghulam has come running, avoiding the returning Baluchis, and taken Pervez to a hospital in the city by taxi. He has reported the assault at the city police station. An armed posse of police has picked up not only Pir Gul, but several of his companions also.

They are now in the police lockup.

This is serious business. The police are undoubtedly corrupt. They will proceed to milk not only Pir Gul and his companions dry, but they will milk Pervez and Ghulam dry, too. The lawyers will move in and compound the situation. My donkey-walas can be on strike for weeks, even months, and the excavations, already far behind, can drop to zero. Dislocation of the grocery shop routine will make things difficult for all the labor.

I thunder at Ghulam. *"How dare you* go to the police with such a report! Who is in charge on the site? Is it the police, or is it *me?"*

He agrees.

Does he realize what he has done? Does he realize that it is now necessary for me to close down his shop? He has insulted me by going over my head to the police. Do I not have power to deal fairly with any assault? Does he think I will not give justice to Pervez and without *any cost?* Does he think I will favor a gang of Baluchi donkey-walas assaulting unprovoked a single, unarmed and innocent Sindhi shopkeeper? How can he think he can continue business when there are a thousand sympathizers to Pir Gul in the labor colony? His only chance is to close up and flee for his life *unless* he shall choose to go to the police and withdraw the case against Pir Gul *immediately.* I will do my best to protect his shop and deflect the anger of the labor gangs. The Wazirs and Mahsuds are blood brothers to the Baluchis, but he must act *without delay!* He can be assured there will be a fair trial.

My office does not make an impressive courtroom, but I have done the best I can. I shift furniture around, sit sternly behind my desk, have the plaintiffs on the left and a quite unrepentant Pir Gul and a couple of his accomplices on the right. This is a multi-language courtroom, for streams of communication flow and intermarry in Brahui, Sindhi, Urdu and English. Zaidi and Mehtab assist with translations and courtroom management.

Pervez is a pitiful figure. His head is wrapped in bandages, leaving only just sufficient space for the necessary functions of hearing, seeing, breathing and speaking.

Haltingly, he tells his story. It is as Ghulam has said. He has been sitting in his shop when, unprovoked, Pir Gul and his men burst in, abusing and assaulting him. He has suffered serious injury and intense pain.

Pir Gul is asked for his story. He does not deny Pervez's account, but there has been provocation. The Baluchis have sent a boy down to the shop to get sugar, milk and tea. The boy has no money with him, but that is customary. The Baluchis take their supplies on tick and pay when they themselves receive pay for their work. Pervez refuses to let the boy have the supplies on credit. It has been more than two months since they have paid anything. The boy reports back to the donkey-walas, repeating, perhaps embellishing, the florid phrases Pervez has used to describe their ancestry. How can any self-respecting Baluchi accept that from a Sindhi? He has brought the consequences upon himself.

I turn back to Pervez. He has heard Pir Gul. If he will assure me, by placing his hand upon the Holy Q'ran, that he has made no such remarks, I will accept without question his affirmation, for he is an honorable man. I will then deal with Pir Gul as he deserves. Zaidi brings the Holy Q'ran and places it on the table.

a boy and his lunch

There is silence. A long silence. Pervez looks at Pir Gul and then at the holy book and licks his dry lips. He looks back at me and says, "I feel unwell. I need to sit down."

He does so. I realize his evidence is over and I turn back to Pir Gul.

"The case against you is proven beyond doubt and by your own admission you assaulted most violently the shopkeeper Pervez. My sentence is that you are fined three hundred rupees damages."

I hold out my hand toward Pir Gul. From a full wallet, he takes with considerable distaste three hundred rupees, a sizable fine, and hands the notes to me. I place them on the desk in front of Pervez.

I turn to him. "I have observed that you are a sharif man who will not give his word before God lightly. You deserve the three hundred rupees as compensation for the suffering you have received. It was an appalling act. However, I believe that you will not wish to benefit from another man's misfortune. I surmise that you would rather see the fine that Pir Gul has just paid used to benefit the whole community and that you would prefer to see it donated to the mosque fund. Am I right?"

Pervez nods without enthusiasm. He is as able as I to see that to receive money at the expense of Pir Gul might lead to another unruly visit to his shop with possibly even worse consequences for himself.

I take the money back into my own custody as Treasurer of the Mosque, insist Pir Gul settle up his account with the shopkeepers before me then and there and dismiss the court.

Visitors in the Desert

December 1954, Hyderabad, Sind

I did not know Marie well when working on a factory near Taxila. I knew the Browns and Christys better, they have children and I enjoyed telling them stories. Marie has returned from America to her work at the hospital not long after I have arrived in Wah. My fellow travelers on the church bus have told me about the tragic loss of her husband from polio at the beginning of the summer. He has been their pastor and they have dearly loved him.

I am invited to attend a conference of Frontier missionaries at the hospital that February of '54. This is my first encounter with other than the hospital missionaries. There are about forty of them. How they sing! I can not recall ever hearing such singing, fit to raise the roof! They are men and women—mixed American and British, one or two Scandinavians—from probably half a dozen different missionary societies serving on mission stations across the North West Frontier Province and the northwestern areas of the Punjab.

They are a close-knit group of friends, clearly enjoy being together, laugh a lot, play jokes on each other and are not impossibly ethereal. I gain from them a glimpse into the way missionaries think about their impossible goal of bringing Jesus Christ to the Frontier and even into Afghanistan—and how serious and committed they are about it.

I transfer to Hyderabad and Taxila becomes part of a distant world I once passed through. However Marie writes in late November to say she is coming to Hyderabad soon with a team of literacy experts and there may be chance to meet.

Marie spends the first part of December in Karachi meeting her team. Apart from Dr. Laubach and his wife, there are a young and very intense honeymoon couple, a relaxed newspaper reporter and an authoress of children's books. All are American.

In Karachi, they work in Urdu, using the Arabic script, so Marie is demonstrator for the lessons they teach.

Marie stays at the Brenton Carey School and Orphanage with a missionary friend, Marian Laugesen, from New Zealand.

At Hyderabad, the old capital of the Sindh Government, they will be working in Sindhi. Nearby at Kotri, a great new river barrage is just being completed across the Indus. It will have an immense economic effect as its feeder canals develop and feed water into the desert. It will also provide the vast quantities of water that Karachi is sure to be needing as it grows.

Marie tells me they will be arriving early in December; they will be staying at the Canal Rest Houses. I drive down to the city to make sure there are no initial problems they might need help with.

When I find their accommodation has been cancelled on them at the last minute I offer our humble two-room shack on the edge of the desert. In an emergency you can't pick and choose.

My announcement to Stuart that we are having guests in an hour is met by outright unmistakable rebellion. "*We* are not having guests; *you* are having guests!" Stuart will move over into Hagen's house *right now*. Has he not been telling me he thanks God he is an atheist? Now I am swamping the house with missionaries. That isn't in his contract, and he isn't staying. I am talking fast. I totally rely on Stuart; he is my right hand man. He can't do this to me—leave me all by myself with five missionaries on my hands. They will make mincemeat of me!

Allah Buksh is sent running for extra beds from the labor colony; they will all be infested with bed bugs, but this is no time for niceties. The honeymooning wife will have near nightmares each night fearing her husband is being eaten by cobras or jackals or hyenas or tigers or whatever wild animals this country possesses, but she should just count herself fortunate she is inside.

As a concession, Stuart can keep his own bed. The thought of Stuart losing his own bed has not occurred to him, and he states that plainly. He is unhappy, no doubt about it, but by now he is swilling white paint over the bedroom windows so generously that it is obvious we will have to replace the panes of glass when it is all over if we want to see out.

I tell Allah Buksh to get the donkey with the broken leg out of the garden. We have a small, walled garden in which we have been trying unsuccessfully to grow grass. He must make sure Donald, the duck, is out of the house when the visitors arrive and that his mess has all been cleaned up; we don't want to give a bad impression.

"Allah Buksh, we will have dinner at half past seven prompt, and don't you dare make it curry."

I am off to pick the guests up.

Stuart has warmed to the guests by the time Christmas comes. Each day they have been collected from the construction site after breakfast and taken to the Literacy Demonstration Centre at the Canal colony. They are gone then until just before regular teatime. Stuart is more gregarious than I, has more energy and is willing to stay up later than the regular 9 p.m. to chat—as

a boy and his lunch

long as it isn't about religion. The pair of us have pretty well exhausted subjects of conversation other than work and normally spend any free evening silently listening to classical music and writing letters or doing office work. He appreciates the different company, and Hagen also helps provide variety for our guests. He pops in to visit and offer around his vile smelling cheroots. His wife is particularly interested in the Danish Pathan Mission based in Mardan, so Marie and he have common interests.

There are frequent major site injuries, often quite bloody and gruesome. I ask her to accompany me on rounds and carefully watch her reactions. As a nurse, Marie has been trained never to usurp the authority of the doctor, but on this site I am the doctor! I make rounds to the labor barracks of sun-dried bricks and corrugated sheet roofs daily. I have pills of one kind or another for every ailment a man might legitimately possess and probably some beyond that. I dispense medicines and pills liberally on the assumption that anything is probably better than nothing and thus have gained a quite unwarranted reputation. I suspect many of the men have tuberculosis.

After she returns to Taxila, I upgrade my medical equipment with a large-capacity hypodermic syringe with a needle of robust dimensions. I then seek from her by mail advice about what part of the buttock of my trusting patient I should select and how to apply the injection. Although I always boil the needle and syringe before using it, this does not seem to ensure the ready flow of the penicillin or sulfa or whatever alternative of my limited stock I am using. Frequent blockage of the needle during any injection is just one of the industrial hazards we all face. By the time I leave the site, the needle itself has become seriously blunt. But scores of patients have benefited, and I have a vast reputation as a healer among the Pakhtuns.

Allah Buksh, the cook, excels himself during their stay. He has been an undiscovered maestro in the art of cooking. When he has come to work for me in April, I have given him the day's menu. It has not occurred to either Stuart or me to change it, although the cause of the severe-blurry-eyes problem and the inability to focus the eyes is later laid clear at the door of vitamin deficiency.

The challenge suddenly placed before him taps all his latent qualities. He has no refrigerator in which to store perishables, he has previously only had wood for his fuel. My desperate shopping has included a small tabletop kerosene oil cooker, so he feels like a king in his smoke-filled kitchen.

Expense is no object, so he turns out roast chicken, steak and kidney pudding, sirloin, roast hump, steak, and Yorkshire pudding. Fish and vegetables of the country that we have previously refused ever to allow in the house are garnished in ways that almost make them edible when hidden under gravy.

His puddings are superb. Custard with every meal, apple pie, bread pudding and suet and steamed puddings of every ilk, spotted dick, golden pudding, treacle pudding, roly-poly pudding—you name it, he knows it.

Christmas Day arrives and only Marie and Chesley are left. We do our best.

On the edge of the city, almost overlooking the Indus, is one of the Victorian gothic brick churches of the British Raj. It is now in disrepair, but old Father Lavery, an Anglican missionary suffering from severe elephantiasis, is still there, living on his own. Bats fly around inside the dusty church. The priest's congregation fills little more than a couple of rows, but the communion service makes the day really feel like Christmas Day.

We have Christmas lunch with the Petersons. They have a lovely modern home with Danish linens and table service and decorations, floor carpets and modern furniture—a different world to our own. We move back over to drink tea in the garden until the sun slips down and it is time for our evening meal.

As the roast potatoes, the Yorkshire pudding, the sprouts, the carrots, the cabbage, the peas, the turnips, the beans, the gravy and then the roast beef keep coming in there seems to be no end. But there is yet to come—a beautiful brown roasted-to-a-turn piece of poultry on a platter.

It looks like duck. Duck! Stuart and I both blanch. Donald? We haven't seen him today, where is he? "Where's Donald?"

Allah Buksh points to the plate.

That's Donald? But Donald is family!

"Allah Buksh, what did you kill Donald for!"

"I no kill Donald, Sah'b, snake bite him! He die, over there, beside the hand-pump." He bustles off quickly to the kitchen before we can ask more questions.

Stuart and I look at Donald with sadness and a distinct loss of appetite. I doubt that a snake has killed Donald, but I hope that, if it indeed has been a snake, it was a python and not a kreit or a viper. We who know cannot eat: it seems akin to cannibalism.

Stuart's sadness is not yet complete. When Allah Buksh brings in the Christmas pudding, it is burning—one might almost say blazing—with a bright blue flame. No sooner does Stuart see it than his eyes jerk to the sideboard beside the door on which he keeps his treasured bottle of Cointreau. In the morning it has been almost full. It is now almost empty.

As soon as the train door to carry them north is opened, Chesley steps back instinctively, but Marie, like a real trouper, does not hesitate. Forcing herself into the melee of women and half naked children, she smiles sweetly

a boy and his lunch

at the horrified Chesley behind her and says, "Come along, Chesley." Chesley dreads twenty-four-hour journey in a female-rattling Black Hole of Calcutta only less than one other thing—being left behind in Hyderabad without Marie. She looks at me desperately, like a trapped animal, and I offer my arm to help her up into the train. The guard is blowing his whistle. Marie's hand is stretched out to help her. The cases quickly follow Chesley's launch into the compartment; the door slams and the train is on its way.

Hagen drops in to check they made it onto the train and asks, out of the blue, "Why don't you marry Marie, Ken?"

I laugh at the question. We are so different—different worlds, different lives, different goals—but the question lingers. What on earth (or in heaven) has prompted Hagen to ask?

This 'interesting and unusual Christmas', as Marie phrased it, proves in hindsight to be a critical experience for both of us. Neither of us recognizes it at the time, but *it* leads to our marriage just one year later.

I have promised five years earlier that God can have the rest of my life (if He will give me three years to myself first!) Things are beginning to percolate.

This impromptu visit of Marie to Hyderabad is to prove part of my journey towards His goal for my life.

Fireburst

The world's on fire -
Not with disaster,
Hate and war,
Love's flames burn
A thousand bushes
Across the face
Of a dry world
Without consuming.
When the flames touch
One bush to the other
A circle of fire
Will compass the world.

Fish Curry

Karachi 1956

During the first year of our marriage, we move from our lovely home in Mauripur in Karachi to an orphanage more near the heart of the city. Marie will run it during the absence of Marian on furlough in New Zealand.

It would have been easy for a stranger calling in at the orphanage to assume Marie has been there all her life. During her time on the Army hospital train in Italy during the war, she and Lundy had made frequent visits to Casa Materna, a Protestant orphanage on the south side of Naples. That little sanctuary was their recreation and relief from the horrors of conflict brought back with the wounded soldiers from Cassino. There was a sense of permanence and practical holiness and the presence of God to be savored in those few snatched hours.

Now for a while, her own orphanage challenges her qualities of love and compassion. Marian leaves an easy legacy. When women run things without interference from men they usually thrive. The orphanage operates to set patterns and routines and virtually runs itself.

Besides the girls in the orphanage, much of Marie's time is given over to managing the school, dealing with parents of the girls coming in from outside each day, looking after her own household and caring for the steady flow of incoming missionary guests.

The women, whether the teachers, the cooks, Janebai or the matron Jhaggoo, are dedicated and loving. The resident children—between fifty and sixty of them—are happy children. It is not only because they have regular meals, adequate clothing and tender loving care; they are a close-knit family who have fun and play games together and who enjoy being with each other. There is nothing soulless about this institution. The compound of the orphanage is not large, but it is their world. They rarely go beyond its walls except to cross the road to Trinity Church in a neat little procession for Sunday morning worship or for a walk with Poppa (in groups of ten or fifteen) down to the shops as a special treat.

A taxi driver asks me if all these girls are *my* children.

"Ask them."

"Is he *really* your Poppa?"

The girls giggle at such a silly question. "Of course."

He looks back at me accusingly, shakes his head sadly and seriously and goes back to his cab, reflecting on what the world is coming to.

I change my job. I am working for the first time with Americans and enjoying it. The U.S. Government has started in the spring a huge aid package to Pakistan for the construction of military and airfield facilities.

As my three-year contract with my British employers ends, we are moving into the orphanage. I decline an offered renewal and take instead a one-year contract with the U.S. Corps of Engineers. I am given responsibility for developing the optimum design of the concrete mixes to be used in the extension to Mauripur runway on the western edge of Karachi. This will allow a more regular daily routine to assist Marie at the orphanage and will cover our commitment to Marian until she is able to return or obtain a replacement for us. After that, we will pop north to Sialkot for a few months to do a children's ward at the hospital and then go to England and find God's will for the next stage of our lives.

I quickly discover that, contrary to the British custom of freshly brewed tea at appropriate but distinct intervals of the day, the coffee pot is put on as soon as work starts and simmers all day, and coffee is decanted from it until it is time to clean up and close down.

There are five of us working in the laboratory. Bob and Orval are two of my colleagues, and they travel in daily from the Columbus Hotel where they stay, picking me up along the way. Like most of the men they work among, they are hard-living, hard-drinking men with hearts of gold.

During the autumn of 1956, I am like a child in school, discovering the rock solid reliability of God. Running the accounts of the orphanage is not without its difficulties. Our pockets are rarely more affluent than almost empty. However, I am finding that, without money, without major donors, without bank balances and savings, it is still possible to manage financially. Because you have no credit status, there is no one who will lend you money even if you should be tempted to try to cover a need temporarily. An ability to borrow makes us captive and gives us a spurious alternative to dependence on God.

This is liberating to discover. It means that we have to take seriously the way to pray. Give us *this* day our daily bread. If we have today's bread and save it for tomorrow, it will be stale and inedible.

The story of Moses and the manna in the desert tells us that the manna was to be gathered enough for the day and no more. The excess would go bad. There was always enough for the day. Gather and use that. There was a weekly exception; on the day before the Sabbath, two days provisions were to be collected and, because this was the way God had arranged things, the Sabbath supply remained fresh.

The heart of the situation is that, to be sure of the bread for each day, we need to stay close to the heart and will of God.

a boy and his lunch

The children are teaching me. As needs become apparent, I tell them, and they pray, and it happens and keeps on happening. It has been happening for sixty years before we came to the orphanage, and it will go on happening after we leave. *Sufficient unto the day* . . . Of course the six hundred rupees Marian had passed over to us has been quite enough for Marian to run the orphanage on. She has had an endowment fund and a bank balance, but it hasn't been written in ledgers.

We will hand over exactly the same amount—six hundred rupees—to Edwy and Pat Naismith when we leave the orphanage, giving the same assurance to them that Marian has given us.

They in turn will discover the same thing.

One night—it is after two in the morning, for even the open-air cinema across the road has at last closed—the watchman wakes us up. One of the men I work with is downstairs. He needs to talk with us. It is urgent. Rubbing the sleep out of our eyes, we come down. John, a site engineer, is there.

"Do you want a fish?" He has been out night fishing and has caught a fish a few miles off the shore.

"Oh sure, it will make a change; we can have fish curry. Bring it in."

Then we see the fish!

It must have been a younger brother to the one that swallowed Jonah! It takes all the strength of John and his driver and the watchman and me to manhandle the fish into our kitchen. I had been thinking of a ten-pounder perhaps. This is the biggest fish I have ever had anything to do with. Whether it is a marlin or a tuna, I don't know. To me, it is the next size smaller than a whale!

John takes his leave soon afterwards and leaves us to it. It takes Said and Marie and me the rest of the night to cut it up and salt it down. Marie's Montana backwoods knowledge of preserving meat guides our labors. As dawn comes, we get more salt, several bathtubs are filled with fish, we feel and smell like fish, and Bob and Orval move to the other side of the van when I go to work.

Christmas at the Orphanage

December 1956

There are differences in character and culture between Americans and English other than their choice of tea or coffee. Marie and I are both enjoying discovering those differences on a personal level, but there are other differences, too.

One of them is the way the British and Americans give help to others. The model of aid for the developing countries and for Britain is the Colombo Plan, developed to help struggling members of the British Commonwealth. Every project put forward is carefully scrutinized by project specialists, planners and accountants. Feasibility studies are done and redone. Sums are checked and rechecked. Projects are divided into phases, subsequent phases being dependent upon the previous performance. Common sense is applied and reapplied. Money is not going to be wasted if human foresight and caution can have anything to do with it. It is a successful and inevitably a slow process.

American giving is different. It seems to flow out of the generous heart of a nation blessed with abundant resources and a willingness to share them. There is an acceptance that is refreshing that not all aid will go where it is intended. Inevitably, there will be corruption and mismanagement. While minimizing whatever losses you can as you go forward in a hurry, what is important is to move quickly because time is often not an ally.

Both ways of giving are valid, and both are justifiable. The story that follows will demonstrate not only God's providing but also the generous hearts of the providers.

Time moves on to the beginning of December. I am worried. I am still learning how to relax. I have just found out that the custom is the staff of the orphanage receive their wages for December on the fifteenth of the month. Not only that, but the property tax and the water tax are also falling due. Marie will have to buy the blue and white cloth for the children's Christmas clothes and get the tailors busy soon. Then there will be the copybooks and the pencils and the ribbons and the oranges and, of course, special food for Christmas. I will need two thousand rupees by the fifteenth of the month. Where on earth is that going to come from? I am pressing God in prayer, maybe He already knows, but there is no harm reminding Him He only has half the time He usually has to arrange matters.

Bob broaches things one morning after they have picked me up for work. They have become used to this strange father who has scores of children clamoring at the gate when he comes home. "The boys and I have been thinking it might be kinda nice to give your children a Christmas party. How would you feel about that?"

What a wonderful idea! How the children will enjoy that!

"Go ahead!"

And then several days later, they drop the bombshell, and I spoil it for them with the most thoughtless reaction.

The bombshell is that the party is on and that they have collected two thousand rupees. *Two thousand rupees!* I can't believe it! Two thousand rupees! For a party?

Hardly have they finished telling me, and they are both looking so pleased, than I break in with a plea. Would—could—it be possible that, instead of spending the money on a party, they would let me have it? I promise the children will still have a party, but with the money I can also pay the staff, pay the taxes, buy the cloth and the presents and . . .

I stop short, realizing the enormity of what I am asking. I am spoiling everything for them—their generosity, their enthusiasm to do something nice for people, their own plans for a party for Pakistani children at Christmas when they are so far from their own children. Words are like arrows; once loosed they cannot be called back. I am sincere in my apologies. How can I have been so thoughtless, so . . . well, so brutal. I am really sorry. Please forget what I said. The party is a wonderful idea, this will be the high point of our children's lives. We should make it on Christmas Eve. All the words that stumble out of my mouth can't undo the damage. I can see that written large on their two faces.

Bob mumbles something about "Asking the boys." I urge him just to forget I'd ever said anything, but I know I have spoiled Christmas for them.

Only a couple of days later, while I am working in the concrete laboratory, Bob hands me an envelope. I open it. Inside are two thousand rupees. I look up at him, my heart full.

"The boys said it's okay, you can have the money."

I know this is God providing, but oh, at so large a cost in human happiness. I can't say anything and just turn away so that they shall not see the tears in my eyes. It shouldn't be like this.

I give the money to Marie. She, too, is sorry but takes it as from God. She buys the white and blue cloth, bolts of it, and sends for the tailor and his assistants. She buys white satin ribbons for the girls' hair. She buys sandals. She buys copybooks and pencils in the bazar. She pays the wages of all the staff on the fifteenth. She sets aside money for the taxes. She buys provi-

a boy and his lunch

sions—extra provisions—for Christmas and invites Bob and Orval and all those who have contributed to come for the party on the afternoon of Christmas Eve. We will have it in the garden.

On Christmas Eve the girls, ready for our party, look just lovely. We are both so proud of them. Their hair is shining, washed and braided. Earlier they had been sitting in a large circle braiding the hair of the girl in front of them. The ribbons shine. The new clothes have been washed and ironed and are being worn. We are waiting for our guests to arrive and then . . .

It seems for a moment as though the roof has fallen in, for a large bus draws up outside the orphanage gates. Bob and Orval, dressed in their Sunday best, come bounding in. "Tell the girls to get in."

Words stumble off my tongue. I have really fouled it up! I have misunderstood. I have not understood that they had given me the two thousand rupees merely to keep safe. They have gone ahead and arranged the party after all, and I have gone ahead and spent the money that was to pay for it! What a mess!

"I'm terribly sorry, Bob; I misunderstood. I'm afraid I've spent the money."

Bob cuts me short, grinning. "We knew you would. That's okay. We gave you the money, and then we had another collection and collected another two thousand rupees. We decided that this time we'd better not tell you about it in case you'd want that, too. Now will you tell the children to get in? Everyone is waiting for them."

What a party! Only Americans could have put on a party like this party! For the children, just the bus-ride up Bonus Road and over the Clifton bridge is Christmas festivity enough, but as the bus turns in to the Columbus hotel, it seems as though all the Americans in Karachi are there celebrating Christmas with our girls. The band (does any country have better bands than Pakistan?) starts playing as the bus comes into sight. The children pile out of the bus and into the hotel with eyes as big as saucers. Barbara and Lily clutch hold of Marie's hands. Others clutch Barbara and Lily. I carry the baby and hold Akhtar's hand.

The largest Christmas tree you could hope to see decorates the foyer. Where have they got that from, Quetta? There are wreaths and tinsel decorations, holly, baubles brought from Hong Kong, clowns and Santa Claus, paper hats, snappers, cakes on a laden table and presents flown in from Goodness-knows-where heaped under the tree. They must have had a special flight from MATS to fly it all in. Now I understand why I have been plied with questions about the ages of our girls. Obviously, the women have helped choose the gifts. The youngest girls all have dolls. Many have never ever possessed a doll that was their very own. Lily had never even touched one when she came to us. And for Shamim, our one little boy, there is a Tonka truck.

All I can say to myself is, "What a wonderful God! He not only gives us the two thousand rupees we asked for, but He throws in a Christmas party we'll never forget for good measure!"

And now to some stories of missionary life.

The Christian Training Institute

Lall Moti Lall, the headmaster of the Christian Training Institute (CTI) in Sialkot, and I are good friends. He is probably a few years older than I and a leader of the "layman's movement" within the Synod of the Punjab. Marie and I, although not very senior, are now the senior missionaries living at CTI.

Lall is a village boy that Clemmie (E.V. Clements), one of the greats of the Sialkot Mission, has touched on the shoulder one day out in the Punjabi boondocks.

"Hey, boy, do you want to go to school?"

Lall jumps at the chance. Since then he has gone through CTI, through Gordon College and then studies in the United States.

The Fosters, who have spent decades at CTI, have turned this small boarding school into the unchallenged Number one basketball training center for Pakistan. This brings opportunity to the star players to play in top-flight teams like the Army, the Railways and the National team. Bob Foster and Lall also make a wonderful team. Their wives, Aurel and Harriet, make another.

Lall gives me an insight into a role Bob Foster must have had with him and that many missionaries have with their national colleagues and close friends. We are sharing some confidences in normal conversation. He remarks, "You know, Ken, we are talking about things I cannot even tell Harriet. We all have family, and family connections spread far and wide. I have to watch my words even across my own dining table. You have no family here, so my confidences with you are safe. Sometimes I just need to talk about things to someone. It has to be a missionary I talk to because only he is safe with some of the things I want to talk about."

The Fosters have retired. They have waited until we return from furlough. There is no way we can ever fill their giant shoes, but at least we live in the Lal Kothi, the red house where they have lived so long. It is important the big house not be empty. CTI very much has its own life but much depends on what goes on in the Lal Kothi.

The Lal Kothi is the largest house we have ever lived in. It has twenty-one outside doors, one hundred windows and more than twenty rooms, some very large. Before the 1857 mutiny, it had been the Deputy Commissioner's office and probably also his home. There has been a property exchange leading to the Sialkot Mission acquiring the property and many acres around it. This creates the opportunity for a training institute where illiterate men and boys can be given the rudiments of education to equip them as preachers and evangelists.

Later, when the seminary moves to Gujranwala, it develops into a straight boys boarding and day school.

The CTI is not only famous for its basketball. It has been and still is famous for the Sialkot Convention. This is the father of annual Christian conventions and dates back to the beginning of the last century. From all over the Punjab and from as far afield as Peshawar two hundred miles away, Christians come at the end of September, often on foot, for a gathering of praise, worship and teaching. Several thousands will gather. In its heyday from 1900 to 1910, Praying Hyde and Kanaya and others of like mind would be all night on their knees in the prayer room. Marie and I are involved with the youth meetings of the Convention while Marie is also hostess in the Big House to the eminent speakers who come to participate.

It is at this time that I am building a science block of classrooms and also working on a design of a permanent convention building to replace the great twin pole tent that from the early beginnings housed the full meetings.

Although a couple of other missionary families often live separately in their own arrangements in the house, Marie still manages a busy, bustling household.

Our two boys, lusty and active four and five-year-olds, are in the convent school in the cantonment. They go off on Daddy's bicycle early in the morning. Marie also has the short-termers, a couple of young Americans, who are working in the school. The Carlsons come to stay with us for a first year's language study. Audrey, a teacher at home, supervises additional schooling for the boys, and Ed teaches Tim piano.

In addition, we have, as the school year is drawing to its end, four boys at a time from the CTI graduating class come stay with us for about a week. For these boys, it is the high spot of the five years they spend at the boarding school.

The Fosters have started the custom, and we continue it for the four years we are here. The boys just become members of our family. Marie writes each of the boys an invitation requesting that he come and stay with us as our guest at the Lal Kothi. The boys write formal responses in their best handwriting, in English, accepting the invitation. They arrive with their bedding. Marie welcomes them warmly and shows them to their rooms. When they have made their beds and have settled in, I take them to the toilets and, amongst other things, explain the use of toilet paper and the western way of using a toilet. At meals, Tim and Colin help keep the talk around the table

a boy and his lunch

going when they are home. We haven't realized that conversation, too, is a learned social skill.

Our intention is to help the potential leadership of our community glimpse and experience some of the transitions that will be necessary as they grow on through possible college to post-graduate work and overseas journeys in addition.

We really only have problems with one boy who is unable to stop stealing things, often insignificant items. The other boys are just excellent, try their best to adjust to our very strange foreign ways and to benefit from their stay. They love the change from boarding hostel food, and Marie makes sure there is plenty of spicy food for hungry boys.

One of the boys who stays with us in November 1962 catches our particular attention.

Yaqub is from Thatha Chima, a village in the Gujranwala district. His father had been murdered in an affray, and his widowed mother struggles hard to get her son into CTI. From his first admission in sixth class, this boy has been remarkable.

Disadvantaged in comparison with the other boys, he nevertheless soars to the top of his class and stays there. He is possessed of an iron determination that no minute of his five years schooling is going to be wasted. He knows what awaits him back in the village if he doesn't succeed. He is not going to fail if human effort can achieve success. He is going to be a surgeon and work in America. It is an impossible goal to everyone except Yaqub. He is going to make it.

Make it he does!

His name is inscribed on the CTI Student Achievements Board as Top Academic Achiever. From CTI, he goes on to Gordon College for pre-Med. After that, he cannot get a place in King Edward Medical College in Lahore, but he applies for a place in a medical college in Karachi.

He is working as a surgery assistant to the Director of the United Christian Hospital in Lahore, not knowing a place has been granted to him at Dow Medical College as a minority student. If he does not take up his seat by the next day, the place will be forfeited. Karachi is eight hundred miles away!

George Tewksbury, who has never met Yaqub, comes to hear of it and recognizes the critical time element. With a helpful friend he rushes to the UCH, literally grabs Yaqub out of the operating room, gets him onto the last plane to Karachi at 9 p.m., and Yaqub is a medical student the next day.

We are told that when no one else will work in the stench of the mortuary in virtually 100 degrees Fahrenheit and almost 100 percent humidity, Yaqub is in there by himself working, a handkerchief wrapped over his nose and mouth.

He graduates with a degree in medicine and becomes an intern at United Christian Hospital, Lahore. Before leaving Karachi, however, he takes the USA medical qualification exam. He passes it on his first try while some of his own professors have been regularly failing that same exam for years.

For many years now, Yaqub has been running a successful private practice that he established from scratch in Michigan, U.S.A. He has not failed to remember his roots in the Punjab.

The Christian Youth Club

1962, Sialkot

Our involvement in the youth programs of the Sialkot Convention leads me one day not long after Convention to tackle Lall about something on our hearts.

"Lall, we want to start a youth club. We have lots of young people in our local community, and they just don't have enough to do to occupy their time. Let's try to give them something. We have the space here in the Lal Kothi for a club and its activities."

Lall concurs. Christian Town, the adjacent basti leading from the Wazirabad road to Hunterpura, is full of young men—our young men—who are becoming loungers and no-goods, wasting their parents' money on the cinema and cigarettes. Then I spring my bombshell.

"Lall, we don't want it to be for the boys alone, we want it to be for the girls, too. How are our young people ever going to develop balanced relationships with the other sex if they never get a chance to meet them in normal social circumstances?"

Lall is caught off balance. He doesn't want to tell me outright that it is a stupid preposterous idea, yet it undoubtedly is. He picks his words carefully.

I am well intentioned but don't I realize the cultural differences between the East and the West? The Christian community is too fragile to stand unnecessary scandal. Don't I realize what happens when boys and girls get together? It isn't in the culture of Pakistani society to have mixed gatherings of young unmarried people. Marriage arrangements are best left to the parents. Look at the divorce statistics of the United States. This proposal, if it goes wrong, could destroy family relationships built up over generations. There are enough family feuds already. Girls have to be protected. Young men turned loose become wolves, and this will be a golden opportunity for them.

I listen carefully. I agree with everything Lall says, and more. Nevertheless, we want a youth club of mixed young men and women. We believe we can handle the problems and that the benefits will outweigh the problems. We aren't trying to westernize. We merely want to create a healthy, normal environment where young men and women can meet. There are many young women teachers over at the girls' boarding school at Hajipura on the other side of the city. They are away from home and have no entertainment open to them except that which they create for themselves in a closed environment. This is an abnormal situation. They are in their early twenties. We could do something for them at the same time as we are integrating them into the Sialkoti Christian community. They would get to know more about the families from which their pupils come.

Lall represents the community around us. Well, he can set the rules under which we will operate the club.

Lall can see that I am pretty determined and that I am giving him a chance to block it through rules of his own making. He has two lovely daughters himself, and the older girl will want to be involved when she is home from college in Lahore for the holidays. He begins setting the rules out, starting with the girls at their own front doors.

He states a principle. "You can't trust their brothers, whether they are cousin brothers, village brothers or even real brothers.

"Girls either have to come here to the Lal Kothi chaperoned by their own parents, or you yourself have to fetch them, not from a common meeting point but from their own front doors. You can't delegate this to anyone else. They are to remain in your sight or in Marie's sight the whole time until they go back in through those same doors when it is all over. You don't leave them at their front doors, you wait with them until the doors open and they go in through those doors and the doors close behind them.

"You always have an older woman, a Punjabi, present as chaperone.

"In no activity are the girls in physical contact with any young men in any way.

"There is to be absolutely no touching between the sexes in any of your activities and no dancing.

"Whatever you do is done with decorum so that you do not invite criticism.

"At the first sign of scandal, you close the club down."

I agree to all Lall's conditions. They are reasonable. Lall knows his people, and it is only wise to try to work within commonsense precautions. He is going a second mile in just presenting a framework of rules instead of condemning the suggestion outright. Now to make the whole idea work.

Marie and I gather together some of the young men in their late teens and early twenties, Sammy Ramnit, the Tufail boys, Morgan Karam Illahi, Washington, Pola and a few others. We outline our ideas for a weekly youth club. Their eyes sparkle! Something of their own! We will have it on Saturday nights, starting at 7:30 p.m. and running until 10 p.m. We will have elections for the three officers every three months so that everyone who wants can show what he can do. Memsahiba will provide the refreshments for the first night, but after this, they will take responsibility, including wash-

a boy and his lunch

ing the dishes afterwards. Each member will pay one rupee a week to cover refreshments and program expenses. The girls will be their guests, no costs for them. There will be five minutes for devotions at the end of each program. That, together with the actual program itself, will be my responsibility until they themselves get into the swing of things when they will take over the program. The girls will sit on one side of the room and the boys on the other. There will be no messing about and no hanky panky, they will police themselves!

They do. We have *fun*. It is just childish fun, and we laugh uproariously. There are sometimes more than thirty of us. I go around and collect a vanload of young women dressed in their sparkling best. Sometimes there are two vanloads. Pakistani women are some of the most beautiful women in the world, and these are in the bright flush of their beauty. They look just lovely, dazzling.

They must have spent all afternoon getting themselves ready. Some wear saris and the others shalwarqamiz in bright color combinations. They sit across the large room from the boys, who themselves are wearing their best clothes and are on their best behavior. They banter chitchat across the room, but there is complete decorum. The chaperone has no cause to raise an eyebrow. We play party games using newspapers, balloons, elastic bands, and blindfolds—just silly silly party games with no sense to them at all. I am M.C. and enjoying myself as much as anyone else. Boys and girls play the games alternately so that there is no touching. We have skits. The girls do theirs, and the boys do theirs. We even find some relay games where the boys and the girls safely compete on the same teams! We are out to enjoy ourselves, and we do. I have a couple of books of party games, and we ring the changes.

We have refreshments—samosas and pakoras, savian and sanf, cookies and barfi, cake and chai—and then before breaking up for the evening, a short devotion that settles everyone down for home.

This club continues as long as we are at the Christian Training Institute. It is a trailblazing innovation, yet never once do I recall any untoward incidents or any serious criticism of the mixing of the sexes by the elders of the community. Rather, they realize this is providing a valuable and well-supervised channel for their children's energies and interests. The schoolteachers at Hajipura love their Saturday evenings and look forward to it all week. Its success encourages us to establish years later a High School in Gujranwala with boys and girls; and again, this operates successfully within our eastern culture of single sex activities and schooling.

Lall never has any cause for complaint or concern. When Rani comes home from Kinnaird, she, too, comes to the Youth Club.

Ten Rupees for Lakhi

Autumn 1968, Christian Hospital, Taxila

We learn many times of the generosity of the poor to each other and often to others much more wealthy than themselves. If you want hospitality, go to the poor. Here are a couple of brief tales about the very poorest of the people who work with me on the building crew at Taxila.

My mother, when visiting us in Taxila, sees a group of mountain men and women from Kohistan coming up the concrete path toward us. Several are holding something—something small—in their hands. They are ragged. The long overcoats against the winter cold that we gave them at Christmas are frayed and the sleeves torn. They have no socks to guard their feet against the cold, and the chapplis with which they are shod are worn almost beyond use. I recognize them; there is Samela and his wife, Rustum, who has an extra finger on each hand, and others of my laborers.

"What are they doing? Why are they coming here?" my mother asks curiously.

We walk down the path toward them. Samela is hardly recognizable. On his way back home he has visited a dentist in Abbottabad who has created a monstrous set of dentures for him. The dentist must have been a frustrated monumental mason, and he has created a memorial to be remembered. I am not sure that Samela has even been able to get the false teeth out of his mouth once they have been first inserted. I never thereafter see him without them, although I vastly prefer the *"before"* to the *"after"* side of the transaction. I am sure he must be in continual pain, but he seems determined to grind value out of his cosmetic enterprise even at the cost of much discomfort.

We can converse only a few words since we have little parity of languages. However, words are not needed. Samela takes from each of two others a small chicken egg (the small eggs, from chickens allowed to forage for themselves, have bright orange yolks and are preferred to the larger eggs from battery hens) and, producing a third himself, offers all three to me. His companions have approving and happy smiles. I take them, ask mother to hold them and embrace Samela, who grins delightedly with that awful fixed grimace, and I thank them all for their gift.

Mother gasps. "You can't take that, Ken; it's all that they have got."

Yes, that's right, and that's why I take them. The poor have dignity, and we must allow them to keep it. They have a right not only to take but also to give, and we must never deny them that right.

Rustum and Samela come hurrying up to me not long after work (building the operating block in Taxila) has started for the day. They and all their fellows have been absent from the attendance roll call. I soon hear why. Will I come to the Men's Ward? Ghajju has been hit by a bus, and he is likely to die!

Ghajju does not actually work for me, but he is part of the Kohistani community that comes down from the northern mountains to Taxila in the winter.

Ghajju is out of the operating room, a mass of bandages amid all the medical paraphernalia of drips. Clustered around him are Lakhi, his wife, and half a dozen children. Around them are all the other Kohistani laborers who work for me, together with some of their wives. They want me to pray for Ghajju, and I do so. They are bearded men with their own language who come down for work on the plains. I know them all.

We are good friends, and, despite difficulties with their language, they often come to me with other problems besides work. Although Marie wishes they were elsewhere, we are keeping Rustum's gun and bullets in the house for him until he returns home.

Ghajju and Lakhi and the children have been coming through Hasan Abdal, eight miles distant. The town is a busy junction. A bus passing stationary buses on the wrong side of the road at high speed plowed into pedestrians, narrowly missing Lakhi and the children and hit Ghajju head on. The bus has brought the family to the hospital and dropped them off there before continuing its journey to Rawalpindi.

The driver has offered Lakhi ten rupees, but she has not taken it.

The medical staff confirms that Ghajju has suffered severe internal injuries and it is only a matter of time.

I go back to talk to Lakhi. Does she know which bus hit her husband?

Yes, she describes the bus and the driver. We know the company. Yes, the police at Hasan Abdal were there as soon as the accident happened. She doesn't know whether any report has been recorded; how could the poor woman whose only thoughts are for her husband and her children?

It is unlikely a report has been made, a little money is a useful lubricant to grease forgetfulness. I send a couple of the Kohistani men to Hasan Abdal on the bus with a note written in English. It is inquiring from the police station officer the reference number of the accident report and suggesting that proceedings against the bus driver and the bus company are likely to be instituted if the man dies. That will stimulate an entry into the records.

Ghajju dies, and the Kohistanis mourn. What now is to happen to Lakhi and her children? Are they to starve? Does anyone care? I am angry. The oldest child, a son, is barely nine and small for his age. By the recklessness of a hurrying bus driver, they are penniless and without their breadwinner. The bus company should at least be liable for enough money to the family to enable them to return home and survive until the nine-year-old is ready to work.

Bilquis suggests I contact Mamu Mumtaz, her mother's brother, in Campbellpur. That is where the courts with local jurisdiction are located. Campbellpur is forty miles away, toward the Indus. Mumtaz is a lawyer.

I write to Mumtaz, telling him I am coming to him to discuss a problem of injustice with the hope that he may be able to help and setting a time after court hours when I will call at his house.

I take with me Lakhi and two of the men. Mumtaz, whom I have met on one occasion previously, listens to me with patience and interest. There will be no money to pay any legal fees, but I ask him if he will represent Lakhi without a fee and institute a case for compensation against the bus company. He has certainly seen more of this kind of injustice than I and knows it will be hard, if not hopeless, to obtain anything for Lakhi. He is, however, a courteous and a compassionate man and agrees to help. We provide him with dates and details, and he tells us when next to come back to Campbellpur.

Now develops a routine of many months as the mills of justice grind their slow and tortuous way forward. At 4:30 in the morning, Lakhi, two of the men-folk and I catch the first bus out of Taxila to Campbellpur and go either to Mamu's house or to the courts themselves for a hearing. Often there are adjournments due to the failure of an advocate or a witness to appear. I am serving my own apprenticeship in court procedures, for I shall become well acquainted with many Punjabi courts in the days to come. Most visits are abortive, but occasionally we move forward a step or two before we catch a bus back to Taxila.

One day toward the end, the judge trying our case asks me to remain behind. When the court has cleared and we are alone, he leans forward and asks "Mr. Old, why are you involved in this woman's case?"

I explain that by the recklessness of a bus driver, this mountain woman is widowed away from her own country and people with a cluster of little children and no breadwinner, and I have a concern that she be enabled to survive until her oldest son is able to work to support her and his siblings.

The judge sighs.

"Mr. Old, I am ashamed, ashamed that you, a foreigner, should need to be an advocate for justice for one of our poor people when surely we ourselves should be moved enough to do what you are doing for her. It should not be necessary for you to teach us how to give justice to our poor.

"However, I regret to tell you that I will be unable to help the woman in this particular case. The owner of the bus in question is an advocate of this very court, and he is very powerful. I dare not cross him. I am sorry I am unable to give you the response that you seek."

Events prove him right. There is no judgment in Lakhi's favor. Lakhi would have been ten rupees and many journeys to Campbellpur better off had she accepted the first offer made by the bus driver. So much for the value of a life!

a boy and his lunch

Taxila Hospital

This is a busy general hospital. Six babies a day are being delivered in an obstetrics unit designed for two. It is for the treatment of eyes, though, that the hospital is internationally famous. Over the twenty years since 1969, the number of cataract operations performed has exceeded one hundred and twenty-five thousand. The annual total over that period has risen from just under seven thousand to thirteen thousand. The present Superintendent, Dr. Ernest Lall, and his wife Pramila have served there for more than forty years. Their work, carrying on an established tradition of focusing on the needs of the poor, has constantly struggled to keep costs within the reach of very poor people. Yet its standards are remarkably high and infections after surgery very rare. Taxila Hospital has been, in this year of writing, approved by the Government of Pakistan as an ophthalmic teaching hospital for the College of Physicians and Surgeons.

People come to it by bus and by rail and on foot from the Frontier and from Afghanistan, from the hill states and territories of Dir, Gilgit, Chitral, Swat, Hazara and Hunza and from the Punjab even as far as the Sindh. Occasionally, people with Mongolian features from Kashgar and Sinkiang China will turn up. It is known as the "eye hospital" throughout the mountain areas of the Karakorums and the Pamir Knot. Its charges to the patients are some of the lowest in the world, and it has no government subsidy. Friendly overseas organizations finance a continuous building program.

How did it all start?

The Sialkot Mission works in much of the northern area of the Punjab drained by the three most westerly of the five rivers—the Jhelum, the Chenab and the Ravi. In addition, it works in areas drained by the Indus to the west of them.

At the end of the first world war, there was a searching reappraisal of the activities of the Mission. Mission records observe:

> *The Jhelum river marks the division between two markedly different types of work. To the west of the Jhelum lies considerably more than half our territory and we have only two occupied stations, Jhelum and Rawalpindi, in a predominantly Muslim area marked by roadless territory, inadequate forces and equipment. Only three per cent of the people are literate.*

The era is marked by:

> *hard times, the high cost of administration, debts of the mission board, restraints in expenditure that amount to retrenchment and a feverish rush to raise funds.*

There is a call for more prayer for this field of mission, and the church at home in the States begins to respond. In 1920, the greatest number of new missionaries in any one year arrive—twenty-one. New funds begin to arrive.

The next year sees the move out westward from Rawalpindi along the Grand Trunk Road to Taxila, a railway junction about twenty miles nearer the Indus. The apostle Thomas is reputed to have preached the gospel here to King Gondophares. The Sialkot Mission has approved the location. A mile or so along the Grand Trunk Road, beyond the obelisk of Nicholson's Monument, is an old caravansarai. Several furlongs to the northeast, just short of the ruins of a Buddhist civilization that flourished here in pre-Christian days, is the site selected. A mission hospital is to be established. The land—thirty acres—is bought from twenty-three different owners gathered together at the same place and time to receive their payments in silver rupees from Dr. Greg Martin.

About nine miles beyond the rail junction at Taxila is a junction of roads. Straight on northwestward is the Indus river crossing and then Peshawar and the Khyber. To the right is the road to Abbottabad, and beyond that city are the upper Indus valleys. Beyond the Indus, the road from the north—from Swat, Dir and Chitral—meets the Grand Trunk at Nowshera. Taxila is a strategic location for roads to the roof of the world.

Inevitably, the early years mark the struggle to build up the hospital. The first major operation is performed in a tent.

The 1930s Depression leads to hard times for missions. The hospital needs to become and remain self-supporting. Special gifts from all over the world designated for the hospital's work become a major source of additional income, permitting the purchase of equipment and the construction of buildings. Missionary doctors are few, and there are not many Indian Christian doctors yet available. Associates from other missions—Bergsma, Vroon and Karsgaard—help out.

In 1948, a young American general practitioner and his nurse wife who have been helping with refugee relief join the staff. Language and surgical skills grow together. They have a summer of language study in India under their belts but can hardly be fluent in communicating with patients who do not speak the language they have been learning. Medical school also never

a boy and his lunch

taught Norval what he now finds he's needing in surgical skills. Like a hawk watching prey, he watches Andy Karsgaard as he operates, hoping he will forget nothing of what he is seeing. He is an apt student. His skills and reputation burgeon as the years pass. Andy leaves, and OA Brown pairs with Norval. Later, another brilliant surgeon, an Indian woman, Pramila Lall, joins Norval. By the time Norval becomes certified in 1968 as an ophthalmologist, he is performing hundreds of operations weekly. Most of them are cataract surgeries, and his total so far is close to twenty-five thousand, less than a quarter of the final total when he retires in 1986.

Let another member of that early team, Marie herself, describe what happens at this remarkable medical establishment that she calls and continues through her life to consider home:

Spring and fall herald the eye season. When it is neither too hot nor too cold and the accompanying men folk are free from their urgent agricultural labors, thousands of patients flock to the hospital for cataract surgery. They come in battered buses, by train or by walking for many many miles. They are required to bring their own bedding and someone to care for them and cook their meals while they are at the hospital.

When the wards are full, beds are placed on verandahs and in tents, even under trees—anywhere a bed will fit. Latrine facilities are an almost impossible challenge to people, both relatives and patients, who are accustomed to the great outdoors and village customs.

Cataract surgery, as it flows, deals with sixteen to twenty patients an hour. Lying on old fashioned operating tables in the clothes they arrived in, patients' eyes are washed and their faces draped with sterile towels. The surgeons, Norval and Pramila, alternating surgery day-by-day, use the intracapsular method to remove cataracts. With this procedure, the clouded lens and capsule surrounding it are removed together.

It used to be in the early days that we would try to immobilize the patient's head to avoid an eye hemorrhage. They would be carried on stretchers back to the eye ward. However, their prayers of thankfulness would be accompanied by body and head motions in the Muslim fashion. To our surprise, infection or hemorrhage was extremely rare,

and now patients get off the operating table and their wait-
ing relatives walk them back to their beds.

   Ken's work on building the new operating theater begins
at 7 a.m., but at 3:30 each morning, he joins us in the oper-
ating theater to wash patient's eyes and lift early morning
patients on and off the tables until he has to leave when his
construction crew arrive.

When Norval was fifteen, at New Wilmington Missionary conference in Pennsylvania, he committed himself to be willing "*to do anything the Lord wanted me to do*." After his retirement from Pakistan, he continued to serve the world's blind in his role as an ophthalmic surgical consultant, making many trips to China to train eye surgeons.

a boy and his lunch

If you know Him

In the wasteland seeking shelter
I cry for aid and stumble on,
I thirst for drink but can't drink brine
And starve for bread but can't eat stone.

I am tired of all this teaching,
How can it ever make me whole?
I am tired of all this searching
It's time for home but where to go?

Doctrines deaden, laws condemn me,
They bring no comfort in my need
They are buttresses around you
How can I know you cry like me?

Don't just serve me, come and love me
And put your arms right round me, friend.
Show me Jesus if you know Him
And if you do not, don't pretend.

Eye Patients at Taxila

1969

I drop down from the steel frame of the operating block that we are erecting and wander over to the adjacent men's eye ward. I stand outside among the relatives and others looking in as the doctor leads his entourage past the beds. There is no wall between what goes on within the ward and those of us outside. On cold nights, bamboo chicks (curtains) are unrolled. The string beds are almost touching side by side, and the heads of the patients are toward the center aisle. Norval is approaching. With him is the nurse (today it is his wife Dorothy), another carrying charts and behind them others with drops and dressings for the patients' eyes and two others who do the re-bandaging.

There are abrupt pauses in the low murmur of conversation in half a dozen languages going on among the bystanders. The patients have brought their own bedding and food and a relative to care for them. For $10 they are getting an eye examination, a cataract operation and up to ten days stay at the hospital. Very occasionally, a patient from the other side of the Karakorums will stump the various linguists among the hospital staff. The relative will be called for and additional attempts made to communicate with the patient.

Almost all of the patients are at various stages of recovery from eye surgery—cataract extractions, most of them. Norval examines the eye for signs of infection or inflammation and notes the progress of healing. Dorothy gives information from the patient's chart and awaits to write an additional doctor's comment.

The doctor lifts his hand in front of the patient, and all fall silent. The routine is well known. Everyone waits to hear. You can hear a pin drop. This is a precious moment, repeated hundreds of times during the morning rounds, when suddenly you realize what the words "a common humanity" mean. You are meeting it face to face; that you are Christian and white and they are Muslim and brown has suddenly become irrelevant.

You quickly look round. Pathans and Afghans, Punjabis and Hazaras, rich and poor, men and women, literate and illiterate, old and young—you are an unnoticeable part of a merged cluster that has lost individual identity. All are listening as if the only thing in the world they, and you, want and need to hear is the right answer to the question that confused old Swati from beyond Kalam is trying to articulate. You suddenly realize you have a lump in your throat, and your own eyes are watering. "Come on, Baba; you can see, you can see. Try a little harder, you can see!"

Everyone who stands around is silently willing the old man on. It matters not that they have never been anywhere near where he has come from or that he speaks a different language, that before a moment or so previously, they didn't know he existed. He is everyone's father, son, brother, husband. He *has* to see. "Come on Baba, you can do it, please! Please, God, let him see!"

Norval is holding up three fingers a couple of feet or so from the old man's face. His other hand covers the good eye so that it cannot assist. "How many fingers can you see, Babaji?" His voice is kindly and patient. He may have several hundred to see, but for this old man, as for all of the others, he has just now all the time in the world.

This old man has perhaps walked several days, leaning on his stick or the shoulder of his son until he gets eventually past the landslide to Bahrein and then the series of buses to Mingora and Malakand and Mardan and Nowshera and then by train to Taxila. He has never seen a train before, but he has heard about trains from others; and his son is with him and reassures him. They have waited until the harvest is in and his son is free to accompany him.

Back home in the hills, across the Indus and to the north, his wife, almost as blind as he, waits and prays. If it works for him—this immense journey—he has promised to take her also to Taxila and give her the same opportunity that he is getting to see once more. He'll try it out first, and then it will be her turn.

You take another quick look around you. The others are also holding their breath, almost as though they are afraid to exhale lest they disturb the old man's concentration. The old man has not seen through this eye for years. He is having a little difficulty. Through the blurriness, he can see something. He blinks to try to clear his vision, but his eye has no lens. There is something there, moving slowly, waving in front of him like twigs in a light breeze. He ventures an answer, uncertainly. "Three?"

"Shabash, Babaji, very good, now once more. How many this time?"

He is no more sure than previously.

"Two?"

"Shabash!"

The collective sigh of relief tells the old man what he needs to know—he has passed the test. Soon, with a green bandage over his eye held in place by steel-rimmed, thick-lensed cataract glasses, he'll be on that train going back to Nowshera. For scores of miles around, cataract patients bound for or

a boy and his lunch

leaving from Taxila can be recognized instantly by those who know. Norval moves on and his circus follows him.

The crowds are no longer strangers. We look around, congratulating each other and the old man by our relieved smiles, but fall silent almost immediately as once more, at the head of a different bed, Norval raises his hand, sticks out fingers, and asks a question.

It is Sunday morning. We are in chapel. Padri Anwar Allah Rasi is preaching and is in the middle of his sermon. The chapel is full, for most of the staff of the hospital are Christian. The door to the outside, at the opposite end to the pulpit, has been left open. There is a stir in the congregation. Our heads turn. Standing in the doorway is a Pathan tribesman wearing his distinctive puggree headgear and a purple waistcoat. It is apparent at once he has not come to create disruption or exercise violence. He is wearing no bandolier of bullets. In his left hand, held by the two feet, is a live chicken. The pastor's voice trails off into silence.

The visitor walks forward with long strides and steady tread until he is immediately below where the pastor stands. He is completely relaxed and assured in an alien environment. No one else moves. Not a word is being uttered by anyone now that the pastor is silent. The stranger stretches out his hand towards the pastor. The chicken flutters its wings and looks around anxiously. The pastor responds and takes the chicken from the visitor. The visitor turns on his heel, and without a word, walks back down the aisle of the church, does not look back, and is gone. An elder comes forward and enables the pastor to continue with his sermon as if there has been no occasion for a break in it.

There is no need for words. They are superfluous. This particular Muslim has wanted to say and has said publicly to the Christians in Taxila ,"You have a different faith than mine, but thank you for your service to a member of my family. I am grateful."

The full total of cataract surgeries at this quiet little hospital, from its tiny beginnings in 1922 to this year of 2005, is 400,000, and they are only part of the total surgical load. The single constraining principle behind it all is the compassion of Christ for those in need.

Water for Jhokund

May, 1969

Byron and Barbara Haines of our mission are working at the Christian Study Centre in Rawalpindi. This is a kind of think tank and research unit for the minority Christian community to understand itself, its faith and its relationships with an Islam expressing itself in the context of Pakistan.

One day they ask me if I can use an extra volunteer from the States. Byron's cousin, John, from New England, is visiting and would like to be useful. Mine is the kind of job at Taxila where I can usually find work for people.

Young foreigners show a high capacity for initiative, innovation and adaptability. They don't have the language, they travel by public transport, they suffer all kinds of sickness stoically, they have little money, they accept discomfort and are prepared to do anything they are asked. Usually they succeed in their assignments. They love having Marie as a surrogate mother, and she loves her surrogate children.

John moves in with us in Taxila and becomes one of the family. He is lean and lanky, quiet and reserved. He lives much within himself. Through his life, he has suffered from epilepsy but has learned how to live within the parameters of that affliction without becoming a burden to himself or to others. He accepts that he will necessarily have a more restricted life than his peers.

He has not been long with us when one day in March we have two German visitors. Taxila has no hotels. Pakistanis usually stay with their own friends. Non-Pakistanis passing through stay with whichever missionary family happens to have a spare guestroom at the time.

Brother Klinger—middle-aged, astute and joyful—is the leader of a German Protestant group of men and women known as the Christus Traeger, the Christ Bearers. They are committed to bringing the Presence of Christ into a situation by dedicated Christian service. Uwe is another of the Brothers.

They had first come to Karachi almost three years previously. They are concerned for lepers and have been working at the Leper Colony at Mangho Phir and in the leper colony near the Governor's House. Some of the Sisters working in the bazars off Elphinstone Street have talked with a curious shoe-seller. He is very interested in what they are doing. He tells them his name is Ashraf Khan; he is not from Karachi but from Amb, a tiny area northwest of Abbottabad in the northern mountains. There are many lepers there, but no one cares for them. No foreigners come there, or at least they don't come to his own village. There are no roads. All the help goes to people in the towns, yet the lepers there are able to beg in the bazars and make a living. What about the people in the mountain valleys?

Brother Klinger accepts the invitation to visit Jhokund, Ashraf Khan's village perched high above the Sirhan river. It is close to a thousand miles from Karachi to the hills of the Karakorums.

Ashraf Khan meets him when he arrives at the hotel in Abbottabad. Early the following morning, they go north by bus to Mansehra and then several miles westward in an overcrowded taxi on a diminishing road track until that peters out. Now it is horseback the rest of the way, hired horses. Normally the villagers walk the twenty miles, using mules and donkeys and horses as pack animals. Ashraf is apologetic for the path. The government has promised to open up a road link as far as Jhokund. His brother-in-law is the chairman of the village council, so it won't be too long now, within a couple of years.

Brother Klinger, unaccustomed to his form of transport, dismounts slowly and painfully when they arrive. He is expected, garlanded and given tea, then a huge meal of mutton and rice. He is accommodated in the house reserved for visiting wedding parties from other villages. The night is eerily beautiful. There is no reflected light, for there is no electricity in the valley. The stars in the sky seem almost an inverted pavement of dots of light; there are so many more stars than Klinger has ever observed before. He sees to the west a bright light moving through the sky and realizes it is a satellite.

The following day is exploration. Only Ashraf speaks any English. Klinger himself is fluent in English.

Jhokund is a Shangri La, though not all is idyllic. Far below the ridge flows the Sirhan river, south and westward to its confluence with the Indus. Do the women get the water from the river? No, their custom is to walk four miles to a spring and then wait their turn to fill their water pots; there isn't a strong flow of water. Ashraf has gathered patients for him to see. There are many old cases of leprosy and new cases also. In the other villages — Ashraf points across the valley toward the western hills where clusters of dwellings break the green of the slopes — are many others but they have been unable to walk to Jhokund.

Klinger and Ashraf, accompanied by the inevitable crowd of curious young boys (Klinger is the first white man they have seen), clamber down the steep path to the river. It is a long way down, but the cool, clear water is refreshing. Some men are fishing. They are waiting for their visitor's arrival. Usually they fish with nets cast into the water and quickly pull tight, but today is a special day. This time they throw in a stick of explosive (gunpowder is readily available in the bazar at Abbottabad); a wonderful bang and a plume of high water, and then the boys, too, are splashing in the water, collecting Klinger's supper for him.

Klinger isn't looking forward to his horseride back towards Mansehra when his visit ends, but he has only the alternative of walking; so with some reluctance, he chooses the horse. He has seen enough to convince him that this might be a God-given opportunity that might not occur again, and despite the risks, it will be worth taking.

That was two years ago.

The Brothers, particularly Uwe and Otto, have gone up and, with the assistance of gathered labor, built a room for themselves a hundred yards from the village and then accommodation for the Sisters. Even before that is ready, the Sisters have arrived, initially four of them. Then come the clinic rooms, a small ward, and TB wards—almost a third of those requiring attention also suffer from tuberculosis.

There are two things needed that can be mutually beneficial—a piped water supply and electricity. A generator could supply lighting and power to a pump if a pump can be found to lift water maybe four hundred meters.

One of the Brothers outlines the need in a draft scheme proposal to Brot fuer die Welt (Bread for the World), a generous German donor to Third World countries and causes. They send out an engineer who drafts the scheme in technical terms, a submersible pump, an auxiliary piston pump, a three-phase generator, pipes, fittings, valves, cables and controls.

By the time the wooden packing cases of equipment arrive at the railhead of Havelian, the way has been opened up for four-wheeled traffic to get as far as Jhokund.

Brother Klinger hears that Taxila has a European engineer working at the hospital. Can I give the technical help and advice the Brothers will need with the installation? I smile ruefully. I would like to help, but I have my own labor force working on the new operating block, and they depend upon me for daily instructions and supervision. I am doing the drawings as I go along. There is no way that I can get away for more than one day. Maybe John can help. He can act as my representative and contact me if there are any problems that arise.

We agree that we will go up together with John to Jhokund and look things over.

Apart from the road to Bamburet in Chitral it is the worst and most terrifying road I have ever traveled; but nevertheless, it is a road, and the equipment has now arrived at the village

John Haines' Diary

Thursday, March 20, 1969

Went with Ken and two German missionaries to Jhokund to see about installing a water pumping station there for the little leprosy hospital. The trip from Taxila took five hours - two hours by car covered fifty plus miles and three hours by jeep covered twenty miles (my bottom will never be the same!)

I thought that Taxila was peaceful in relation to Pindi but Jhokund has it beaten by a thousand miles. A motorized vehicle is a rarity there and the mountains and the green valley are exceptionally beautiful. When I go up to install the water pumps for the hospital I am not sure I will return when I'm finished. The quietness is deafening!

Ken and I were the first English and American citizens to go to Jhokund.

Wednesday May 7

We arrived at Jhokund today at about 1:30 p.m. After consuming three or four glasses of water and a couple of cups of tea and some biscuits (cookies) Ken, Uwe and I set out to check the work already done for the pumps and also to measure the true vertical distance that the water needs to be pumped. The vertical distance is about one thousand feet.

Ken and Uwe left about 5 p.m. for Taxila.

My stay started by trying to fix the present plumbing system at the leper hospital. The faucets in two bathrooms leak and so does one of the toilet tanks. What a job and what a mess!

As I sit here on the verandah overlooking the valley at 8 p.m., I hear a baby crying in the distance, a murmur of conversation from the German Sisters washing the dishes and the peacefulness of nature. What bliss.

There is a newly acquired member of this household, a dark skinned (Dravidian?) little girl about four years old with no known parents except for the German lady doctor in charge here whom she calls "Mommy." When asked if the German doctor was her only mother she said that she had another one also. The sad fact is that neither is the real mother of those dark brown eyes.

Thursday May 8

Brother Otto has arrived to stay for two or three days. I started opening the crates, building shelves to store the stuff and trying to figure out what it was via its German name.

My only interruption this morning in the little room where I was working was the discovery of a small snake (small by Stateside standards). It looked like the viper Ken had killed in Taxila, so I got some assistance, flushed it out and it was killed by one of the men. Heavy shoes are better on a job like this, as are shorts, but Darn! It gets hot!

Friday May 9

I have opened almost all of the crates and unloaded them. Now to see how well they check with the list (in German!). I dove off the rock which juts into the river and into which we also want to put the pump. I'll have to go in again tomorrow with a safety rope and try to measure the depth. As the rock seems to be an overhang it will be interesting to see how far back it is washed out.

Monday May 19

Today has started out as a very bad day. Ashraf Khan has been very upset that little Sarah is not getting a Muslim education but is, 'as he thinks', being taught Christianity. This poor child has been given up by her mother and after trying to let her live with a Muslim family she was retrieved and put to live with a Christian family. Because the Chris-

a boy and his lunch

tian family is going away for a while she has been put in the care of Sister Wanda here at Jhokund. She has been here about three weeks.

This morning about 7:30 a.m. Ashraf Khan came once again to argue his ideas of Sarah's welfare with Sister Wanda. Being a 'typical' Muslim man he does not like a woman not to obey him. Sister Wanda, German bred, does not.

When Sister Wanda said "No" to his taking Sarah and called for one of the other Sisters to take her, Ashraf Khan sprained her thumb by prying her hand loose from the door and had one of his servants take Sarah.

The servant, unknown to us, was waiting as were about twenty villagers that Ashraf Khan had brought! He then informed me (I was working outside) that none of the villagers would work for me and that all work was to stop.

Right after Ashraf Khan left for Mansehra or Abbottabad his sister and her husband arrived. About six or eight hours earlier the sister had taken poison. Now, it is 1:30 p.m. we still don't know the outcome but the hospital was closed upon Ashraf's departure and his sister would be dead if Sister Wanda had not taken care of her.

We have been told by Ashraf's cousin and also by his brother-in-law that men and cement will be provided to finish the work. The brother-in-law is chairman of the local government organization in this area.

At about 11 a.m. the generator was dropped on the three bare middle toes of my right foot - Ouch!

And, of course, the Sisters are in a mild state of shock!

At least I got everything out of the generator room so that we can lay the floor. Now to see what happens this afternoon.

By this evening Ashraf Khan's sister had regained full consciousness and recognized people. She was sent to her cousin's house for the night and is to report back tomorrow.

Brothers Otto and Uwe arrived about 3 p.m. for making the underwater hole for the pump. After being informed of the state of affairs here they drove to Abbottabad to send a telegram to Brother Klinger in Germany asking him to come out immediately. I trust that upon his arrival things will be straightened out!

I accomplished nothing this afternoon except to hobble around and feel sorry for myself and somewhat for the rest of the situation here also.

PS Having taken a shower this evening the Sisters all said I looked a lighter color and I have been given clean sheets for my bed!

Tuesday May 20

Due to the situation brought upon us by Ashraf Khan I have moved out of the hospital and into one of the T.B. bungalows so that no gossip can be started. The rule of the country (culture) is that unmarried or non blood-related persons of different sexes do not abide in the same house or even go to the other's abode. It has been established that even though the Sisters are not married they will have male visitors from the Brotherhood and these gentlemen will sleep there at the hospital. However, due to this crisis, gossip could be slanderous and therefore all precautions are being taken to prevent it.

Brother Uwe and his men started chiseling the hole today and made good progress, I think.

A couple of the German Brothers and I went to Mansehra for supplies. While returning we came to a fork in the road and weren't sure which way to go. We spotted an elderly gentleman sitting on the porch of his house. The three of us approached and, with what little Urdu that between us we could muster, we tried to ask the road to Jhokund. After we had finished unraveling our question, he said with a twinkle in his eye, "Yes, and where is it that you would like to go?" in very crisp English.

This evening we, the Brothers and I, had great fun trying to cook on a kerosene stove that had a clogged fuel line. Unable to clear it, we solved the problem by throwing kerosene on the fire at set intervals causing great flare-ups. The results were tasty, more or less.

a boy and his lunch

Four other Brothers came to review the situation and we all sat up and watched the stars. I accomplished nothing. Saw two satellites.

The four Brothers left this morning. I went down for a swim as I did yesterday. Again, I accomplished nothing.

Ashraf Khan did arrive this evening as we three were getting ready for dinner. He came around to be sociable but was given a cold reception! I didn't have the guts to do it myself but Brother Uwe responded with "What do you want?"

Yesterday we found out that most, if not all, of Ashraf's family was against his action. This includes most of the village as most of them are cousins (1st, 2nd, 3rd etc.) or some other relation.

Maybe the picture is not as bad as we first thought that the hospital might have to close.

Brother Klinger, head of the Brotherhood, arrived tonight.

Thursday May 22

Saw two satellites tonight within five minutes of each other. Brother Klinger presented himself to Ashraf Khan this morning just in time to prevent a fight and possible bloodshed. Ashraf and about twenty men had gone down to the river to stop the work of Brother Uwe and his men who are chiseling the hole. Many were armed and, as I understand it, when Brother Klinger arrived Brother Uwe was holding a 20 - 24 inch chisel and getting ready for a fight.

I know not the results, if any, of the subsequent conversation between Brother Klinger and Ashraf.

My only accomplishment of the day was the drilling of some holes for light sockets and feeling sorry for myself. Why?

I started to put wire clips up but, as the Sisters were cleaning house, I gave up.

Brothers Otto and Uwe were planning to leave today and at 3:20 p.m. I was informed that I was going too. As my possessions were spread out between the hospital, the T.B. bungalow and even my swimsuit by the river, it took a little time to collect my stuff. It seemed (probably my imagination) that the fact I had to take some ten minutes plus to collect my stuff made Brother Otto mad - tough luck! If I had known in advance that I was going I would have packed. As it was I had to leave my swimsuit and my sandals by the river.

Brother Klinger said he will see Ken in about a week's time.

I didn't check out with the police in Abbottabad so I will have to go back and do it. I may be going back in a couple of weeks if everything works out okay.

Got a prescription from Dr. Christy for dysentery and then went to Pindi.

The hospital staff has been pulled out from Jhokund and is here at Audrey's leprosy hospital. I said hello to Dr. Wanda and gave her a list of items that I want back from Jhokund.

The water pump for Jhokund is still being put in. I hope (I think) that they don't expect me to go up and work on it.

Sarah is still in Ashraf Khan's hands.

Note from Ken

Brother Klinger calls in at Taxila in early June. He and his group are pulling out of Jhokund. He is unsure of the safety of the Sisters if they are to be left. He has, however, a responsibility to the donors of the generator and the pumping equipment. The Brothers have been close to completion but have been unable to get the water supply operating. Please, will I go up and make one last effort to try to get the water moving? He is sure Ashraf Khan will not cause any trouble and be most cooperative. I write to Ashraf Khan and tell him that John and I will head for Abbottabad as soon as I can after paying the men on Saturday, Midsummer's Day.

Saturday June 21

After work at 12:30, Ken and I drove to Abbottabad to meet Ashraf Khan and go with him to Jhokund. The trip to Jhokund was uneventful.

Upon arriving at Jhokund, I saw little Sarah who looks very good and seems to have adjusted to her change of life. She recognized me and smiled shyly, but a little later she cried. I assume that was due to some subconscious memory I revived such as the loss of the Sisters in her life.

We started the generator and, after setting it to the correct output, we went down to the river to see what would happen with the pumps. The submersible pump didn't work so we took it up the hill to the hospital to see why. Everything seemed okay so we had dinner and then took the pump to the pump-house for a direct check. It worked! And so to bed.

Sunday, June 22

Up at 5. Breakfast and down to the river after having started the generator. After blowing and then shorting out the fuse we hooked up the submersible pump and it worked - even to bringing water up to the generator house which it had never done before.

While Ken worked on putting it back in its case and locating it in the river, I looked at the wiring diagram for the motor of the piston pump and realized that three wires were not hooked up. So, hook up, plug in and away we go.

It worked! Why the Germans had problems I don't know, except that they were in the process of pulling out when they hooked it up so their hearts (and thus their minds) weren't in it.

We had to lubricate the pump because the flywheel was very difficult to turn. We finally were able to get it loose enough so that the motor could drive it. We then hooked the two pumps together and Ken went up the hill.

Water beat him by two or three minutes! Hooray!

The first water ever to be pumped at Jhokund was pumped today!

Now off for a quick swim and a ride back.

We had no brakes for the latter part of the journey to Abbottabad and the jeep kept stopping for some unknown reason.

Dave Morrison (an English VSO volunteer) and I will go to Jhokund next weekend for about one week's stay to tidy up the job and arrange that the pump can be started from above without going down to the pump house.

Note from Ken

Sad that the German Brothers who have worked so hard and so patiently did not have the final pleasure of seeing and hearing the water steadily mounting the hill in the pipe; hearing the deepening grunt of the piston pump as the load on it steadily increases; joining with the excited little boys, men and, towards the top, women as we follow foot by foot the rising water in the pipe. When the water finally gushes out in reckless plenty in the village itself, it seems like a wild torrent set loose. Women and children scattering to bring pots, kerosene tins, canvas water bags, goat and sheepskins with all orifices tied are capturing as much of it as they can lest it suddenly stop forever. Someone has grabbed a tabla and another a dholki and a third a wooden flute, and a dance of triumph and joy is underway.

John and I are kings for a day while those who had earned the crown are no longer there to receive the thanks due to them.

From now until August 8, John will go to and fro between Jhokund and the outside world sorting out various problems. He gets water to the hospital as well as to the village, and electric light from the generator at night shatters both darkness and silence. I do not go back again because John is coping okay. The German Sisters do not go back to Jhokund. Some stay for a while at the Leper Hospital in Rawalpindi, and others go, John thinks, to Vietnam.

a boy and his lunch

Gujranwala

September 1970

I first visit Gujranwala in September 1955. A few days after Marie and I become engaged to marry and before she takes up her duties at the hospital, she takes me thirty miles to Gujranwala from Sialkot. Although I don't know it at the time, this is the destination to which my mysterious voice of six years previously has committed me.

The floodwaters are still piled against the raised canals that run between the Chenab and the Ravi along the contours. We slow and watch for a while the many snakes swimming in those waters.

Perhaps she might wonder whether as an engineer I would be interested to work in the Boys Industrial Home and Training School. After all, I had trained initially as an electrical and mechanical engineer. I am not interested. Apart from the fact that I am going to take my new wife back to Britain as soon as my contract is complete and then ask God to show us what He wants us to do with our lives and where He wants us to go, I am not impressed with Gujranwala.

The Finance Minister of the Pakistan Government once called Gujranwala the "dirtiest city in the world." It is certainly not as bad as he suggested, although the land is level and the monsoon rains do not know where to go and therefore stay where they fall.

Gujranwala lies in the heartland of the Punjab. The greatest of the Sikh rulers of the Punjab, Ranjit Singh, was born here. Guru Nanak, founder of the Sikh religion, had himself been born in Nankana Sahib about fifty miles distant.

Punjab means "The Land of the Five Rivers." The most westerly of these five tributaries to the Indus that derive from the Karakorums, the Pir Panjal or other sub ranges of the Himalayas is the Jhelum river.

Further east, between the Chenab and the Ravi—the middle river of the five—lie both Gujranwala and Sialkot. Lahore lies on the east bank of the Ravi.

The two remaining rivers, the Sutlej and the Beas, join courses in India before flowing into Pakistan downstream of Lahore. Alexander's Macedonians and mercenaries revolted at the Sutlej during the torrential rain of the summer monsoon of 326 BC. This was the "river too far". The advance came to a halt, although it was the last of the rivers flowing westward into the Indus; and beyond, on the other side, all of India lay before them.

The land of the Punjab plain is flat. In the distance is observed the curvature of the earth like a sea horizon with villages rising on mounds built up through centuries.

The Grand Trunk Road from Calcutta to Kabul, running from southeast to northwest, and the railway line parallel to it divide the old city of Gujranwala from the new. It had once been a walled city, but now only a couple of its old gates remain. Inside, in one square mile, live about two hundred thousand people. As well as the clustered houses and scores of little iron and steel foundries and machine shops, the old bazars are there, the cloth markets, the brass bazar, the vegetable markets, the spice and cooking oil bazars, the sweet shops and the tea shops.

Curiously, in front of the station, in English only, is a large sign reading "NO HAWKERS."

Across the road choked with traffic and past the level crossings that seem closed and cluttered with tongas and oxcarts and bicycles as frequently as they are open, on the northeast side of Gujranwala, are the civil administration, the police, the courts, the jail, the civil surgeon, the Deputy Commissioner and the Commissioner, the cricket stadium, a satellite town and the suburb of Khokherke on the Sialkot Road.

On the east side of the Sialkot road in Khokherke are brick-built dwellings connected by tiny alleyways. Here live many Christian families as well as many Muslim families. It is said that you can buy a passport or a visa for any country in the world in Khokherke, all with the proper stamps, if you have enough money. A whole colony of Christians has grown up and continues to develop there. There is a Protestant Christian cemetery along the road and a Catholic one not too far away across the fields. Cemeteries are a very important aspect of community viability. Several Christians own shops; there is a Christian dentist, and there are even one or two small Christian factories. There are four churches. The two earliest are adjacent to the police headquarters, the Catholic church fringes Satellite town, and the Protestant Khokherke congregation meets in the chapel of the technical school.

The institutions of the Sialkot Mission headquarters that Marie shows me are the Mission Treasurer's office, the United Bible Training Centre (UBTC) for women and girls, the Boys Industrial Home (BIH&TS), which is indefinitely closed because of staff problems (the boys have been sent home), and the Theological Seminary that trains pastors for the Protestant churches.

I become more acquainted with Gujranwala when, several years later, after joining the Sialkot Mission, I serve on the management body of the reopened Boys Industrial Home and Training School and appreciate the efforts of the missionaries, from the United States, Holland and Germany who are working there.

Now we are to get a much closer look at both problems and opportunities, for we have been appointed by the mission to work at the school. It has been renamed the Christian Technical Training Centre.

Munawar

August 1971, The Christian Technical Training Centre, Gujranwala

Marie is in Murree with the boys, and I am in Gujranwala. It is Sunday afternoon. It is Sundays that I miss her most. I am writing my daily letter to her. A knock on the door. Don't they know that nobody, simply nobody, goes calling on a Sunday afternoon at 2:30 p.m.? Who is it this time? I pull back the curtain. A young man, a stranger, stands on the verandah.

Ah well, no rest for the wicked!

I greet him. He is well-dressed and neat. He has a pleasant style and manner and is duly diffident. He looks like a Muslim boy rather than a Christian. Am I Mr. Old? "Yes, I am." and then he introduces himself. He is Munawar Khan, and he lives in the old town of Eminabad not far from the railway station. Eminabad is about six miles towards Lahore on the Grand Trunk Road. He has come because he needs help.

I invite him in. He tells me his story.

It is a story of domestic discord. His father is under stress at work. He has a very responsible job at the Pakistan Railway headquarters in Lahore. He takes his tension out on his family, particularly his wife. It has just come to a head with the latest row. His father has now given his son an ultimatum. Either he stops interfering in the domestic differences between his parents or the father will not send his son on to college as the son has been expecting.

Munawar has also come to the end. The home is full of disharmony. He has made up his mind. He is going to leave home. He'll make it somehow.

Now he comes to the point. Will I help him get to America? All his life he has been interested in America. He wants to make a life for himself there. He doesn't know how to go about getting there. Can I please help him? He looks at me expectantly.

My heart has warmed to this young man. I am not sensing any guile, only sincerity. He thinks I am an American. I don't bother to correct his impression. Doesn't he know or realize that probably half the young men in Pakistan have the same dream?

"Munawar," I answer, "I'm certainly not going to help you to get to America, but I will give you a piece of advice." The boy listens intently.

"You go back home, and when you are alone with your father, you say this to him: 'Father, I'm your son, and I know that you love me. While I am in your home, I am under your discipline and guidance and under your authority. I know you want the best for me. If you don't want to send me to college, that's perfectly okay with me. You must do what you feel is right.'"

Munawar sighs with disappointment. This is not the kind of advice he has come for. He wants to know how to get to America. He thanks me and takes his leave. I think that I have seen the last of Munawar.

A year has gone by.

The government has just passed nationalization orders for all privately operated schools and colleges. We are trying to digest the implications and discover whether we have any options.

Over at the office, I am having admissions interviews. We have it all down to a routine. First, I talk to each boy and then pass the lad and his application papers on to staff sitting at several tables. They conduct in-depth interviews to try to sort out where a boy might best fit. We are not out to exclude boys but to find out ways to allow them in and the best places to put them. Boys who bring important mentors or relatives to influence their admissions soon discard them when they are warned by the head clerk that all such "safarishes" are listened to with patience and interest but that it is my practice that no boy with a safarish is granted admission.

The admissions are almost over for the day, and there is a lull. The staff has left. I will deal with anyone else who is late. Two young men come in. I do not at first recognize Munawar, but he reminds me who he is.

He has brought his friend. He wants to go to America. Munawar has brought him to me for advice!

I look, large-eyed, at Munawar. For advice! I have not forgotten the visit a year previously. "What happened to the advice I gave you?"

"I went home and did what you said, sir."

"You did?"

I am amazed that the young stranger had swallowed such unpalatable advice and had responded to it. That was one thing I had not expected.

"What happened?"

"Sir, I waited until my father and I were alone, and then I told him just what you told me to tell him. It was amazing, sir. He didn't get angry as I had expected. He stood there for some moments still as a stone, and then his eyes filled with tears. He came over to me slowly and put his arms around me and couldn't speak for a while. I could feel he was sobbing inside, and then he said, 'Munawar, of course I'm going to send you to college.' After that he turned away, and I left him to himself.

"I'm in the Law College at Lahore and have just completed my first year. I'm top of my class. I'm studying to be a lawyer."

I do not recall the advice I give his friend, and his friend never comes back. Munawar does, often.

Seeking to understand what makes us tick, why we had left our own lands to come and work in his city, he begins to attend our regular Bible Studies held in our home and to join in discussions as they develop. We have no agenda for him except to share friendship and search together for understanding in the Scriptures of the nature of God and to understand His purposes for us as individuals. He is like us—searching, but within a different framework; a traveler on the same journey but on a different road.

Some time later—by this time he has graduated with honors—he asks me again if I will help him get to America. He wants to continue and complete his law studies abroad. This time I agree, but with three conditions. As we apply for admission to the law schools of various American universities, we will tell no lies, use no safarishes and pray over each letter before we send it.

Munawar is a frequent visitor in those days. He becomes, over time, another dearly beloved son to Marie and me. He brings to the house the addresses to write to, I draft the letters and then we pray over them before he takes them down to the post office to mail. There are many disappointments over many months.

Eventually, one day Munawar arrives, beaming fit to burst and holding a letter with a Canadian stamp in his hand—an admission into the law school in Edmonton, Alberta. We look on the map together to make sure where Edmonton is. It is a long way to go to school!

When he returns home from Canada, his student visa having expired with the successful completion of his course, he soon comes to visit and share his news. Something wonderful has happened, entirely unexpected, while he had been in Edmonton. He has met and fallen in love with a Canadian girl of Sikh background and she with him. Her name is Samina, and her family has emigrated from Bombay in India to Canada and has settled in Edmonton. He shows us photographs. Isn't she beautiful? Yes, she is, but we, too, can see there will be major difficulties ahead. There are considerable faith differences between Muslims and Sikhs, far more so than between Christians and Muslims. There are immense cultural differences. Is there any way this can work its way through into successful marriage?

I suggest that Marie and I host Samina on a visit to Gujranwala so that Munawar's devout Muslim parents can meet her. Munawar is grateful. When she does arrive, Samina has to stay with the KleinHesselink family since Marie is away in the hills, but all who meet her are charmed with this very westernized Indian girl who so clearly loves Munawar. They are confident love will find a way through all the difficulties somehow.

It does. The couple marries and settles in one of the Toronto suburbs where Munawar begins a law practice. He is a good son and brother. Gradually all of Munawar's siblings and his parents move also to Canada or the USA, where they settle and establish their own roots. A far cry from dusty Eminabad in the early seventies.

The marriage between the couple is a happy one. We do not know how they have sorted out their religious differences. As the years pass we acquire several more surrogate grandchildren through them.

Munawar Visits England

July 2005, Sellindge, Kent

I am long since retired, happily married to Patty and sharing an idyllic life on a farm in the beautiful Kentish countryside. This May, a gathering of family and friends celebrated in a very special way my eightieth birthday. It was poignant for us all; for at the end of last year, I was diagnosed with lung cancer. There is also a growth on the kidney. It is only a matter of time before I shuffle off this mortal coil. Each day has extra savor now that its limits are perceived more clearly.

When Munawar hears the news of the illness of his old friend, he thinks back over the years of our association and shares with Samina and his children the thought that he'd like to visit us in England before it is too late. One last time. He is thinking he would just make a brief trip over. The other four are unanimous. "What about us? Don't you think we need to visit, too?"

From that point on, it seems to be a miracle the way things fall into place, almost as though there is a divine agenda being fulfilled. Samina is a head physiotherapist, and there is no way in which her absence can be covered by other staff available; and yet a way opens up. For only the first time since their marriage, Munawar's parents are not accompanying them on their annual holiday.

They do not want to be a burden on us, so they arrange to rent a car at Gatwick, stay overnight with us, go across by ferry to Europe, rent another car there for a few days and return for one more night before heading elsewhere.

I take the opportunity that first evening they are with us for a private talk with Munawar about Ephesians 6:4 and a burden I have about modern fathers failing their children.

"Munawar, in Christian belief, the Bible places squarely upon the shoulders of the father the responsibility for bringing up his children in the nurture and admonition of the Lord. I believe that applies even across faiths. It is your responsibility, not Samina's but yours, to bring up your children the best you know how. They need to know about God, and they need to learn it from you. It is not right that because you are a Muslim and Samina a Sikh that you let your children grow up in a vacuum until some later time as they move into adulthood they need to and will find their own faith position. You cannot and must not neglect their need. You are a Muslim and you have a duty. Take the very best of your faith's understanding about God and give it to your children. You cannot give what you do not have, no one can expect that, but you must give the very best of what you do have. In a similar way, Samina must give to your children the best of what her faith gives her about God. You must not neglect your duty because of sensitivity to each other and end up ignoring your children's needs. God will bless to your children what you share with them about Him. Don't neglect your responsibility."

Munawar is thoughtful as he ascends the stairs. The children, nervously harbored in three bedrooms that are each more than five hundred years old, find quiet ways to sleep in company with each other or their parents. He shares our conversation with Samina.

Next morning, as they are departing for Dover, Samina arranges time for a private conversation. She is earnest and anxious. The family needs to sort out its faith. "This is the opportunity for us to do so. We don't want to miss it."

I respond "Samina, you have *Walking the Way* with you. Read together the chapter about the Orphanage and the three lessons I learned there. Discuss it with the children as you journey. Share each other's ideas and make sure you are listening to each other. We'll talk about what you have just told me after you come back."

Days later, it is about 8 p.m. before the family returns. To avoid us needing to get a meal for them, they have had pizzas in Dover and have brought along some for us. They themselves are not interested in eating or even drinking tea or chocolate. They want to talk, both parents and children. They want to talk about miracles along the way. They are insistent. Over and over they exclaim "It was a miracle, that's what it was, it was a miracle!" They share their experiences.

They are in Frankfurt. It is 1 a.m. They have been sightseeing since they have arrived, and time has run away from them. Now they are looking for their hotel. They know it is adjacent to the airport. They are hoping it is not so late that their rooms will have been given to others. There is no one around to ask. A car pulls up beside them. The driver is rebuking them. Remember, they are driving a rented French-registered car. Without a word to guide him that they do not speak French or German he addresses them in English! "What are you doing here? Don't you know this is restricted airport property?"

Munawar is full of apologies. They are so sorry. They are looking for their hotel and are lost. Can the driver please tell them where the Hotel Meridien is? The driver laughs. The Hotel Meridien! That's not at this airport, it is across the city near the main Frankfurt airport. They are at the wrong airport. The right airport is almost 40 km away! Consternation. How on earth are they even going to get there before dawn? The driver smiles. " Do not worry, my friends. Follow me! I'm going there, anyway."

He leads them all the way across the city in the middle of a silent night in a journey they will never forget and leaves them at their hotel. It's a miracle, isn't it?

And then, earlier today, another miracle. Munawar is trying to get on the autobahn towards Brussels and Calais. He drives up the *off* ramp onto the autobahn, heading for certain collision. A driver leaving the autobahn in an instant takes in the situation and swings his car across the ramp road to block traffic in each direction. It remains blocked until Munawar has reversed and is leaving the ramp in the correct direction. Isn't that another miracle?

The adventures are not yet over.

Munawar has parked his family car in the airport parking lot at Toronto airport. It has one of those keys that can do almost everything except ring out the Westminster chimes or take photographs. You may be able to effect entrance to the car, but without that wonderful key, even Houdini couldn't get the car started. Going up the ramp to the ferry, checking his pockets, Munawar finds the key is missing. Consternation again. It's going to cost $100 to replace and probably a week in time. They'll need to take a taxi home, a journey of many miles! Where did he last have it? In the car as he left Frankfurt. He leaves the family, hoping they will be able to hold the ferry for him. He runs back to the car hire agency. Have they yet rented out the car he has turned in. Then can he please have the keys, he thinks perhaps . . . ? He runs to the parking lot, finds the car, opens the door. He searches. Not where he first looks, but there, hidden in a crack, is the key! Again, as far as the family is concerned, a miracle.

Another is perhaps yet to come. Samina bursts out "And we as a family all want to be baptized before we leave here tomorrow morning. Well, the others can answer for themselves, but at least I do." Munawar answers "And so do I." The two girls join in, and the youngest, the son of eight years old, answers "Well, I'm not sure." His sisters have told him it will be difficult, and he fears this means painful. Both of the girls say they hope to become missionaries, the older one a missionary doctor and the younger a missionary nurse.

The following morning, in front of other witnesses, I conduct for the first time a baptismal service. I had been an observer at Bilquis' baptism, but I ask Munawar, Samina and the two girls the baptismal questions and receive the affirmations and give the assurances. I trust God will turn a blind eye to some of the shortcuts in due procedure.

I think and hope that He sometimes does that. It is the way He works.

a boy and his lunch

Marie Allison

Marie Allison has come out in the early fifties. She is from Pennsylvania. She is one of the last of the Sialkot Mission missahibas. She has all of the six character attributes essential to survival–

> *C*ommonsense, a sense of
> *H*umor, a
> *R*esilient spirit,
> *I*ntegrity,
> *S*elf-discipline and
> *T*enacity.

These qualities are not necessarily welcome to some of those who are slowly replacing their American predecessors. She and Gene Purdy, her friend and colleague, work in Hajipura, the girl's boarding school in Sialkot.

They are fortunate to work under the tutelage and influence of a remarkable woman who is coming to the end of four or five decades of service, Eva Hewitt. They could not have a wiser mentor to introduce them to a changing Punjabi culture.

Moves by people who look to benefit from the change in mission organization and management are afoot to get Marie Allison out of Hajipura. The requirements of financial probity belong to a past age. Marie's presence is superfluous and inhibiting.

In April 1971, Louisa Habib Khan, Pasrur's headmistress, becomes matron at Kinnaird High School in Lahore. Let her serve out her last few years in relative calm and obscurity. She has lost her battle to try to clean up Pasrur. Will her successor do any better?

That same month, in replacement, Marie Allison is appointed interim Principal and Manager of Pasrur Girls Boarding School. She is horrified and almost panic-stricken. She can remember when Joe and Marjorie Alter lived in the men's bungalow and Marie Cash and Ruth Ardrey and Jean Black lived in the women's bungalows. All have a lifetime of Punjabi experience. Now she is there alone, a sole representative of light in a place of increasing darkness and threats of violence. Her nearest missionary friends are more than twenty miles away in Sialkot.

Later, she takes courage from the story of Esther. *"Maybe it is for such a time as this that you are here."*

Lari, one of the teachers, is leading the opposition against her. The next fourteen months become for Marie an endurance nightmare. They are both the most awful, frightening days of her life and the times of deepest and sweetest spiritual consolations. She is driven to the deep reserves within her, drawing courage and support from Scripture, particularly the Psalms. Her private devotional times become her times of encouragement and renewal. She keeps a journal. It is a diary of satanic attacks on this lonely beleaguered woman and the tender provisions and protection of a faithful God. It is a diary of the loyalties of her missionary friends, particularly but not only the women, both married and unmarried, who come to stay with her and encourage her. She is supported by a great canopy of prayer from missionary homes across the Punjab. It is a diary too of the few loyal Punjabi Christian friends who are willing to incur the hatred of their neighbors and even their families in support of righteousness over craven accommodation.

It is also a diary of the failure of men and women, even godly men and women, when they are in authority and under pressure. It is the victory of expediency over principle. It is a diary of our vulnerability to the subtle cultural and personal pressures that subvert us. It unwittingly becomes a handbook of the godly life that puts righteousness before convenience and even survival, and it holds out no promise that good causes necessarily triumph.

Trouble really begins for Marie in September of 1971. The Pasrur teachers have obviously been stirred up during the summer recess and come back primed for trouble. The occult is being used in both Sialkot and Pasrur. At Hajipura, there is "an out-and-out attack of demons on some of the girls."

Before it can build up to a crescendo of discord, the same war that brings relief of staff hostilities to us at the Christian Technical Training Centre brings similar relief to Marie at Pasrur. The war between India and Pakistan breaks out at the end of November.

Pasrur is vulnerable to Indian attack; the school is closed and Marie ordered to leave. Army officers request and are given permission to occupy the missionary houses. Soldiers occupy the girls' dormitories. During the '65 war, three thousand refugees have occupied the school. In this '71 war, the Army units are careful tenants. They return the property to Marie in good shape the following January.

During the war period and until January, Marie comes to Gujranwala and stays at the United Bible Training Centre. She will be going home on furlough in June, so she needs somehow to survive that long if she can.

Her stay in Guj out of the oppressive atmosphere of Pasrur and her long talks and prayers with her missionary friends stiffen Marie's resolve. There

a boy and his lunch

is a principle of spiritual warfare she can't get around. If you earnestly desire the blessing of God, you must deal with the sin that stands in the way. You cannot go around it, you cannot pretend it isn't there and ignore it, you deal with it and let God take care of the consequences. Yet it is not as though she were on a mission station with half a dozen others minded like herself to back her up; she is back off to Pasrur, and she is alone.

She summarizes her situation in her book *Jewels in the Dust*.

> *Immediate action was held back by fear. I was terrified of what the GANG could do to me. In the past year a missionary had been killed for less! From the human standpoint all the disadvantages were on my side. I was a white woman and a foreigner. I was able to speak the language to a certain extent but I did not know the colloquial language. They were on home territory. They had a formidable backing in their Christian brotherhood and even in their Muslim friends. They had access to a spy system, a part of their culture.*

After reasoning that she should do nothing, she concludes that nevertheless she is in a better position than anyone else to do something saying, "I have no family in Pakistan they can touch, I cannot be bribed and my reputation is above reproach so I can't be blackmailed."

Her first step is to replace the cook Lari has brought in of her own free will to cook for the girls with a needy young widow.

The new school year begins in April. Marie wants to have things sorted out by then. On March 6, she calls Lari into her office and hands to the young teacher a notice of dismissal. It does not have the placebo explanation of "services no longer required" but dismisses her for "conduct unfitting for a teacher."

Lari rallies the teachers, all of them. They demand an instant meeting at night with Marie. She refuses. Eva's advice to her has been, "Never have a confrontation at night, because the potential for danger then is so much greater." The teachers go and beat up the school clerk's wife. It is getting uglier.

Lari brings a court-case against Marie in the Sialkot courts.

The backing from the Education Board for Marie's action to dismiss Lari is to transfer Lari to Sargodha!

Lari returns to the school, boldly and threateningly going about her business.

Lo and behold! About 5 p.m., Ken Old, Bob Meister and Lall turned up. Marie Old had called Ken who was in Sialkot to tell him I had been surrounded so to get out here and help me. A short while later, Wilbur Christy arrived with three other men from Gujranwala. It did strengthen my heart to realize all these busy men had taken time to drive here to help me.

Marie is doing her best to hold back her tears from distressing encounter to distressing encounter until she is alone at night behind her bolted doors.

At the beginning of April, on Easter weekend, with just two more months to try to hold on, she is in Guj. A message comes telling she has to be in Sialkot at 9 a.m. the following day to see the Inspectress of Schools with the school books from Pasrur. Marie is close to breaking. Just thinking of the bus trip back is enough to put her under at this point.

Marie Old saw my need. "I'll talk to Ken about taking you back by car." Oh, blessed angel of mercy! She not only took me home but stayed to take me back to Sialkot the following day. Then she stayed with me at the Inspectress' office and then took me back to Guj that night.

I send up from Guj Sain Ahmed, one of my completely loyal Muslim workmen who has come down from Taxila with us. He is totally reliable. He is to be there for Marie and to hotfoot it back to Guj if there is any emergency where she needs immediate help. She needs someone she can rely on.

By now Marie is getting encouragement and help from her missionary friends and from some of her outstation Pakistani friends. Dorothy Wilder, Vivienne Stacey, Marie Old, Eva Hewitt and Gene Purdy each go and stay a while at Pasrur with her.

Court cases against the secretary of the Education Board, the headmistress of Sargodha School, and the school clerk by Lari and other teachers proliferate. The teachers are saying, "Miss Allison is going home this summer, but she is not going without our mark on her." As the end of May approaches, Marie is virtually under house arrest. She does not go out unaccompanied. She is longing for permission to close the school for the summer.

a boy and his lunch

> *Marie Old was staying with me. We believe the whole matter will be over by Saturday (and we can close). Marie plans to leave by Thursday but I frankly hate to see her go so we prayed about this.*

> *Ken Old sent word the head of the Education Board was away so getting permission to close the school will be delayed. Then Ken came along. He assured us that things would probably go on as they were so I should be patient. This just made me angry. I told Marie afterwards I felt like throwing a brick at him! She laughed. God had shown us the end must be near.*

> *Marie Old and I cast out by prayer the Satanic powers in those teachers and the three men involved with them. Then Marie suggested we walk around the school, praying as we went so we did this. After our excursion of prayer together, Marie O. and I had breakfast and then went to Guj in her car.*

The end is indeed near. Vivienne Stacey returns with Marie. The school is to be closed.

> *I had to get away from Pasrur before the teachers heard the news. Vivienne was with me because the whole missionary community feared for my life.*

They leave undetected in early evening on a direct bus to Guj. She never returns. Within two weeks, she is on her way home to the States. It is early June,1972.

> *By the time I reached home, I was utterly exhausted. Aunt Dot came to see me. I saw a look of shock on her face*

for my own face was literally gray from exhaustion. It took
at least two weeks for my body to get rested and two years
for me to begin to feel like an American again.

Marie feels that without God's intervention and protection she "would either have come home in a straight-jacket or in a box!"

Although she would normally have returned for several more terms, she never goes back to the field.

Lari becomes headmistress of the Pasrur Girls Boarding School. It is nationalized in September 1972. She is still there when we leave the country in 1990.

A Church in Kabul

June 1973, Afghanistan

Christy Wilson is the son of missionary parents serving in Iran. All his growing years he looks with longing eyes and heart eastward towards Afghanistan with a strange desire. After he has gone back to the States to complete his education, he wants to come back—not to Iran, but to its eastern neighbor.

Afghanistan is a closed country and zealous in its defense of Islam. It is a country of many tribal groupings and languages. Its two primary languages are Dari, akin to old Persian and used in the west of the country, and Pushtu, used by the Pathan tribes in the east toward India. North of the capital, Kabul, are the Tajiks with their own distinct culture and language.

In 1951, Christy Wilson and his wife Betty are en route by road from Pakistan to Kabul. Christy has an appointment there as a high school teacher of English. How will these two young people be able to live out their faith to the glory of God in a country whose doors are closed? Those doors are barely opening—not even a crack and hardly a squeak. They covet the continuing prayers of friends outside its borders.

The years speed by, and the love of the Wilsons for Afghanistan and its peoples continues to grow. After completing his terms as a high school teacher, Christy is allowed to remain in the country as pastor of the international congregation of foreigners working in Afghanistan. There has been a Nestorian church in Afghanistan in the early centuries, but, apart from church facilities for the British army garrison and its families during the late nineteenth and early twentieth centuries, there is no trace of Christianity outside the diplomatic enclaves.

The years see growth in the international interest and influence in Afghanistan. The number of foreign experts continues to grow. Increasing numbers of wealthy Afghans are being educated abroad and bringing foreign ideas and frequently non-Muslim brides back home. Slowly, changes are beginning to occur in society. The mud walled forts and homes of the villages immediately around Kabul are being ruthlessly bulldozed to make way for modern, western-style buildings in an expanding city. There is an American school for children of American nationals. Even a Christian academy develops for foreign children whose parents desire their children to have a distinctly religious orientation to their education. Many of these foreigners are devout Christians determined to live their lives in a way that bears witness to the qualities of their faith.

The changes towards modernity are resented by the staunchly conservative Islamic priesthood. Many of the women, under the liberal influence of the reign of King Zahir Shah and the example of his womenfolk, are even wearing short skirts and black nylon stockings. Their arms are bare and their necklines disgustingly low.

In 1959, President Eisenhower, while visiting Afghanistan, asks King Zahir Shah for permission to build a church. There is a mosque available for the use of Muslim diplomats and others in Washington DC, so it is a reasonable quid pro quo request and one acceded to in many countries.

Christy has had his dream for more than a decade. Betty and he have moved house several times to enable the growing congregation to continue to meet in their home. The dream is to build a church in Kabul to house his congregation. He has discussions with the owners of land near his house. The congregation has a building fund.

On a trip down to Lahore on a holiday break in the autumn of 1970, Betty and he call in to visit with us in Gujranwala. Can I come up and look the property over and perhaps prepare some initial drawings for a church?

Although I have by this time worked on a number of church designs, I am aware that my designs leave a great deal to be desired architecturally. As an engineer, I tend to design things for function and for minimal cost, not appearance. This always leaves a great deal lacking in the beauty of the building.

We take Tim and Colin with us at the tail-end of their winter break from school. They love the trips to Kabul, for they represent adventure. There are specialties such as electronic goods readily available in the Kabul bazars at much less cost than home in Pakistan. Marie loves any cloth bazar anywhere. I enjoy the tea bazar where it is possible to buy unlimited quantities of long-leaf Darjeeling tea.

While staying with the Wilsons, I hear the sound of muted voices in the garage and look in. Betty Wilson is sitting on a cane-bottomed chair talking quietly to a group of men. What a wonderful vignette for the memory to capture and hold! The men are listening intently, but most of their hands are busy. They are Afghan men, probably half a dozen of them. They are not well-dressed. Most are obviously poor. The color of their clothes is dominantly black. They are bearded. All are sightless. They are weaving baskets caught at different stages of evolution. There are various little heaps of basket weaving canes and supplies. Several baskets, already completed, are stacked behind the men, who sit crossed-legged on red and black rugs spread beneath them. There is a steady hum of good-tempered conversation.

a boy and his lunch

They are talking to each other, and Betty, fluent in their language, is joining in with them.

After a few fascinating moments watching, I slip quietly away.

Some of these men are beggars from the Kabuli bazars. Betty has felt led to try to help them. This group has been meeting for more than a year, and the men are now close friends. Gathering together for them means a bowl of curry and naan bread, baskets to make and sell, somewhere out of the cold to sit and have conversation. Naturally, talk turns to religion and belief. There are only two worthy topics of conversation for a group of men (and several unworthy). After the various politics have been brought up to date, then the conversation turns inevitably to religion.

I produce a rough plan of the church for Christy, choosing for initial construction a simple imported, prefabricated pitched roof building such as I have used a number of times in Pakistan. Later, when the idea of a church building has been accepted and the dust has settled, a slender, freestanding, campanile tower akin to a mosque minaret can be added.

An excellent church architect in New Zealand now volunteers his services and takes over the task of design, and things move ahead rapidly. We hear the building is almost complete. The dedication date is set.

Marie and I have opportunity during '72 to see the completed building before it is dedicated. It is superb, with a soaring church roof of Herat blue. Christy delightedly points out a natural patterning in the marble floor that suggests clearly the dove of the Holy Spirit.

The congregation is already using the church, and Christy's joy is contagious.

Trouble, though, is on its way.

In September, a section of the compound wall is broken down by government troops. It is repaired, again damaged and again repaired. In February 1973, the wall is again attacked and then entirely demolished before a stay order can be obtained.

The Prime Minister sends word to the church board asking permission to tear the church down. On June 14, 1973, city government bulldozers come onto the church site and, despite international protests at the action of the Afghan government at their embassies around the world, the church is completely demolished. The congregation is permitted to remove various fittings and furniture and the organ and piano. The under-floor heating is ripped up lest it prove to be espionage equipment. It takes a month to clear the debris.

The reason given for the action is that there has been no planning permission.

The blind school is ordered closed immediately.

The Wilsons, after twenty-two years working in Kabul, are given three days to leave the country.

Later that year, King Zahir Shah is overthrown in a Soviet-backed coup, and his cousin, General Sardar Daud Khan, takes over as president. He himself is assassinated in 1978 in a military coup. After intervening political changes, there is a further Soviet-backed coup in December 1979 when Babrak Karmal takes over. The guerrilla war starts. In a few short years, there are five million refugees in Iran and Pakistan—one third of the whole population. The Hezb-i-Islami leader, controlling the Pukhtun mujahideen from Peshawar, is Gulbuddin Hekmatyar. Later he will become Prime Minister of Afghanistan.

a boy and his lunch

Smoking and Drinking

July 1973, The Christian Technical Training Centre, Gujranwala

Marie urges me not to go. I have received a request from "the enemy" to come over to Khokherke; they have a question they wish to ask me. The opposition from within the Christian community has been hot recently. Reports are going to the government and to various church authorities trying to get us thrown out of the country on the grounds of running a spy network, stealing church property or infringing various civil and criminal laws. There is a clique of our opponents in Khokherke. We are fairly sure, from their peculiar use of English idiom, which ones are writing these diatribes.

I receive an invitation from them to come over to Amanat Pervaiz's house at 7 p.m. this evening to meet a group of Khokherke men who are seeking an answer to a particular question. They will tell me what the question is when I arrive.

Marie is understandably uneasy. This is at a time when I have rigged up an alarm bell system from our bedroom to the servant quarters where several of our Muslim employees who have come with us from Taxila live. We can rely on them to come immediately when the bell rings. Marie has under the bed the boys' baseball bat. There has already been one attempt at a break-in.

Marie asks me not to eat or drink anything I am offered since it might have been doctored. Will I not take a companion?

I assure her that nothing untoward will happen. I might receive an ultimatum, but there is no risk and there will be no harm in my going. I am going at their invitation, and I will be their guest. They have a duty to protect their guest, and they will observe the conventions.

There are about a dozen men waiting for me when I arrive. I know almost all of them. Those I know are Khokherke residents. Among them are, I am sure, the authors of the spurious complaints and reports about me. Amanat, who speaks fluent English, welcomes me, shows me to a chair and gives me a cup of sugary tea.

I look around as I drink. The men, none of them employees of the Seminary or CTTC, are sitting down in the other chairs and on the settees arranged in a circle. One or two remain standing. The air is thick with tobacco smoke. There may have been a huqqa (a smoker's bubble pipe), but most are smoking cigarettes.

The normal custom in a Punjabi home is to talk about trivia until it is time to leave. Then as you are leaving, you raise the purpose of your visit. I choose to breach convention and open the conversation. "Gentlemen, you have invited me to meet you here because you have a question to discuss. What is your question?"

Amanat is obviously their spokesman. He comes straight to the point.

"Mr. Old, is it alright for Christians to drink?"

The question surprises me. Whatever question I might have surmised they would ask, it is not this. Yet this is a relevant question. The government of Pakistan is introducing legislation to prohibit the sale and use of strong liquor under its understanding of Q'ranic injunctions against drinking. However, owing to the observed practice of British troops taking wine at communion during church services, it is believed that the Christian faith requires its adherents to drink wine.

The government is willing to grant liquor permits, with undoubted commercial value to black marketers, to Christians who apply for them.

I look around. The men lean forward, the better to catch my answer.

They are serious. This *is* their question, but I wonder why they have chosen to ask me to answer it. There are seminary professors living just across the road, and they could give authoritative answers by chapter and verse. I am, after all, only an engineer and in particular the man they love to hate.

I begin by answering the unasked question about Jesus' own practice.

"Some believe that when we read about Jesus drinking wine or the fruit of the grape or when we refer to the water turned into wine at Cana, we are talking about an unfermented non-alcoholic grape juice. I don't think that is so. I believe that when these references are made, we are referring to fermented alcoholic liquor with the power, if enough is drunk, to intoxicate.

"However, if we want to determine whether Christians can drink alcoholic liquor, we need to look elsewhere.

"The key verse to guide us is Romans 12:1. Amanat, will you please look that verse up for us and read it to us?"

Amanat takes down his well-used Urdu Bible and reads the verse I ask and the following one, also.

I beseech you, therefore, brethren, by the mercies of God, that ye present your bodies a living sacrifice, holy, acceptable unto God, which is your reasonable service. And be not conformed to this world but be ye transformed by the renewing of your mind that ye may prove what is that good, and acceptable, and perfect, will of God.

The whole group goes silent, looking again at me. There is no animosity, only curiosity.

"It all hinges for each of us on whether our bodies, affected by the effects of alcohol, or for that matter, nicotine and tobacco, can be considered a living sacrifice, holy and acceptable to God.

"God created each one of us. He created both man and woman, and he created the manner in which our bodies function. Our bodies have a delicate and intricate nervous system, controlling when and how we blink an eye or raise a finger or thread a needle. We are delicately and wonderfully made. When we introduce voluntarily into our bodies substances that affect the way our nervous and emotional systems operate, we are interfering with the capacities of something that God created perfect. Can we offer that back to God as an acceptable and holy sacrifice? If we feel that we can, then we will find no restriction on taking drink or smoking. Let me ask you a question. Can I smoke?"

I am amazed at the response. Unanimously and without a moment's hesitation, with one voice, they answer, "No!" as though the very thought of it is unthinkable.

I laugh at them. "What are you talking about? Almost all of you are smoking, and yet, you tell me that I cannot smoke! What do you mean?"

Amanat speaks for them all.

"Mr. Old, you don't understand. We can smoke! We can drink! Father Paul down the road at St Joseph's—he can smoke, and he can drink. But *you* can't drink and *you* can't smoke!"

"And pray why not?"

"*You* are our missionary!"

I begin then to glimpse and partly understand the strange relationship that missionaries have—the strange love/hate relationships—with the communities they seek to serve. It is quite all right for Amanat and his fellows to seek by every foul means open to them to get me thrown out of the country. That is all part of the rules of the game as they play it. It is, however, not acceptable for me ever to try to get down off the pedestal on which they have placed me, a pedestal I have not sought, and show that I have the same weaknesses that they themselves possess.

I, willy-nilly and without choice of my own, am to be their exemplar of what is right. They do not expect me to lie, to cheat, to steal, to become angry, to be humanly fallible just plainly and simply for the reason that I am their missionary. I am to operate under completely different rules than the rules they live by. It is to be expected I will oppose what they are doing, but I am not allowed to use the weapons that they are using in retaliation against them.

We part that evening amicably. Marie is relieved to see me home again. She has been praying.

My Khokherke friends continue to try to get me thrown out of the country, and I play within the rules they allow me to use and, eventually, after all the dust of conflict has settled, survive.

a boy and his lunch

Monsoon

August 1973, Gujranwala

A dramatic novel of my childhood memory is *The Rains Came* by Louis Bromfield. I have not reread it, but the whole fascinating tale is, as I recall, the drama of the monsoon in an Indian setting. Now I am watching that story myself.

For three days, the rain has been almost incessant. As the levels of standing water move towards and from the high spots on the ground, each eddy leaves its traces in straw and seeds like a receding tide. Plinths of buildings are always higher than ground level to accommodate minor local flooding. Some of these plinths have not been made high enough.

Fortunately, unlike most towns, Gujranwala is not subject to flooding from rivers overflowing, but the city used to flood from trapped rainwater. In rains like these, every roof leaks. The hammering staccato of the rain—thirty inches in three days—will have penetrated anything. Fortunately, the schoolboys are home for their short summer break. Inevitably many, helping to clean up, will be late back. Brend and Marjet, like Marie, are up in the hills with the children.

The little "nanga pangas" have long since tired of dancing naked in the rain. Everything is soaked through. More bricks are needed to raise canisters and containers above the invading waters or the accumulating roof leaks which cannot drain past the high doorsills. Umbrellas are futile. It is simpler to get wet through and enjoy it. My days are occupied in patrol duties to locate leaks and prevent damage. Accompanying the rain are violent gusts, thunders and lightnings. Trees in softened ground uproot and fall. Limbs tear and scream as they shear. The electric power lines short onto the steel pylons with blue flashes. Sometimes the pylons are live and lethal. Vehicles plow great water furrows through empty streets. All the irrigation channels are full. The playing fields and front gardens are covered with six inches of trapped water that has nowhere left to flow and cannot seep through the sodden ground. Sandbags guard the main doors of the workshops. The machinery is covered with plastic protection against leaks. On and on the rain continues!

Radio Pakistan is reporting disaster not far away. Our nearest major river is the Chenab. It is an untamed giant. Pakistan has no capacity to dam and control the river before it emerges from the mountains, for that area is in Indian hands. Two tributaries emerging from the Kashmir hills, the Musawwat Tawi and the Jammu Tawi, have overflowed toward each other and totally covered the wide Vee that they form before merging into the Chenab. Eight feet of water have swept over the land and downstream. The trees that once had been plentiful have been cut down during the Indian occupation of early 1972. There is no refuge. Screaming wildly to the helpless observers on the bridge families clinging to housetops or other buoyant matter have been swept downstream through the wide open gates of the barrage at Marala.

Scores of thousands of village houses, mostly comprising mud walls and, for roofing, earth covered clay tiles on four by twos, have collapsed and are still collapsing. For many, the devastation will require immense effort at recovery.

I begin to wonder about the house replacement process. To rebuild in the same way gives no long-term remedy. The same thing can happen again next summer. What is needed is some kind of rigid-framed structure where the walls can be washed away but the roof will survive and remain in place and intact. The walls can be of mud, but they should not be carrying the weight of the roof. The roof must have easy access from the ground and be capable of providing a human refuge until rescue can be arranged or the floods subside.

The roof should sit on an independent concrete frame. It should need only manpower for erection, no machinery or equipment, so everything should be kept as light as possible. It needs to be susceptible to mass production and to transportation on trucks that have body length capacities of only 13' 6". It will be needed urgently. Long delay in organization and production will not be acceptable if it is to be of any value in the present situation. Its own foundations must load the wet ground with less than one half ton per square foot. It has to be structurally stable and be braced against collapse from a force—floodwater, coming from any sideways direction.

I start sketching. Do calculations, sketch again. The basic framework is not difficult. Everything will be precast concrete. There will be no concreting on site, just assembly. Columns and beams are necessarily limited to 13'4" length, just short of the length of a truck. The columns, in X section to reduce weight, will have holes every fifteen inches to allow steel pins to act as steps to the roof. Main beams will carry subordinate beams at half span and at the points of support. Crossbeams will be 6'8" long. They carry arched concrete tiles limited to the weight a woman can carry. I judge this to be 58 lbs, the weight of the filled water pots the women regularly carry so gracefully on their heads, and work out the size accordingly. I avoid using women as laborers, but obviously in this task, the men will carry the heavy loads and women and boys will move the roofing tiles. The assembled mod-

a boy and his lunch

ules, 13'4" square, can be coupled together to form continuous lengths or double or triple widths.

Initially, I am thinking I will fix the columns onto the foundations with a hinge of a steel pin but discard this in favor of a foundation pad with a tapered socket into which the column drops and is anchored with sand. The various heads of the columns initially are loose heads, but this is discarded in favor of several columns with different fixed heads. Beams are anchored onto lower beams or onto columns with vertical steel pins. Sway braces are 3/8" diameter steel bars. There is nothing particularly ingenious about this solution; it is all quite obvious and straightforward.

Next, I design the shuttering molds that will be needed. I try to arrange that the difficult, most expensive parts of each mold can be used several times each day, even if the products themselves are not moved for a week.

I have learned that if we are within God's Will, then He provides the means to enable that Will to come to pass. This is a divine principle. When man's search for God becomes serious, then it becomes in addition man's search for God's Will. It is this latter search that never ends. We, His servants, do not act with a divine blank check, but we are constrained to locate and identify that divine will and then remain within it. Once there, we are secure and confident and, essentially, unlimited. I am confident that, in this matter of housing for the homeless, He has compassion on them and further that, like the loaves and fishes, He will act to respond to their need.

Somehow He will provide the finance that will be needed. That is His business, not mine. If this sounds like a risky charter to operate under, all I can say is that in thirty-four years, from the early days in the orphanage until the time we leave on retirement, I never once find this presumption to fail. There are matters that are our business and then there are matters that are God's business.

I put the carpenters onto making the shuttering, begin to purchase the steel reinforcing bars from Lahore, the two types of sand and the limestone aggregate from Taxila and Wah. When the carpenter trainees come back from their holiday, I set them to work also. After the wooden prototype molds are made and the initial concrete elements cast, I start the welding crews on making improved steel molds. Cement, often in short supply, is temporarily plentiful. No one wants it because, with 100 percent humidity, it is almost impossible to use before it air-sets into lumps and becomes unusable. Later, as the weather improves, the rains cease and humidity drops, general repair work rapidly gets underway throughout the flood-affected areas, and cement again becomes in short supply.

Within little more than a month, about a hundred men are working on making precast houses. The large garden field in front of the school is one great precasting and curing yard and storage area for accumulating concrete pieces. Trucks seem to be continuously loading. We are developing multiple designs — for grain stores, for village schools and for housing colonies — and working flat out trying to keep up with the demand.

Aid agencies have projects of flood relief; this is a product that is available and that they can use. Teams of men and boys go out to erect the frames and become proficient in setting out and erection. Most of them are Christians, and this is needed work for them. Some of the housing units are taken to the Marala barrage and there ferried by boat to the Vee area between the rivers in order to be flood refuge platforms in any later flood. Lee Reed comes across from Thal to help. Brend runs the school, and I manage the housing project.

A missionary friend drops me a quiet hint that $30,000 has been given by the One Great Hour of Sharing Project of the Presbyterian Church in the United States for use in the housing project under my personal direction. This is a complete surprise to me; I do not recall that I have asked for money. However, it has been fed through the World Council of Churches Pakistan Flood Relief Fund and has become lost and "stuck" in Lahore. It stays there until Marie, down from the hills, goes to battle with Geneva. If the World Council of Churches (which is not at fault) is unable to remit the money to us, we will need to refer the matter to the donors. The money arrives!

There is good cooperation between Catholic and Protestant agencies in the Punjab InterAid committee. Catholic and Church of Pakistan bishops and Presbyterian and other Christian leaders work actively together. Six weeks after the floods occurred, the committee comes to Gujranwala, where the work is still gaining momentum, to see the housing. It undertakes to purchase virtually all of the houses we can manufacture and erect until the immediate needs ease. This continues until we are close to going home on furlough early in the following summer. The yard and all the work are then transferred to Lahore, where it continues for several years under other management.

Before that, though, I am to become acquainted with a worried senator who has a problem and be called to the Prime Minister's house, but that is another story.

a boy and his lunch

The Senator in Trouble

October 1973, Gujranwala

Work has just started for the day. The first trucks are loading the houses. The shipment lists are now down to a routine and take only a few moments to prepare. Nek Alam is checking the loading.

I have not met the stranger previously. He doesn't appear to be a local man. He is wearing a smart, light gray suit more suited for a metropolis than our kind of town. He speaks fluent English, appears edgy and anxious. He is interested in what is going on. How many days does it take to build a house? Well, we can assemble a frame and its roof in a day or so, not more than a day and a half.

We usually leave the floors, the walls, the doors and the windows to the people who will one day live in the houses.

"Could you build a house, fully complete, by Thursday, Thursday morning?"

"Today is Monday. I suppose we can, if it isn't too far away."

He appears relieved, as though a great burden has been lifted from his shoulders. He is obviously more than a sidewalk superintendent, there is some purpose to his visit.

Over tea in the office, he confides what it is. He gives me his name, he is the senator from Gujrat. He belongs to the ruling People's Party. He has a very serious problem. He hopes that I can help him. As I will know, the Chenab river passes through his district. There has been appalling damage along the course of the river. Great loss of life. The gates of the barrage at Marala have been fully open. There is no impeding or controlling the raging river. The link canals carrying water between the Punjab rivers to compensate for the loss of irrigation waters from the Sutlej and Beas make the situation worse. The earthen canal embankment, perhaps ten feet higher than the land itself, has been breached. The whole force of the released waters along the full length of the canals has discharged into the flat fields still carrying the summer crops of sugar cane and fodder. Great scoops of soil from the breach areas have been distributed over large areas and into the villages. Some villages have been virtually washed away.

The Prime Minister is deeply concerned. He is a man of immense personal energy. In this matter, he seems tireless. The Punjab holds a greater population than the other three provinces combined. Much of the land is as flat as a chapati. The rain has not had a chance to drain before it is itself supplemented by the floodwaters from the rivers. All kinds of emergency operations have been established. The immediate concerns are first rescue and then food and also prevention of cholera and dysentery and typhoid. Now they are beginning to deal with the problem of rehousing. The Prime Minister has made large sums of money available to the government organizations in the affected areas, working through the commissioners and deputy commissioners and the elected representatives, the members of the National Assembly and the Senate.

Naturally, the Prime Minister has been requiring progress reports on work in the flood areas. The senator explains with an expressive shrug of the shoulders how it is possible for him to know what is going on in every corner of his large area. It is possibly the worst affected area of them all. The Prime Minister has been probing and insistent. He has satisfied the Prime Minister with detailed reports. The rehousing is progressing well. Rannmal, one of the worst affected villages, is being rehoused, and the rehabilitation is now extending to the neighboring villages.

Then the Prime Minister has sprung a bombshell. The senator has not slept at night since!

"Mr. Old, the Prime Minister's wife is coming to Rannmal to inspect our progress on Thursday. She is coming by helicopter. She will preside at the hand-over ceremony of the new homes for the villagers but . . ." here is the confession, "no work has yet begun there, let alone be ready for hand-over! Can you help me? I am in much trouble. Can you build a house for me in Rannmal by Thursday morning, please?"

He does not have to explain his problem further. We both have problems, but at this moment, his are much worse than mine! He shows me where Rannmal is on a map. It is about sixty miles away. He assures me it is possible to get close. If I can spare the time, he will take me there now. We will pick up the local deputy commissioner in Gujrat and travel on from there in his four-wheel-drive vehicle.

I make no promises whether we can help, but time is obviously beginning to tick away if we are to be able to do anything. I send a message to Marie that I will not be back for lunch, tell Brend where I am going, tell the foreman, Nur Zaman, to prepare a pair of doors and several windows in a hurry, and then the senator and I are on our way. I need to see whether our loaded trucks can get anywhere near the village.

It is tragic. The canal has broken during the night. It must have been plain terror. Rannmal is about one mile from the breach, across dead flat fields. Part of the village has been scooped away into a large, still wet crater. The Land Rover remains on the village road a furlong away. We walk across to the village. A number of the houses have been washed away. Some of the houses are still occupied. All the villagers are crowded into those that remain, managing somehow, sharing what they still have left. The ground is wet and spongy. The truck will be able to get no nearer than the Land Rover. Everything will need to be carried from that point. The villagers bring tea and rusks for their visitors and produce cane-bottomed chairs and a table-cloth for the table.

The deputy commissioner begins to organize the reception for the Prime Minister's wife. She will arrive about mid-morning. There will be a marble plaque for her to unveil. He will arrange that. The senator agrees with the villagers on where we will build the first house. We will, he promises them, build at least twenty more after the first one. The village will be responsible for all the unskilled labor that will be needed and for the meals and accommodation of the workmen.

I break into the conversation. Can the villagers get bricks for the walls and, if there is still time to lay them, for the floor?

Yes, the brick-kiln at Ghutke has been flooded, but the stacking of the new sun-dried bricks has now been completed, and firing will soon start. There are still some of the unspoiled pre-monsoon stocks, and they will have them brought by donkey-wala. How many will I need? They will be here by tomorrow evening.

The senator assures me that there will be no difficulty about payment; I can have it all in advance if I wish. We settle those details on the return journey home. I think he would have raided his children's moneybox if necessary to keep me happy; he is so anxious everything go smoothly. He himself will be meeting the Prime Minister's wife in Gujrat and will travel with her in the helicopter to Rannmal. He will see me on Thursday morning, Insh'allah. Khuda Hafiz - God be with you.

If I can deliver, I will have a friend for life!

Rannmal

October 1973

We have Tuesday and Wednesday to build a house sixty miles away. We have to keep it simple to keep it quick. Although it can be done with six, we will have nine columns for a room 13'4" square with an outside porch of half that size where the wife can do her cooking and spend much of her time. Because of the wet subsoil, we will need additional pads under the foundations to spread the load. We dare leave nothing behind; there will be little time to go back and get anything we forget. We have to remember tools, ladders and scaffolding, steel pins and tie bars, spares in case of breakages, the doors and windows, a roll of plastic, paint and brushes. Nur Zaman will stay behind and supervise the yard. We won't have time to train an erection crew from the village. That can come with the later buildings. We will take a team with us. I will take Munir, Caleb and Mohammed Hussain with me. I check carefully the two trucks on Tuesday morning after Nur Zaman tells me they are loaded and put on half a dozen more spare tiles; the men climb on to the trucks, and we are on our way!

Munir organizes the unloading at the road near the village and the order of the transfer of materials to where they are needed. Foundations will be needed before beams and tiles before copings.

While the trucks are being unloaded, I make my way over to mark out the column foundations. This is simple routine. Two steel pins are put in the ground for the centers of the first two. Two tapes, a side and a diagonal, fix the third and fourth positions. A check that three and four are the right distance apart. Now mark the two intermediate columns and then the three front porch ones. Draw a circle eighteen inches radius around each pin. Nine men are now frantically digging holes. Our Punjabi soil is wonderful material, an alluvial soil of consistent characteristics. You can cut a vertical side for ten or twenty feet, and the odds are that it will not fall. We aren't even going three feet deep.

With a dumpy level, I level in the excavations.

Let me tell you about Munir and the level. Munir is from the Murree hills. His father and his uncle are carpenters working with me in 1958 in Murree. When Ali dies, Nur Zaman needs, according to custom, to marry his brother's widow to provide a home for her and her children. He already has his own wife, but I have no hesitation in lending Nur Zaman money to take a second wife as well. The three boys—Munir, Aziz and Javed—now have an uncle who is their stepfather. They are like additional brothers to Tim and Colin, of a similar age and growing up together.

They are all still working with the building crew when we retire. By this time, Munir has replaced Nur Zaman as the building foreman.

For many years, from the time when he was a little boy, Munir holds the staff which I will read with the level. He has perhaps had two years of schooling. All the time he is watching carefully, thinking. When I leave the level in position and go elsewhere for a while, I will release the screw that locks the rotation so that it will swing easily. That way no casual person will force the level and break it. At such times Munir will sneak up and peer through the telescope. The picture is always upside down! While he holds the staff, he studies it, trying to understand the meanings of the horizontal stripes, each 1/100 of a foot broad. He learns to read Roman numerals. He watches the way I level the three screws to bring the bubble in the right position throughout the circle. He watches the way I focus the telescope. He sees me rotate the eyepiece ring to bring the graticule lines into focus. He never once asks a question about what I am doing, just watches.

Then one day, I come around a corner and catch him by surprise. He has become tired of waiting for me to level in some foundations and is doing it himself! This time Caleb is holding the staff, and he is behind the telescope. He steps back, a guilty look on his face like a boy caught scrumping apples. I check what he has done. Perfect! I would have said that it is not possible to figure out how to use a surveying level by watching, but he has done it.

Women, girls and boys stream from the unloading point about a hundred yards away from where we are building, each with a roofing tile balanced on the head. The women walk with an easy grace and straight back. Two men in file carry on their shoulders a crossbeam, each end resting on the loosely wrapped puggree cloth (turban). There is something incongruous about it all, and yet, at the same time, it bridges the centuries. This is the way it has been done forever. In the adjacent field, a peasant is plowing with a pair of oxen and a wooden plough. The winter wheat has to go in, flood or no flood.

The older women prepare bread and vegetable curry for us all. So good and so hot!

By now the pads are all in, and the bottoms of the column sockets have been brought level with sand in a final adjustment. When the first four columns are in and plumb and secure, the cross-bracing of steel bars is fitted and tightened. Now it can't collapse like a pack of cards. The foundations are back-filled, the extra soil left over raises the floor level and the beams are hoisted with much shouting and pinned into position. By the time the next pair of columns is erected, I am standing on the roof of the first section, adding my voice to the exhortation.

Modern mechanism and lifting and winching equipment has taken much of the joy out of teamwork. The old sea shanties were born by crews on a four-master working together to raise the yards or lift the anchor. In Hyderabad, building the cement factory, some of our concrete pours are continuous, lasting more than twenty-four hours. Unnoticeably, men drop out, and others fill their places. The work keeps on going. The key men in such a pour are the callers. I am pretty sure that not all their cries or responses would have met with my approval if I had understood them. The conversations would go on to the same steady rhythm hour after hour. The foreman is a rascal–Y . . . e . . . s Lord; So is his father–Y . . . e . . . s Lord; As for his mother - Y . . . e . . . s Lord; And as for Old Sah'b - Y . . . e . . . s Lord.

By the time it is dark, the roof tiles are all in place with several left over. The back of the job is broken.

There is no better breakfast than a Punjabi village breakfast! There is something wonderful, at least to the stranger, in the rhythm of each day. The cockerels crowing before light creeps through the crevices and cracks of the shutters and doors. The hushed background conversation of the women who have risen while it was still dark. The walk across the fields. Traditionally, the men have one side of the village and the women the other. The men find private, separate places to squat, in amongst the sugar cane. The women, in an open space, squat in a circle, facing towards the center and sharing the gossip. The slow walk back. Salaams along the way. Then the ablutions under the hand-pump. Shaving without a mirror. A shared towel. The smoke twisting slowly upwards in a dozen lazy strands from courtyard fires. Piping hot parathas (unleavened bread with butterfat from water buffalo milk) porridge, yogurt, sugary tea. Since you are a special guest, there also may be scrambled eggs.

Throughout the day, we waste little time. Baskets of freshly dug earth are carried up the ladders on heads or lifted in two stages via the scaffold platform. The seams in the plastic are lapped over several times before the earth is spread and leveled. The copings are located and fixed around the edges of the roof.

Below, the walls, one brick thick in mud mortar, are keyed into the rebates of the columns. There won't be time to point them with cement mortar. The mud is just trimmed neatly. When the walls are complete, the doors and windows are wiped clean of mud and stained brown just before dark falls. They will be dry by morning. The dirt floor is dressed with an inch of local gray sand.

While we are finishing off our assignment, the local authorities are completing theirs—a glorious, five-panel, tented pavilion in bright red and yellow on bamboo poles. The memorial plaque is set in brickwork on its own separate plinth. Our little building is appearing increasingly more humble and insignificant with every addition to the extravaganza. It's the way men work.

Thursday morning. No helicopter. A convoy of eighteen vehicles snakes along from the canal bank up to a well-organized parking lot near the plaque. The Prime Minister's wife is very gracious. Behind her back, the senator puts his hands together in a silent appreciation. Tonight he will be able to sleep after all.

Naudero

November 1973, Gujranwala

Just before dark, Marie and I return from a shopping trip to Lahore. Marie drops me in Brandreth Road at nine and will meet me there at 4 p.m. By the time we have picked up all the purchases left in the shops along the road, we have to hurry to get off the road before dark. In times past we rarely traveled the roads after dark, but things have changed. However, unlighted oxcarts, narrow roads and undipped lights coming straight at you make journeying after dark no pleasure.

Brend comes over soon after we are back. A message has come from the Prime Minister's house. Will I call back as soon as I return from Lahore? No, he isn't joking. It is a phone message that the head clerk has taken. No, the caller has left no details as to reasons. Just a request that I call back upon my return from Lahore. What trouble am I in now?

All my life I have detested telephones. The only time we have a telephone in our house in Pakistan is when we use a doctor's house that already has one installed. I can't stop people phoning in, but I hardly ever initiate a call out. The world would be better off without telephones. This time there is no wriggling out of it.

I go over to the school and call the operator. Will he please connect me to the Prime Minister's house in Rawalpindi? The operator takes his job seriously. He probably has ten starving children and a wife in the hospital having the second set of twins. No way is he going to connect anyone to the Prime Minister's house. What do I think he is, a nut? It will be more than his job is worth. I ask him, beg him to call his supervisor. This is a serious call. He will not. I call him Bhai jan, lalaji to sweeten him, it makes no difference. He is not going to connect me to the Prime Minister's house, now or ever.

I call again, will he connect me to the Superintendent of Police? Yes, he will do this. Now I am talking sense at last. I explain to Qamar that I need his help to persuade the telephone operator to connect me to the Prime Minister's house. Give him five minutes and then call the operator again, he suggests.

I have wondered what happened in those five minutes. Did he send a squad of police over to the telegraph office? Did he use gentle persuasion over the phone or the threat of immediate arrest and a flogging in the bargain?

I ask the operator if he will please connect me to the Prime Minister's house? "Yes sir, yes sir, at once, sir." Clicks and noises, urgent conversations on the line and a bell dinging. "You are connected, sir."

I explain to the voice at the other end that I am Mr. Old of Gujranwala and I have been asked to call. My call is expected. He will put me through. It is the Prime Minister's cousin, Mumtaz. "Thank you for calling. We are very interested in your housing. Will it be possible for you to come up to Rawal-pindi, at your convenience of course? We would like to discuss it with you." We agree on a date several days hence and a time in the early afternoon. Yes, I know where the Prime Minister's house is—behind the golf course near the old Murree brewery.

Marie has a house-full of people to be looking after, so she stays at home. Although the journey is only about 135 miles, it is always wise to allow four or five hours. Marie deems it safer to travel by train, but usually I travel by bus. Today, however, I am taking the car.

Mumtaz, middle-aged and likeable, is cordial. The Prime Minister's wife has recounted to the family her visit to Rannmal where she has met me. I have a novel form of house. Can I describe it to him? I show him photo-graphs. I show him the booklet of designs for houses of various sizes and the plans for grain stores and various school designs. Here is a dispensary. You can even use it for a police station. He is intrigued. He supposes it would be possible to build a whole village out of such a concept.

The Prime Minister is wishing to improve the housing of his own villag-ers in Naudero, near Larkhana in the Sindh. He has had an eminent Karachi architect prepare plans for a new village. However, it seems as though the Rannmal-type house might offer a rapid and economic method of building a village on a virgin site; there is plenty of land. Do I have any designs for villages?

I have been knocking around plans for Kanaya New Town, a dream town to be set at the junction of the planned Gujranwala circular bypass and the Sialkot Road. This location would enable rural poor, migrating to the cities for work, to live at a bus hub that can quickly deliver workers to the factories in and around Gujranwala. However Kanaya Town is much bigger than a village. I will prepare a special set of drawings for Naudero.

I am an engineer, not an architect. Although I do architectural work and my own building designs, I never delude myself by claiming I am an archi-tect. Some of my buildings are downright monstrosities. My village design is equally unimaginative, purely functional. It is the shape of a bicycle wheel laid flat, divided into eight sectors with linking roads along the spokes with another circular road at mid radius. About one thousand people. I keep check-

196   a boy and his lunch

ing the progress with Rawalpindi to make sure I am doing what is needed. School, dispensary, police station, shops, and a mosque—all are there.

The plans are approved. What will it cost? I have worked in Sindh. I know how costs there compare with costs in the Punjab. Presumably, for this particular project, there will be no difficulty getting cement. I work out the cost—well under a million rupees, a real bargain. I contact Sadiq Mirza. We have worked together in Hyderabad. He now has his own contracting company. He is simply the best concrete engineer I have ever encountered. He agrees to go down to Naudero and build the village for the amount I have estimated.

With his agreement in my pocket, I make a last journey up to the Prime Minister's house to hand over the plans and to tell them that I have arranged for a contractor to go down and build it for the estimated cost. Mumtaz is pleased with both designs and estimates. There is no question but that the Prime Minister will want it to go ahead. When can I go down to Naudero?

This takes me aback. I have had no intention of going down to Naudero. However, I have arranged for a superb Pakistani engineer in whom I have total confidence to go down and do so. I am prepared to go down two or three times during the construction period to check, but I have responsibilities for a boys' school in Gujranwala, and this takes precedence.

Mumtaz is unhappy. The Prime Minister won't be liking this. Can't I make time? Can't I find a substitute to run the school? I assure him that Sadiq will do an even better job than I could or would do. That isn't good enough. He is sure the Prime Minister can't let the project go ahead unless I am willing to go down and do it.

I am not, and although we part friends, the project doesn't go forward.

The Poetic Policeman

Spring 1974, Lahore

A number of my friends among the Government officers are interested in English literature and poetry. The Deputy Superintendent of Police (DSP) in Gujranwala would happily change the conversation of his crowded office, when I entered, to a discussion of the motives of Macbeth and his lady or to the animus that Shylock held against Antonio. Much to the puzzlement of the assorted thugs who seemed to gather in his office, he would throw in a quotation such as, "Love's not time's fool though rosy lips and cheeks . . ." that bore only strained relevance to the conversation going on around him.

The commissioner, on the other hand, reads the Concise Oxford Dictionary for pleasure. He practices new words on me. He also seems to know everything written by Joseph Conrad almost by heart. Because Joseph Conrad has lived at Pent Farm, only a couple of miles or so away from our home in Sellindge, he considers me to be God's gift to him as one of England's experts on Conrad. He gathers up his philosophical questionings from his latest reading of "Heart of Darkness" until we shall next meet.

This story, though, is about another literary person, a poetic policeman who saves my bacon or whatever alternative is appropriate.

I begin by sharing a piece of wisdom I learned the hard way. Take any references or recommendations of the high personal character of particular individuals given by fellow missionaries with a generous seasoning of salt. They won't, of course, be lying, but they might, perhaps, because of their trusting natures, be just a little too easily led up the garden path.

Nek Alam (it means Righteous Counselor) is a Pathan convert. A missionary friend on the Northwest Frontier gives him the highest character references. He needs to be away for his own good. Can I give him a job? Anything to help Jack. The housing project is going full steam ahead with close to one hundred men employed. Nek Alam can be the storekeeper.

Here, right away, I make a strategic mistake when I should have known better. You only ever appoint as a storekeeper someone whom you have known for fifty years, someone who is totally illiterate so that he can't fiddle the books, someone on the lower rungs of your own tribe and family and someone who is convinced that you will extract every drop of his blood by blunt hypodermic needles if he ever loses as much as a nail from his store.

I will soon be needing steel from Lahore, forty-five miles away. Such purchases I do myself. After scouting the various rolling mills at Badami

Bagh for the best prices and looking over the steel—there are many qualities—I give my order to Fazal Din & Sons. I order ten tons in various sizes and pay more than thirty thousand rupees in notes that I am carrying in my briefcase. I take and check the receipt.

Now to arrange to take delivery. I am going to have no mistakes. I will send two men in from Gujranwala next Monday morning. They will be carrying a signed note from me instructing the steel shall be delivered to them. I leave a copy of my signature on the receipt counterfoil. If they do not have the note, there is to be no delivery to them. They will watch the steel being weighed onto the truck and keep a tally. If any price adjustment is needed, I'll sort that out on my next visit. I will personally check the steel when it arrives at Gujranwala. Is all of that clear?

On Monday, I send in Ayub Malik, a Christian, and also Sain Ahmed. Ayub is halfway honest, although he does sell votes at elections. He can keep the tally as the steel is loaded. Sain Ahmed is a Sikh boy who converted to Islam to save his life when Pakistan separated from India. He has come with me from Taxila and is absolutely loyal and trustworthy. I give him the authorization note and money for meals and the truck hire.

By afternoon, they are back in consternation, without the steel! Fazal Din & Sons says that my men have already come in on Saturday and have taken full delivery. No, they don't know the names of the men or the number of the truck that has taken the steel. They have said that Mr. Old has sent them in to collect the steel. One of the men was clearly a Punjabi and the other was a Pathan with a very light complexion.

Sain Ahmed has talked to laborers and the teashop owner nearby. The story is true. The laborers have loaded the steel, and the teashop owner remembers the Pathan, a young man with blue eyes. Nek Alam all right.

I am already aware that Nek Alam has not been in to work today. Indeed he has not been in on Saturday, either.

Thirty thousand rupees is an absolute fortune, and where to start? Unfortunately, Qamar, our local Superintendent of Police and a good friend who used to come for tea and discussions on mystical faith, is in America. He would have had good advice to offer even though Lahore is a different police jurisdiction.

The following morning, Marie and I—Marie loves any excuse for a shopping trip into Lahore's bazars—are at Fazal Din's.

They shrug their shoulders sympathetically. They are so sorry for me. You can't trust anybody these days. They have had similar experiences themselves.

Why have they delivered the steel to people without any authorization from me?

"Why, Mr. Old, we trust you, you are a sharif man. When you send men in without a note of authority, how can we doubt you? They said you were in a hurry and have not had time to give them the note. You knew we would understand, and we did. We will just have to be more careful in the future. You can't trust anybody these days! Do you wish to repeat the order?"

No, I don't want to repeat the order, I just want the steel I have already paid for. It is their responsibility to provide it! They have made the error, it is their responsibility to correct it!

Would we like some tea? Chai lao!

It is about here that my Guardian Angel (G.A.) takes over. I have had many occasions to be grateful to this unseen guardian who over the years has bailed me out of all kinds of fixes, but the convolutions of this particular escape boggle the mind.

We are driving down Ferozepur Road towards Cambridge Circus, swerving between trucks, buses, motorcycle rickshas, pedestrians, bullock carts, horse taxis, cars, and even camel carts. The pedestrians have no particular pattern of movement and no fear for their lives. There are hundreds of them. Horns and curses split the air. Marie, sympathetic, is listening to my distress. I know no one in Lahore. I need a policeman. Suddenly, in all this chaos, I yell, "Hold on!" and swing the truck across the traffic in a violent U-turn that would have brought pride to a ricksha driver. Brakes squeal in every direction. Tonga horses rear on their hind legs. I pull across desperately to a lone man walking briskly through the crowd and yell, "Qamar!"

He turns, sees me and stops. No matter he is supposed to be in America, here he is in Lahore, just when I need him. Quickly, I welcome him back home, inquire about his wife and acquaint him with my problem. Does he know any policemen in Lahore who might be able to help?

He shakes his head slowly, doubtfully. "Meet me at the Judge Advocate General's office at the High Court at 3 p.m. this afternoon. I'll give it some thought."

Pause and reflect that Lahore has more than three million people, that I happen to see on a back street the one person who might be able to help even though he lives in Gujranwala and I thought he was in America.

I take Marie to Shezan's for lunch—this is always a treat she looks forward to—and drop her at Anarkali for shopping. She will go by motorcycle ricksha to the Mission office at Empress Road when she is through and wait for me there.

Qamar breaks away from his meeting of police officers to greet me.

"I don't really have much hope for you," he starts, "but go to DSP Ibrahim at the District Courts. The only information I have that may possibly be helpful is that he writes poetry." He smiles, wishes me luck without conviction and rejoins his meeting.

By this time I am well-acquainted with the District Courts, as a defendant in various cases. DSP Ibrahim's office is adjacent to the road. I knock and enter. I am impressed with the man sitting behind the desk. If I had been looking for a thug to commit bloody murder for pay, I would have put my money on this man. He is florid, burly and bullnecked. His gunbelt and holster and his bandolier of bullets rest on his chair. His hands, like the rest of him, are huge. His eyes are cold and calculating.

There is no one else in the office. As is customary, I begin, after introducing myself, with pleasantries. "I understand you write poetry. Do you write in Punjabi or Urdu or in English?"

I have rarely, occasioned by an innocuous remark, seen such a change come over a man. The man, rock hard and as tough as steel, suddenly becomes butter. His eyes become shifty, flicking to both doors lest he be overheard. His voice softens, even gentles. "Normally I write in Punjabi, that is a poet's language. Sometimes in Urdu, but only occasionally in English."

By now we are friends; the ice has been broken. He confides that he has just written a poem in English for the forthcoming Islamic summit in Lahore. He is hoping that perhaps it might be published in the *Pakistan Times*. He fetches into a side drawer and pulls out a sheet of paper. As he passes it to me—apologetically, it is still just a draft—a crowd of men come into the office demanding attention. I sit back against the wall.

The man is devout, that is clear enough. The Islamic Conference is a tribute to the Prophet Mohammed whom he believes is the Savior of the World. There are about twenty or so lines of appreciation and praise couched in florid terms. I take a pencil and correct a spelling. Then I notice that by reversing two phrases in one line, the scansion is improved; and by switching two lines, it will regularize the rhyming pattern. By now, forgetting that this is not one of my own poems, I am well at it, not altering the content but editorializing, moving lines and sections, choosing different words to achieve rhymes and even-out the rhythm. Occasionally, I will add a new phrase or two to improve the presentation.

Suddenly, as the crowd of men takes its farewell, I realize that I have so messed up this first draft that it is hardly recognizable. I begin to apologize as I hand back the paper. I have just forgotten myself. He asks me to read out the amended version. I do so. He listens, rapt in attention, almost awe. He thanks me. If the desk had not been between us he might well have knelt down and touched my feet.

"You are my guru and I am your chela (disciple)," he announces. "I must come to you and you must teach me."

a boy and his lunch

"Now you must have a problem, what is it?"

He is not optimistic. The fraud, it appears, has not been committed against Fazal Din's but against me. We go and obtain legal advice from the police lawyers. They confirm that since I have paid for the steel, I am from the time of payment the legal owner even though I have not taken delivery. There is nothing legally that can be done to the steel suppliers. Even if Nek Alam can be apprehended, it could take years of court cases with no promise of the return of the steel, which will have been sold off.

DSP Ibrahim says he will see if there is anything that can be done.

Knock in the Dark

Spring 1974, Gujranwala

It is towards the end of the week. The steel has been stolen the previous Saturday, and by now I have little hope that the steel or its price can be recovered.

Marie hears the banging on the front door and nudges me awake. Usually it is the hostel with a medical emergency or someone needing a coffin. It is 1 a.m.

I never have to worry about locking up because Marie just can't trust that I have done it properly. Marie, as always, is thorough. We have had attempts at burglary as well as threats on my life. She checks the kitchen door, two tower bolts. Then the swing door from the kitchen to the dining room, one bolt. Between the two main rooms, tower bolts. The bedroom, one tower-bolt. This is just one way of access, and there are others. Locking up for bed is a regular part of the daily routine.

I slip the bedroom tower bolts and, after I have switched on the porch lights, look at those at the front door. I invite in three or four men—Punjabis, strangers. From their attire I judge them to be town people, not villagers. They are agitated and anxious. Almost immediately, they are talking about the police and asking if I will call them off. They are innocent of any crime.

By now I am beginning to work out that these visitors are from Fazal Din, the steel factory in Badami Bagh. I seat them and invite them to tell me what is happening.

Marie is busy making tea.

They have not done anything, but the police have thrown a cordon around their factory and are not permitting any trucks to come or go. The labor is not being allowed to pass through the cordon. Their reputation is being ruined.

I ask why they have come to me. Because I have ordered the police cordon to be thrown around the factory, and only I can order it to be removed. They have done nothing wrong, they have delivered my steel to my representatives. They are being ruined. Their customers are going elsewhere, and they are afraid for their own safety. The police are becoming increasingly threatening.

Marie serves them tea with lots of sugar and some cookies, but it hardly serves to calm them.

This is all news to me! They don't need to know that. I put on a firm face. I am certainly not going to order the withdrawal of the police cordon; in fact, if I am asked, I will probably choose to double its strength *and* have the principals of the company taken into custody.

The cordon will stay until my steel is returned to me, and they can expect further action by the police to ensure that the recovery happens soon.

Good night, gentlemen!

Two nights later, about the same time, they are back. Not so gloomy this time. Do I not know? The truck has been located, in Sargodha. The steel is still on board. Nothing has been unloaded. It has been held at an octroi tax post. The police are even now escorting the truck back to me at Gujranwala. They have left a man at the Gujranwala octroi post to bring the truck directly to the house. Will I please now call the police off? If I will sign this letter saying that my load of steel has been recovered, then they will be able to get into their own factory. The police have been preventing even the owners getting access to the factory.

Not until I see my steel.

Marie serves more tea and cookies and still more tea and cookies. This is just normal grist to the mill of Marie's day, and she takes it in her stride.

Dawn has broken when news comes that the truck of steel is waiting at the gate. Where should they take it for unloading? The relief on the faces of Fazal Din's men is plain. Mission accomplished. Not quite.

I walk down to inspect the truckload of steel. The sizes I can see are the ones I have ordered. The truck is full of steel.

How do I know that the full weight of steel is there? I am not going to sign the letter calling the police off from the factory until I have had the steel independently weighed. That will mean taking the load of steel back down to the octroi post weighbridge, weighing the truck with its load and then deducting the unloaded weight of the truck. They expostulate. I am adamant. The weighbridge won't open until eight o'clock. Then we will wait until eight o'clock. Can I not accept the loading list? No, I cannot.

More tea and cookies.

Lee Reed from the Thal Agricultural Project is visiting. He is mildly surprised at the vast amount of power I appear to have in manipulating the police forces of Lahore to redress my complaint, but he keeps those thoughts to himself. He volunteers to accompany the truck to the weighbridge.

There is nine tons of steel on the truck, not ten. Suddenly all begins to take shape. Fazal Din's reward, whether in collusion or not, has been one ton of steel not supplied. I hold out my hand. Rs 3,100 please. I will not sign the letter until I receive Rs 3,100. Despair! They do not have it. They will have to get it from Lahore.

I sign the letter thanking the police for their cooperation. I confirm that my steel has now been returned and that I have no further claims against Fazal Din. The police action can now be called off. I give this to Lee Reed who is going into Lahore this morning, anyway. He will hand it over as soon as they give him the Rs 3,100 in cash.

"Would you care for some more tea?"

Leave the Country Immediately!

July 1976, Gujranwala

I have to believe that, compared with other people with guardian angels, my guardian angel works harder and is probably smarter than most. I seem to have a knack for getting into scrapes that can only be circumvented by the most deft and rapid foot and wing work by the various heavenly bodies.

Generally, my life, our lives, continue rather smoothly in the fashion of a bumper car at a fair trying to make its way from one end of the crowded rink to the other. It is never possible in a straight line, and the frequent collisions can severely interrupt progress.

Only on one occasion, though, do I really lose hope. There is a time when I think I have had it. You can't buck the Prime Minister! From the British Embassy in Islamabad comes a message. The Prime Minister's office has instructed that I have outstayed my welcome in Pakistan, and I am to leave the country without delay. Can I find it convenient to come to the Embassy?

It happens about a year after I have returned to Gujranwala the previous June from a short visit to the States. Brend and Marjet have gone on their three-month break as soon as I return. Marie has stayed in England with the boys, but during this summer, she has escaped back to Pakistan for a break with me. However, she is prevailed upon to assist with supervising the missionary language students in Murree, and since it is hot and humid on the plains, she is taking a spell there.

Two uniformed policemen turn up at the Technical Training Centre one afternoon. The boys have already gone home for the day. Will I mind answering some questions for them?

I am accustomed to being questioned by police and by plain-clothes men. Local Christians, some of them our own employees, are still active in trying to get me thrown out of the country. Newspaper articles accusing me of operating a spy ring for "my foreign masters" (somehow linked to or through Germany) will appear in the Urdu press. I am accused of fraud, embezzlement, attempted rape, adultery, tax evasion, discrimination and abuse of labor in verbal accusations or letters endorsed to various authorities or to the press by multiple signators.

"Certainly, Gentlemen, what am I supposed to have done now?"

"Mr. Old, where were you on June 3rd last year?"

A strange starting question! I think back quickly. "Well, I don't quite know where I was, but I was visiting friends in Washington State in the United States."

That answer seems satisfactory.

"Were you in Grandview, Washington?"

"I have no idea, but certainly sometime while I was there I was in Grandview."

"Did you make a speech at Bethany Presbyterian Church while you were there?"

"Yes, I did."

Where is all this leading?

"Did you say 'Pakistan is in a state of riot and turmoil. Its people are near starvation, and there is rioting in the streets?'"

I laugh. I genuinely love Pakistan, and to have made such remarks would have been patently false. "Of course not."

"Then can you explain, Mr. Old, why the Grandview Herald reports that you did indeed make these remarks?"

The policeman shows me a Photostat copy of the Grandview Herald. Certainly the local newspaper is reporting my talk at the Presbyterian Church the previous day in that way. I try to recollect what I had actually said.

Grandview is the center of a very prosperous agricultural area of the mid-Yakima valley in Washington. There are orchards, hop fields, mint fields, vineyards and wineries, fields of corn and wheat. Water from the river provides irrigation right up to and along the hillsides fringing the valley. On the Horse Heaven Hills to the west great dry land wheat fields stretch as far as the eye can see.

I have tried to contrast that situation with the situation of the hungry lands of Asia facing runaway population growth, agricultural economies afflicted by floods and droughts and weak bureaucracies and infrastructure. The previous year I have visited peasant farmers near Shakargarh, close to the Ravi river, whose fields have yielded less grain than the seed which had been sown by hand at the beginning of the growing season. For the first time, I have seen people in our fertile Punjab land close to starvation.

In thirty or forty years, what can happen? Can we conceive that the hungry people of China and India, Pakistan and Thailand, Korea and Bangladesh, possibly two billion people, hit by a string of failed harvests and the ravages of major floods, will be content to sit quietly by while the United States and Canada cut back surpluses to try to maintain prices and markets? There would be riots in the streets of Asia and international unrest that would be hard to control. The time for America to face these problems is now, while there is yet time.

a boy and his lunch

I remember a lady who had been present taking notes. Presumably, in creating her article from those notes, a time slip has occurred.

The policemen ask a few more questions and leave.

Over the next few weeks, it seems that the newspaper article is steadily ascending the chain of authority. The initial police are from Gujranwala and then from Lahore. Now the police are coming from Islamabad. Then comes the phone call. "Will it be convenient for you to call at the British Embassy before too long?"

I arrange to call in on my way to Murree to see Marie the following weekend.

Marie and I enjoy our relationships with the consular and embassy officials of both our countries. They are always helpful. Generally, the U.S. Ambassador stays in Islamabad, and only occasionally do the American consular officials come out to see their nationals in places other than Lahore or Islamabad. The British officials are much more peripatetic. Not only do the officials of the High Commission or the Embassy visit fairly frequently, but the High Commissioners or Ambassadors themselves like to shake off the shackles of office and make excuse to visit Britishers in out of the way places. There is a system of "wardens", local British residents who have a responsibility for the British passport holders within their "warden area". In case of emergency a network of help exists and, on a number of occasions, it has been needed.

The Ambassador himself tells me that the Prime Minister's office has given instructions that I have proved myself an unwelcome guest in Pakistan and that I am to leave the country just as soon as it can be arranged. It is the Grandview business. He will, of course, do anything he can to help, but it doesn't seem very hopeful. What is going to be my response?

I will fight the order to the end. I will go up to Murree for the weekend and bring in my written response on Monday on my way back to Gujranwala.

It is an unhappy, uneasy weekend. Marie can stay a while; she isn't being thrown out, although she eventually will want to be where I am. Her next immediate destination is back to England, anyway. I think of places where I could work instead. I have been asked to work in Nepal. Perhaps that is still possible. There is a Health, Education and Economic Development project in Bangladesh known as HEED; perhaps I can work there.

On Sunday evening, I type a single page reply. The report in the Grandview Herald is incorrect. Pakistan is an Islamic State. It is governed by Islamic principles. Those principles include the provision that a man can only be held guilty on the evidence of two witnesses. I claim that right. There is one witness, the newspaper article. Where is the other? It is the government's responsibility to produce that second witness or else it should drop the charge against me. I sign the paper and leave it with the British Ambassador. He will do his best.

Back in Gujranwala, my heart is not in my work. How can we leave this place? We both believe God has put us here. There has been a Purpose in it all; it will be tragic to leave it unfinished. We have lost my replacement designate, Shafiq, by death in a car accident, and then we lost Brend the previous November. Now I am on my way out. I have no heart to start packing. Marie can always see to that after I am gone. I write to Bangladesh. I wait.

At last the phone call comes from the British Embassy.

The young consular officer is excited. The Ambassador, the doyen of the diplomatic corps, is leaving his Pakistan assignment. He has gone to take his farewell of the Prime Minister. The Prime Minister, as a courtesy, has asked whether there is any one last thing he can do for the Ambassador.

The Ambassador, according to his consular officer, has said "Well, yes, sir, there is one thing. My wife and I once visited a British citizen, Mr. Old, in Gujranwala who runs a training center for poor boys. He is under government orders to leave the country. He has been here twenty-five years . . . If the government could see its way clear to—"

The upshot is a promise by the Prime Minister that, although the order for externment will not be rescinded, provided that Mr. Old behaves himself in the future, he will hear no more about the orders to leave.

I do, and I never do.

Kristel

July 1976, Lahore

A prevalent problem with young foreigners passing through from Iran or Afghanistan to India is drugs.

During the early days of Youth With A Mission (YWAM) Lyn Green and Floyd McClung operated a refuge in Kabul in Afghanistan for these travelers on the hippie trail eastwards. It is here, in a downtown bazar street, Marie and I first observe young people, all whites, with shot minds and blank faces, wandering through a strange world with which they have lost touch and which they can no longer understand. Somehow or other, they are surrounded even in this wild place by a protective shield of holy love ministered by young people like themselves who have chosen a different way to happiness.

George and Anne Tewksbury of our own mission are trying to do the same thing in Lahore even while George holds down the job of Mission Treasurer. George has been a Mission kid in China, Anne is a nurse. Both have an unusual empathy with lost kids in an Asian setting. They are taking more and more of these dropouts into their own home. Just as sympathetic Pakistanis will bring Westerners they find in trouble along the Grand Trunk Road to us in Gujranwala, so local people in the Lahore metropolis will bring troubled foreigners to George and Anne or let them know of a foreigner in need. It is a stream that seems to grow of itself, forcing itself upon them and sometimes almost swamping them. They are just responding with help because it seems better to say yes than no. They have their own jobs to be getting on with. Some of their guests they are glad to see leave. They can see God's hand of mercy, correction and grace in it all.

Kristel's story begins one day when a message comes of a white woman, unwashed and unkempt, high on drugs, sitting on the floor in the corridor of the city Mayo Hospital beside the body of a dead white man on a string bed. The couple, like hundreds along the trail, has been traveling towards the nirvana of Goa in India when his drug abuse — morphine — catches up with him. Kind strangers help her to the hospital with him, but he dies there of the effects of drugs and dehydration. She, hardly comprehending the extent of her disaster, sits cross-legged and hopeless beside the body of her husband, and the crowd walks by or pauses, curious, for a while. The burial is up to the relatives and not the responsibility of the hospital. When after some time the woman has made no move to remove the body — she has no idea what to do—the hospital authorities ask the pastor of the nearby Naulakha Church to see to the burial of this Christian foreigner. George is contacted to conduct the service.

George and Anne take a friend with them as they hurry to the hospital. They push their way through a crowd gazing with quiet and sympathetic curiosity. The woman, weeping compulsive dry tears, looks as though she is fifty years old. Her eyes are glazed and uncomprehending. Her clothing, wet with perspiration, clings to her body in humidity approaching 100 percent. As she focuses on the crowd around her, her eyes take on a hunted look. George pulls back the cloth of the shroud beside her and then replaces it. He bends over the woman. "Would you like me take care of everything here?" She nods gratefully. The friend turns to Anne and says, "You are going to take her home and give her lunch, aren't you?" This thought has not occurred to her, but she sees the need and agrees. The woman will not only need to be fed but cleaned up as well. She is just one of a number traveling the cheap drug trail that will be helped and cared for by George and Anne.

Upon arriving home with the woman, Anne sends the gardener down to stand with the body while George arranges for the body to be kept in the hospital mortuary that night for burial in the morning.

The service is brief. There will be no coffin—only a bed to carry the body—a grave in the Christian cemetery to be dug, a short committal service, and Tony Ralok lies forgotten.

Marie and I meet the woman at George and Anne's home a day or so later. Her name is Kristel. She is haggard and thin, but she has had a bath and is clean. She has had good food to eat and safe water to drink. Her teeth are blackened, perhaps by the drugs she has been taking, and some are missing. Her hair is tidy. She speaks good English.

Initially she just sleeps, retreating into a sanctuary of oblivion that is somehow safer than the cruel and empty world around her. Anne keeps looking in on her until eventually she allows herself to awake. No, she isn't hungry, just thirsty. What she is hungry for is not food. In her cloth bag, amongst her toilet items, are her needles and some of her drugs; she will need to use them frugally until she can get more. She gives herself a fix, relaxes a while and braces herself to meet the outside world.

Anne and George are patient. They begin to talk to her of the only long-term way out of her despair. She has no time for Jesus or for the church. She has had childhood experiences of the church home in Austria that have not impressed her, and they will serve her for a lifetime.

The turning point comes when she agrees to accompany George and Anne to the weekly house church meeting at the home of George Azariah. A young Muslim girl is present who has an evil spirit. She begins to disrupt

a boy and his lunch

the service. Powerful prayers in the name of Jesus are successful in driving out the evil spirit. Kristel senses the presence of Jesus in a startling way and knows, knows for certain, knows for the first time, that He is real. An ex-druggie and George stay up late into the night to talk to her. (Later, she says she thought they wouldn't let her go to bed unless she accepted Jesus.) The next morning, she turns over to Anne all her drug apparatus. It is hard—several times the craving proves irresistible—but she keeps at it. She is at last climbing back uphill.

We see then, as the weeks pass, what tender loving care can do when the stress of an abnormal situation is removed. Over the years, we particularly observe this in several distressed foreign women we become acquainted with. We see them growing younger! Most remarkable of them all is the change in Kristel.

She is not fifty after all; she has only looked it. Her teeth are fixed. Her eyes begin to acquire a natural sparkle. Even her facial wrinkles vanish and her complexion smoothes. She is barely thirty. She is becoming beautiful and beginning to live again. She tries to fathom out what motivates George and Anne. Why do they live the way they do, so simply and so sacrificially? How do they do it and remain happy without recourse to drugs? Anne and she are reading the Bible together. She is finding a renewed interest in life and in her surroundings. She begins to help around the house with more recent guests with similar problems to her own. She visits a German man from off the streets in the hospital and tries to help him.

After several months, her visa and ticket come from the Austrian Embassy. She returns to Vienna. For three months after her return, she attends a Bible school in Germany and continues to grow in spiritual understanding. Her old life, however, still has an attraction for her and will once more gain dominance over her.

Khalid and His Father

September 1977, Gujranwala

Marie is back! Her three years in England, like a prison sentence to her, are over. Even the garden seems to be putting in an extra effort to please and delight. The house has amazingly sprung back to life again. The woodwork shines. The windows glisten. Even the windows in the roshandans just below the high ceilings glisten. The bird nests on the cornices and the black spider's webs in the corners are a memory. Vases of flowers sing in every room. The floors are spotless. The china and glassware sparkle. Every carpet has been out on the lawn and been beaten clean of years of dust. The curtains have all been washed. There are far fewer cockroaches—that war is well engaged. No termite trails creep along the architraves. Even my desk, despite my protests, is tidy. The books in the crowded bookcases have each been separately removed and dusted. The fragile china, boxed away for years, is glowing on the shelves and in regular use. Meals are different every day! It is wonderful, and once more it is good to be alive!

The school is going well.

We are a school that is particularly focused upon giving opportunity to rural Punjabi Christian boys. These are probably among the most deprived in the whole social community. Some of these boys have high aims and strong determination to get to the top. We rarely have to motivate them.

In addition to these, up to forty percent of our boys are local Muslim boys. Generally, they are less interested in the manual trades such as carpentry and welding and are more interested in electricity, electronics and drafting. Just a few are interested in machining and turning. Again, most of these boys are strongly motivated, and where motivation is deficient, our strong discipline helps to rectify that.

One of our least motivated boys is Khalid. In fact, if there had been a prize for that honor he would have been so far ahead of other contenders it would have been no-contest.

His father, an Army colonel now retired, is a surprise visitor. He is quite frank about his son. He won't be any trouble. He is likeable and placid. However, because he will not work, he has been kicked out of his various high quality English medium schools. He—the father—has heard of our strict discipline. That sounds good to him. Will we please admit his son and see what we can do with him? He does not speak Urdu or Punjabi well; the family uses English at home, and that is his mother tongue. I grin at the father's obvious relief that he can send him along tomorrow morning at 8 o'clock. That is when chapel and Bible class are over and Muslim boys join the others for the regular training classes. Khalid had better search me out. After chatting with him, I will fit him into a suitable program.

Khalid is overweight and affable. He is in his late teens. No, he isn't interested in sports or athletics. No, he isn't interested in being a machinist or a welder, a fitter or an electrician. He isn't interested to learn how TV's and radios work or how to repair them. It is a joy to listen to him speak in fluent easy English that many of our boys would have given much for. His grammar is as good as Tim's or Colin's. With English like that, he is a natural for the two-year drafting course. I describe the course to him, take him over to the drafting shop and turn him over to Colin, who, back from a spell in England, is running the shop. I am already beginning to sense that maybe the father has painted his son's portrait well.

Over the next year and a half, I have various contacts with Khalid. He is never a discipline problem. He comes to school on time and is regular in attendance. He just doesn't do any work. He seems somehow to have a block against working. He is friendly, he is intelligent. Everyone is his friend. He likes the school and everything about it. He is learning to speak Urdu and Punjabi and making himself popular. Every three months, I interview boys who aren't doing well, trying to get to the root of their problems and encouraging them to try harder. Khalid doesn't seem to have any problems. He doesn't seem to be discouraged, so encouraging him is easy. He just doesn't work. Eventually, I tell him that he is wasting his father's money. It is only right for us to take his fees if there is some benefit to him and thus to his family. I will give him another three months to shape up and work. If he doesn't produce clear signs of progress by the end of the quarter, we will have to admit failure, and he will have to leave.

At the end of the quarter it is parting time. I call Khalid into the office. I am sorry he is going, but his failure to make any progress through his course leaves no option. He should hand in his various books to the drafting instructor before he leaves today.

He goes around and says farewell to the instructors in the other shops as well as his own.

The following morning at 8 o'clock, there is Khalid, just as usual.

I call him into the office and explain that he is finished. Didn't he understand that yesterday?

"Yessir, but when I woke up this morning, I followed my usual habit to come to school. I like coming here. This is my school. I have to have something to do when I wake up in the morning. You have to find me something

a boy and his lunch

to do, sir. You don't have to pay me, I'll work for nothing, but you just have to find me something to do. I'll do anything."

Well, here is an interesting dilemma. A boy who won't work is willing to do anything? I can't see any place where I can use him in the school; will he be willing to work in the hostels?

"Anything you say, sir."

Khalid finds his niche at last! A beloved son of a well-to-do Muslim family, educated in the best English medium schools, he is the assistant boarding master to Rennie Gold. They care for between three and four hundred village boys, all of whom are Christian. Khalid is happy as a sand-boy. He purchases vegetables in the vegetable market, bringing the sacks back in a tonga. He can be trusted with money. He takes care of the sick. He checks roll call at study hall. He supervises study hall. He checks that the toilets and the dormitory rooms are clean. He checks the beds for restringing and the frames for re-welding. He issues supplies to the cooks. He takes his duties seriously, and to the boys, he is just part of their family. He is accepted without question. Very soon, we are paying him a stipend he earns and deserves. I don't know how we witness to him as Christians, but he witnesses his faith to us in a warm and winsome way. Colin and Khalid become good and close friends.

Khalid serves a number of years as assistant boarding master. Eventually, he is required to supervise the building of a house on a piece of his father's property and so, with regret and several farewell parties, has to leave us.

Through Khalid, I gain a fond memory of an older Muslim enjoying his faith. This is Khalid's father. The young man invites me to his home. His father has just returned from Haj, the pilgrimage to Mecca, the culmination of a life's dream. The return of the hajji is a time of great rejoicing. I welcome this invitation, for it is my practice to seek to elicit from hajjis what has been the spiritual consequence for them of participating in the Pilgrimage.

Khalid's house is not far from the school, in Civil Lines. It is a house befitting the managing director of a large pottery and ceramics company. After we have had tea, I broach my question.

I am not particularly interested in the actual events that have transpired, the mechanics of the Pilgrimage, but rather, in what has happened to Khalid's father 'inside' as a consequence. Which of the various locations has been most significant to him? For others I have talked to, it has been at the tomb of the Prophet in Medina, but for the colonel there is no doubt. It is in the Haram Sharif, the Great Mosque in Mecca that *it* has happened. Both he and his wife are present for the seven circumambulations of the black draped cube at the center, the Ka'aba. They are sitting among the huge crowd, and then quite suddenly, he feels himself alone, totally alone with God his Father.

He turns to me with shining face, highly animated and full of remembered awe.

He is not conscious of the huge crowd around him or the presence of his wife beside him. He only knows that in these few precious moments stolen from eternity, he is loved by God, his Father, as though no one exists in the whole world beside himself, and he is loved simply for who he is—himself.

God, Almighty God, Creator God, Allah, incredibly loves him as though he were his only son, as though there were no one other except him to love. It is as though God has bent down from his place in heaven and has plucked him up for a few moments and has held him, loving him, enjoying him, in the palm of His mighty Hand. Then He places him gently back into the Haram Sharif charged to take back into the world an experience of God that will remain with him for the rest of his life.

"And what difference has it made?" I ask gently and curiously.

Again, excitement and animation. "Oh, I am a different man. I not only live differently, I see differently, I think differently, I speak to people differently. You ask any of my laborers, my work-people, ask my supervisors, ask my family, my friends. I can never go back to being the man I was, I have been touched by God!"

Christians take as their guidance and as their imperative these words of Jesus. "*I am the Way, the Truth and the Life. No man cometh unto the Father but by me.*"

Jesus did not say "No man cometh unto God but by me." He would not have done so, for he would have believed that Nicodemus and his own Nazareth teachers and many other devout Jews whom He knew, including members of his own family, had experience of God. Jesus is saying something equally searching and penetrating; that the way to the Father, and understanding the Fatherhood of God and His love for each of us, the way to being intimate with God, is through himself, the carpenter of Nazareth.

Here we have a story where a Muslim, in the heart of Mecca, experiences the Fatherhood of God and Jesus nowhere appears in the picture.

I surmise the key to understanding these two apparently inconsistent ways to the Father lies in the word "cometh." Jesus is talking of the action of men and women seeking God. The word "coming" implies a voluntary action by the comer. That's where an initiative, not necessarily the first initiative, lies. If I wish to discover the Fatherhood of God, then the door that

a boy and his lunch

Jesus Christ opens for me is the Way for me. It is the only way. I take the action to seek and to move. I come.

But there is another Way by which any man or any woman anywhere, in any condition of soul or search, may experience the Fatherhood of God. It is by the initiative of the Father.

Quite simply, He says, *"I will that I will,"* and no one anywhere can say Him nay.

Paul Speed and the Drains

As I write, we have just had a visit from Steve, the senior pastor of a church in Cincinnati. He left this morning. His is one of the fastest growing churches in the United States. His church believes, and he believes, that many little acts of kindness can change the world. His particular and regular act of kindness is to walk through the picket lines outside a pornographer's shop and go in and clean his toilets.

His story reminds me of the drains at Ahmalpur.

June 1978, Ahmalpur, Sialkot

It begins with Dr. Zafar, the fine young medical superintendent at Memorial Hospital, Sialkot. Apart from his work in the hospital itself, he is deeply interested in the preventive aspects of medical care. He is involved in a rural health scheme in the villages and rural communities within a twenty-mile radius of his hospital. He is developing a cooperative scheme whereby the ill-trained rural midwives work in cooperation with his own visiting team of doctors and nurses. He is concerned, too, about the village conditions where untreated sewage becomes part of the water supply withdrawn by shallow tube-wells. This leads to endemic abdominal diseases that, particularly in young children, can easily prove fatal.

He calls in one day at the Technical Training Centre just as school is finishing.

"Ken, how much would it cost to put drains in a village?"

I could have answered, "Well, it all depends on . . ." but that is not what Zafar is after. He wants a figure. He gets one. I think of a village, imagine drains into it, think another moment or so, assume it would cost about eighty thousand rupees, double it and add a bit and say cheerfully, "Oh, it would probably cost about one hundred and seventy thousand rupees. If you can get the money, I'll help you put the drains in."

I forget all about it. That is close to the annual budget for the school, and I know there is no way Zafar can ever get hold of that kind of money.

I underrate Zafar.

It probably takes him eighteen months, and then he calls in again. How soon can I get the drains into Ahmalpur?

Uh huh! Where on earth is Ahmalpur?

Ahmalpur is just about due north of Sialkot, about fifteen miles, on the left bank of the Chenab a couple of miles north of the Marala river barrage. It is a medium-sized village with the usual one or two sewage ponds (chhappards) at the low points into which the sullage from the village flows. Over centuries, the village itself has become mounded above the flood levels of the river, and slopes are good and adequate where this has occurred. In other parts, there is hardly any slope at all.

Most of the houses are the traditional mud-walled, flat-roofed homes, one or two rooms opening to a full-length, open porch and beyond, an enclosed courtyard. Residents just throw their household garbage over the wall.

These homes are linked by a network of narrow gullies. Standing in the middle of the gully, you can touch with your fingers the plastered mud walls on either side if you don't mind standing in a greeny-gray, thick, gooey mud that is up to twelve inches deep.

Ahmalpur is a "buffalo" village. Daily, milk is carried into Sialkot for sale. The rich, creamy milk is supplied by the scores of water buffaloes that, each morning after milking, make their way with their calves from the courtyards of their individual owners to the grazing meadows beside the river. Daily they tread the narrow gullies into even thicker, gooier mud. Most of the rain that falls stays there, and the urine the buffaloes contribute helps. Each evening they confirm the gooey status as they return home to work the mud a little more on their way.

One man tells me that, although you can usually keep your feet clean by keeping to the sides, he hasn't walked down some of the main gullies of his own village for twenty years.

Zafar promises to get the six thousand bricks and the pit sand we will need to start with by Monday—a week away—and, oh yes, they have a volunteer at the hospital, Jamie Muir; he will probably be happy to come out and help if we need him. I confirm we will.

Paul is my youngest sister's son. He has just completed his English A-levels and is taking time out before going to university. He is one of these grand young people who come to Asia to broaden their horizons and is willing to do anything. Well, almost anything.

Paul looks uneasy and swallows hard when I suggest he might enjoy tackling an assignment away from Gujranwala. He speaks no Urdu or Punjabi and, no, it is unlikely anyone in Ahmalpur can speak English. How will he go about putting in drains?

Well, first of all, it will be helpful to learn how to use a surveying level. He and Jamie can work that together. Crash course for Paul in surveying. Paul's sense of adventure is beginning to be overwhelmed by a sense of impending calamity. Where will they sleep? Oh, Dr. Zafar will take care of

a boy and his lunch

that. What about their food? Oh, the villagers of Ahmalpur will take care of that. Paul wonders whether he will be able to handle a continual diet of hot curry. Aunt Marie knows what volunteers need and like to eat. What about toilets? Just make sure you use the men's fields, not the women's. Follow the men. This is going to be different!

We check that Paul has enough toilet paper and other likely essentials like bedding, load the surveying instruments and drive off to Sialkot to pick up Jamie and head further north. It is little comfort to Paul that Uncle Ken is going to help get them started. After all, he's heading back home in the afternoon.

We survey all the slopes and decide which drains are going to run where and to which chhappard. The bricks are at the ends of the gullies. They will each have to be carried. The drains will be simple brick channels in the center of each gully. They will need to be set solidly in sand because, if they are not, the buffaloes are immediately going to knock them out of shape. Although it is usually best to start laying drains from the lowest point and go uphill, it might be better, to avoid working in effluent from the houses and elsewhere, to start from the high point and work downhill. They can spot-level bricks in the invert and work at laying the bricks to a consistent slope by a stretched string or strings.

We have an eye to leveling the mud below without having to move and replace it. We set a profile to the drain section using half a dozen bricks or so on a bed of sand. We set a similar profile at the point where the gully bends its direction, stretch a string, even two or three. Now they are set to go. If they find they need a mortar, they can use the mud. We have brought shovels and trowels and metal pans to carry sand.

I promise to drop in occasionally to see how they are getting on. I'll try to be back in a week. My last remembrance of Paul and Jamie as I leave them is to think of explorers being abandoned in the Antarctic wastes without supplies by the last of their companions heading north for the ship, for safety and home.

When I last go back to Ahmalpur when the boys finish, it is a different village! It sparkles. Every gully is dry underfoot! Down the center of each gully is a neatly laid brick drain. Water and sullage effluent is running down these drains to the ponds, issuing from newly made drains in the courtyards discharging the water wastage of houses. There is no garbage, litter, mess or filth from over the walls into the gullies. These drains have to be kept clean. The courtyards are neat and tidy and releveled with sand or soil to make sure all the slopes now feed to the little household feeder drains. In some homes, pack horses and donkeys have brought in panniers of sand or earth to raise the floor levels of the rooms themselves so that all slopes concur to the one great end of complete drainage.

Of all my recollections of Pakistan, Ahmalpur stands out most clearly as a successful example of applied kindness. These two crazy British boys, still in their teens, by plain grit and determination and quality of character, have worked a transformation that will echo on for years from village to village in the Sialkot District.

Villagers get angry with Zafar because he has chosen to help Ahmalpur instead of their village. Scores of villages initiate similar schemes with Zafar's help.

I hear the Chief of the Army Staff of the Pakistan Army give a talk at the City hall in Gujranwala. He is talking about the need of everyone to get down to the brass tacks of helping their country. He gives an example of two young foreigners he has recently seen laying drains in a village near the Chenab in Sialkot district. Why are foreigners needed to show us what to do? Aren't our people capable of initiatives, of seeing needs of others and unselfishly responding to those needs? These two young men have come at their own expense thousands of miles just to show us how to help others without hope of any return other than that their kindness will be accepted. That is what service really means, and we should be ashamed that it is taking others to show us that.

It is easy to be proud of Paul and Jamie.

Bags in the Bazar

Gujranwala

Nazir Matthias, the Head Clerk, is upset. In fact, he is furious. I have rarely seen him so disturbed. In his hand, he holds a bunch of paper bags made out of the usual newsprint or something. I examine the bags. The quality of paper is good, very good. Surprisingly good for a paper bag. More than newsprint, obviously.

The writing is in Arabic script.

"Yes, sir, you are right. They are pages of the Bible—here, these are the Psalms. They are turning our Bible into paper bags for the bazar. That's what the Muslims think of our Bible. The shopkeepers are using these bags in the Guj bazar. I've just got them from there. There's going to be trouble over this."

Phew! If you want to sow the seeds for riots, just make pages of anyone's Holy Book into paper bags for shopkeepers. Murder has been done for less. Just imagine what would happen if the pages of the Q'ran Sharif were to be used in this way. The whole bazar would be burned down. Christians may be in a minority, but they feel just as strongly about their Holy Book.

I soothe Nazir. Let's first find out what is happening. I take the bags over to our local governor, the Commissioner. He is a friend and a wise man. He hears me out, recognizes the explosive nature of the situation and picks up his phone to the Superintendent of Police. He will call me back.

By late afternoon, I am back in his office, and he has a full report. Someone has been working hard. All the bags have been confiscated. If there are any reports of more still in use, I have merely to let him know. I quickly pass the word down the line before protests gather momentum.

Several days later, after further inquiries, he tells me what has actually happened.

Some organization in the United States, based in the Chicago area, has been sending, unsolicited, Bibles to Pakistan. The organization called Bibles for Asia or some such, has apparently obtained a telephone directory of the Lahore area. It has mailed Bibles to random addressees selected from the directory. Insufficient postage is affixed. The addressees of course decline to pay additional postage for unsolicited material. The parcels containing Bibles continue to pile up in the main sorting office in Lahore. Eventually, together with similar unclaimed materials occupying valuable space, the whole lot is auctioned unexamined to the highest bidder. That purchaser, without any desire to create a religious affront, uses the paper he has bought to make bags. Some of them end up in the Gujranwala bazar. Will I please advise the senders of the potential dangers of their actions?

I am quick to do so.

My letter courteously points out to the senders the dangers of their actions. Our country is volatile and religiously very sensitive. There are divisions within Islam as well as inevitable tensions between Islamic and non-Islamic faiths and groups.

If a wise administrator had not acted promptly and effectively, the situation inadvertently created by them might well have got out of hand. Lives might have been lost together with injury and damage to person and property. Pakistan has a very efficient and well-run Bible Society. It is an accepted part of the social and religious scene. Bibles can be freely purchased at low cost by anyone wishing to obtain one, there is no covert surveillance of purchasers. Supplies for all needs are more than adequate. Why not use the facilities available? Each donor dollar would go so very much further, and there will be no risks involved.

The response I receive is saddening. The writer from Chicago has no regrets whatever for what has happened. His own father, an Indian, has picked up a Bible fragment in a Bombay bazar and as a result had been converted to Christianity. There will be no change in the organization's policies.

I might as well not have written.

The word "missionary," although it includes doctors, engineers, nurses, schoolteachers and farmers in its range, implies possessing the desire to bring non-Christians to faith in Jesus Christ.

It is an inherent part of the Christian faith that its followers are enjoined by their Scriptures to:

> *Go ye therefore and teach all nations, baptizing them in the name of the Father and of the Son and of the Holy Ghost, teaching them to observe all things whatsoever I have commanded you and lo, I am with you alway, even unto the end of the world. Matthew 28:19–20*

Through the last twenty centuries, that impulse has ever been significant. As the new Middle Eastern faith moves to the outer fringes of the Roman Empire in the west and Nestorian Christians venture ever farther eastwards, so the faith keeps up with the far fringes of land discoveries. With the first colonists into the Americas and Australasia moves the church.

a boy and his lunch

Wherever pagan religions have been encountered, the claims of Christian faith have been presented. Eventually, in many places, Christianity becomes well-rooted and in some places dominant. It is not—and never has been—primarily a militaristic faith, presenting ideally rather the claims of a loving, redeeming Christ upon an individual seeking a closer relationship with God. Undoubtedly, the spread of European colonialism is a major factor in the spread of Christianity worldwide.

Conversion has never been only one way. People leave the Christian faith for Buddhism, Islam, Baha'ism, Judaism, Hinduism as well as traveling the other way. *The Times* newspaper has talked of ten thousand English women converts to Islam. The reasons for conversion are many and varied. They are certainly not always from the highest possible spiritual motives. Marriage to or interest in a partner of a different faith. Personal advantage such as different and easier marriage and divorce laws. Subterfuge and spite. Intellectual rather than spiritual conviction. Disillusion and reaction.

If my own references to conversion are largely relating the stories of individual Muslims becoming followers of Christ, this is because these are the stories that became known to me. Undoubtedly, there is also a reverse flow, but it is not one I am well acquainted with.

Some general observations can, however, be made.

It would appear to be a basic human right that any individual should be able to choose his or her own religious affiliation, even if that might not be the same as the parents' religion. While the family has the right to make its feelings known, there is a legitimate barrier short of violence beyond which disapproval should not go.

Conversion is a rare rather than a common occurrence. Publicity tends to ensure a broad coverage, but instances of movement by individuals into or out of the Christian faith were and are unusual.

We were living in an Islamic country. By and large, Christians are well-tolerated, although certain special laws are onerous. Missionary work is generally appreciated, largely because prime foci are education and health and social welfare. Because, like the Jews, the roots of Christian and Muslim faith are to be found in the Patriarch Abraham, there is an acceptability not accorded to Hindus and Sikhs. What was—is—resented is the proselytizing activity of Christians, particularly Christian foreigners, and the disruptive effects and shame these produce on Muslim families when they are successful.

Although there are many instances of group conversion into Christianity, very few have come from the Islamic community. Almost always, conversion from Islam is conversion of a single individual; not even a single family unit.

The reactions of families affected by conversion of a member of the family tended towards violence, in some rare instances murder. In other instances, there was persecution through the courts by the leveling of large numbers of false court cases. In many cases, there would be complete ostracism and sometimes the divorce of the wife or husband. Inevitably, conversion would require that heavy social costs be paid and many problems be encountered, peaceful resolution sometimes proving impossible.

a boy and his lunch

Dieter

September 1979, Gujranwala

Kristel, the subject of an earlier story, is back in Lahore at the Tewksbury's within a year of having left. This time it is a different woman that Anne meets at the door. The voice aids recognition, but she has changed *so* much. This woman is beautiful—long flowing, well-groomed hair, heavier in weight and glowing with vitality. Joyful reunion with much news to exchange. With her is a male compatriot, slender in build, lightly mustached and of similar age. They have met in Austria.

It hasn't been easy—Kristel's return to a normal world. Back home in Austria, she has worked for relatives in a restaurant, replacing two previous workers. It has proved too much. Long hours and complete exhaustion. Her good resolutions snap. She is back on drugs and moves in with a man who has recently lost his wife and is also on drugs, moreso than she.

Kristel's trips on drugs are proving no answer. Every trip is a bad one. She admits herself to a drug rehabilitation center, and when she completes the course, Dieter admits himself to seek the same help. For neither of them is the cure 100 percent complete. She looks back to her anchoring experience in Lahore with George and Anne, and the couple decides to travel overland to see them. It worked once for Kristel; maybe it will work for them both.

Dieter is wanted by police in Sweden and Austria for robbery and probably also for drugs offenses. He is traveling without a passport. He doesn't explain how he has entered the country.

He, too, is grateful to receive accommodation and help. With passing time, Dieter begins to change. He receives regular remittances of money from his mother in Vienna, so he is not penniless. His disappearances to get fixes or acquire the means to do so become less frequent.

We and their other friends in Lahore do not know how long Anne and George can continue to survive the nights of broken rest and the long hours of emergency care they sometimes need to give their street-wise friends. They are trying to get ready for a short furlough home to Colorado. Their love and patience for these hurting strangers, trapped in a strange land and far beyond extricating themselves unaided from their initial willfulness, is exhausting them.

We offer Dieter a job in the woodwork shop at Gujranwala. We are uneasy about a drug addict coming to us, even if he swears he is now off drugs, but George and Anne are trying to leave for home and desperately need relief. This is one way we can help a little. Kristel decides she will stick with Dieter and come, too.

Only if they are married!

We are quite firm about this. We will take them both, but only if they are married. We cannot have an unmarried couple living together. All right then, they will marry. Easier said than done! George is an ordained minister but is not registered to marry foreigners in Pakistan, especially when one of them does not have a passport. Robbie, the only serving missionary we know who might be able to do this, is not available. We are stymied for a while. No wedding, no move to Gujranwala. Dieter spends his days trying to find someone who will perform the marriage without questions. We insist that no bribes be paid and no lies be told. If this marriage is God's will for them, there *will* be a way, and it will involve no shady dealings. This limits the field of search.

Somehow, we learn of Daniel Samson. He is a Christian who has risen to be a district magistrate in the Civil Service. After his retirement, he has become more active in church life and is currently bishop of a small cluster of believers. He is a good man, and he lives in Lahore. His magisterial powers have given him the right to marry foreigners. He is willing to marry Dieter and Kristel. He will charge no fee. It is the first and only time I have assisted in conducting a wedding ceremony. Their past is behind them, and the couple is like any other young couple in love and getting married. The wedding takes place in George and Anne's house, though they themselves have left for home.

Kristel and Dieter are now forging a new life together. They will live in Brend and Marjet's old house. The missionary community in Gujranwala, like any community of goodwill anywhere, gathers around with gifts of furnishings and utensils, curtains and bedding, towels and tablecloths, whatever they think might be needed.

Kristel works as a typist in our office. Dieter is given responsibility for the commercial production side of the woodwork shop. One of his assignments is to make coffins. As a service to the community, we are the suppliers of coffins and hold a stock available for immediate use. People will send for them from fifty miles away, sometimes in the middle of the night. Inevitably, it is our door they will find.

We hold the price down to six hundred and thirty rupees for the twenty years we are at Gujranwala; we are not interested in making a profit but in providing a service. Burial normally is on the same day as the death. Only once did we sell a coffin for a Muslim funeral, the custom there is a shroud. If Christians can afford it, they prefer a coffin if one is available. Since ter-

a boy and his lunch

mites will quickly consume any wood that is used, the grave of choice has a brick floor and walls and five concrete grave slabs covering the coffin.

Dieter is very intelligent, applies his mind to the production problems of furniture and comes up with ingenious and workable solutions. He is industrious and working hard.

Dieter has a visit from a German friend, a good-looking blonde young man in his early twenties—Max. He, too, is interested in staying a while with us. Unknown to us while in Gujranwala, Max resumes taking heroin. The pair work together in the carpenter's shop. Max has never been to India. He works out that, by leaving early, he can get across the border and to Amritsar by noon, see the Golden Temple and be back at the border before it closes at 3.30. He will be home by no later than 8 p.m.

He is not back by 8 p.m. He is not back that night. Nor the next day, nor the next. We are by now deeply worried. He has left all his stuff behind except his wallet and passport, so he clearly has intended to return. What has happened to him?

Bob Thomlinson, our English bursar, recently back from furlough, decides to go to India to try to find out what has happened to him. This surely is looking for a needle in a haystack! Someone has a photo of Dieter and Max working together. He takes that with him. He leaves at the crack of dawn, covered by the prayers of all of us. He is back before we have gone to bed at 9 p.m.

He has caught a bus from the border beyond Lahore to Amritsar and is there by noon. He tries to work out what Max might have done when he arrived. He had to have stayed somewhere. If he had intended to go on to Delhi, he would have taken his things with him. Max could have received the free meal offered to visitors to the Temple, but the women serving food will not remember one among so many similar travelers passing through.

It is likely Max has been or is staying in a local hotel. Bob decides he will first hawk the photograph around the reception desks of the hotels near the Golden Temple. It is a very faint hope, but he is helped by a chance richsha wala who offers to take him to a good, clean, cheap hotel. Why not? It pays off. It is the very same hotel in which Max has died! When Bob asks the way to the police station, the manager is nervously curious and then excited. The receptionist at that same hotel has good reason to recognize the picture.

Max has been the young man in Room 24. He has booked the room shortly after noon but has not come down. They used the passkey to enter the following morning for cleaning. The young man was found dead on the bed of an overdose of heroin. They have reported it to the police. He is not the first. They buried him the same day.

Bob visits the cemetery, but there are no identifying markers. He brings from the police Max's belongings for return to his parents.

I become aware that Dieter is sending one of our old laborers off on errands to Khokherke. I question the man and then face Dieter. Either the drugs will stop immediately or Dieter will leave. We will be reluctant to see him go, for Kristel is a lovely person with close friendships and a deepening spiritual life. Dieter is penitent. It will not happen again, he promises.

The situation is before too long out of our hands. Dieter disappears and with him the daughter of an ayah who cares for the children of missionaries. In order to legitimize marriage to this girl without the need to first divorce Kristel, Dieter formally becomes a Muslim and takes the girl as a second wife. Remittances from his mother continue to enable him to live without working. Eventually, he acquires his own house in another city and lives with his second wife and family there.

Kristel returns to Austria. What happens to her or whether she is ever able to become divorced from her husband, I do not know.

a boy and his lunch

A Rupee in the Offering

Spring 1985, Gujranwala

The trouble explodes because I am putting only one rupee in the offering each Sunday morning. I have been doing this for some while.

Now it is evident that, at this particular Session meeting in Imran Goliath's office, the Session is loaded for bear. I am the only missionary elder on the Swift Memorial Church congregation session. Attempts to get women added to the Session and the terms that elders actually serve limited to something less than life have not found favor. The current Principal of the Seminary considers the local congregation his own sub-province of patronage and pretty well runs things through his own nominee as pastor. Since the pastor lives in quarters in the seminary, he can't bite back.

The pastor, William, a kindly man whom I respect, is told at the beginning of the session meeting that his chairmanship is being temporarily suspended because of urgent business and that the meeting will be chaired by Imran Goliath. It is uncertain that Imran Goliath is even a member of the church session, but the session doesn't really stand on niceties when something is to be railroaded. In this case, it is the censure of a member of the session—serious business requiring careful management—and maybe the unwilling pastor is not up to the niceties.

The chairman, having taken over, brushes aside the other normal matters of the agenda but does open with prayer led by the Principal of the Seminary (we will refer to him as PS).

Now to business.

"Is it correct, Mr. Old, that in the future you will be giving only one rupee a week as chanda (offering)?"

I confirm it is, and furthermore, it isn't just in the future, but I have already been doing it for some time.

Indrawn breath of shock by the members of the session!

If I had announced that I had become a Muslim, I could hardly have caused more pain. A rupee! A censure is suggested. PS intervenes.

"Perhaps Mr. Old would like to explain his action."

Imran Goliath takes the cue. It is to be expected that a member of session will channel his tithe through the church offering; can I explain why I have chosen not to do this?

I look at the church treasurer as I speak. "For the past four years, there has been no accounting for the church offerings. At the regular meetings, the congregation is urged to give towards the expenses of the Gujranwala Convention and the expenses of the congregation, but there is never any accounting for the funds that have been given. The congregation has no idea what is really happening to the church finances. I have decided that I will place my tithe where I myself know where it is going, and that is what I am doing and will continue to do. When adequate and up-to-date accounts are presented and balances that should be in the bank confirmed, I will reconsider the situation."

Wow! The other session members look aghast. This is tantamount to accusing the Treasurer, a man of great presence and standing in the community. They look at him and then back at me, for I have not finished.

Furthermore, the Session is directing its questions at the wrong person. The way I choose to give my chanda and how much are matters between me and God and not the business of the Session to enquire into. They have other matters they should be dealing with. "Good Night, Gentlemen."

Emmanuel runs after me. I have misunderstood. Please come back. The business of the Session is not finished. As far as I am concerned, it is. "Good night, Emmanuel."

Nazir Matthias, the Head Clerk, asks me the following morning how the Session meeting went. Although he is not an elder, he has an unusual position as Chairman of the congregation, representing the congregation when occasion to do so arises. I imagine he has already heard what has happened. I tell him.

I am surprised by the reactions that follow. Over the next few days, matters coalesce, and other matters become clear. All of the congregation is asking the questions that I have been asking about the church finances, but no one has dared to raise them. So, not so strangely, are all the other members of the Session, but who is going to dare to speak? The Treasurer is a strong man with much influence and many powerful connections. An elaborate charade has been concocted. No one will say anything to the treasurer to his face, but instead they will accuse Mr. Old of defaulting on his chanda and then let Mr. Old proceed to bell the cat. What can go wrong? A wonderful Punjabi solution to a difficult question. Next item on the Agenda, please.

However, as I tell PS when he comes to explain, I am prepared to be nobody else's puppet. In the future, they can play charades with someone else.

Protests by the congregation continue to mount. They ask the pastor whether he is with them or with the Session. He is with them. They disavow the Session. PS orders the pastor to quit his quarters and turns off his electricity.

a boy and his lunch

Marie goes to visit the pastor's wife for a time of prayer and encouragement. They are good friends. A Pathan chokhidar (watchman) patrolling the seminary quarters seeks to prevent Marie from going to see Mrs. William and raises his long handled axe as he stands in her way.

Marie's eyes flash fire. "Don't you dare raise that axe to me!"

The man dare not touch her, and Marie knows it, so she is little concerned.

The next night, at the weekly evening prayer meeting in our house, there is a knock at the door. I answer it. The two young men outside put their fingers to their lips for secrecy and beckon me outside. I know them. They are from Khokherke, two of our ex-trouble makers. They want to talk, privately. Where can we go? I turn out the verandah lights and invite them on to the screened verandah.

Inside the big room, Marie is wondering just what is happening to her poor husband who has disappeared so silently from the prayer meeting, so they pray for God's protecting hand over Goodness-knows-what. She has no need to worry.

The two visitors have heard that their Memsahiba, Marie, has been threatened by a Pathan chokhidar at the Seminary. Is this true? I confirm it is, but it is nothing. Memsahiba is quite able to take care of herself.

They are deadly serious. No deal! They are not going to allow either their Memsahiba or me to be threatened by anyone, least of all by a Pathan watchman at the Seminary. We need bodyguards, and the Khokherke boys have appointed themselves to the position. It is all organized and under control. Now who do we want beaten up first?

I tell them that, rather than beating anyone up, I'd like to see them and their parents in church next Sunday, but that is not an attractive option to them. They are ready for action. They leave, assuring me there is no need for anyone to be frightened; the Khokherke boys have everything under control.

The Rice Husk Field

Gujranwala

Will Ericson is a missionary who lives alongside us in Gujranwala. We first meet him in Kabul when Ruth and he are living there. He is from St Louis and by profession an Air Traffic Controller and is in Kabul as an advisor to Afghan Airlines. They are committed Christians, members of Christy Wilson's congregation and our hosts during our visits to Kabul.

After Kabul they work in the Philippines, and then, like many others of similar heart, take early retirement and look for opportunities to work out their faith in service while they are still young and active.

A mission working in northern Pakistan has a project. The Punjab is a flat, rice-growing province. Its basmati rice is some of the best available and exported to the deep pockets of the Persian Gulf and Saudi Arabia. What of the useless husks generated as the rice is cleaned and polished at a hundred rice mills across the Punjab? Is this possibly a source of cooking fuel for the several million Afghan refugees now housed in camps in the North West Frontier Province?

There is an urgent need to identify new supplies of fuel to replace the twigs and branches long stripped bare from the trees and scrub.

In Thailand, they are producing four-inch diameter logs of rice husks in purpose-made machinery by compressing and heating them until they bind together. A project for Pakistan is developed; funding from aid agencies is quickly assured, and its implementation now becomes a matter of urgency. Machinery is ordered. Again it is a question of Hurry! Hurry!

Gujranwala is the center of the rice growing area. An arrangement is made with a farmer seven miles along the Sialkot Road for the construction of a rice husk fuel logs plant on his land. When the project is complete or no longer needed the whole caboodle will be turned over to him.

By the time Will is appointed to manage the project, there is a field stacked with a brown mountain representing approximately a thousand truckloads of rice husks. Will has to bring the production on line as quickly after yesterday as possible and then begin trucking the logs up to the refugee camps.

Will Ericson has good reason to be suspicious that the startup of the Rice Husk Log project might not have been straight. For one thing, the person trusted—it seems almost implicitly—by the missionary organizers who live a couple of hundred miles away is a person with relatives in the locality.

There has been no in-depth process of checking stage by stage what is being done or what is being claimed is being done. There is no site supervision by the people paying the bills. A wedding has been financed beyond the visible means to do so by the family claiming the rice husks payment. The work—stocking of rice husks ready for production—for which payment has been claimed and made is uncheckable. These circumstances alone—and there are others as well—would have been enough to induce temptation even if not actual fraud.

Will is a new man to the mores of the Punjab, but he is not as naive as others are or as others still would have wished him to be.

When he comes with Ruth to Gujranwala, he takes over a project already much delayed. The machinery to convert the rice husks into fuel logs is not yet working. The pressure is on, for the raw materials are there and waiting. The field adjacent to the new factory is filled with rice husks as far and as high as they can be stacked, from boundary to boundary. It isn't really a rice husk mountain, just a high mound, possibly fifteen feet high at the high point. Just millions on millions of rice husks.

The field is full; they can't bring in husks from the new milling season until some of the current stocks are used up. There is even a question whether the long exposure in the field might have made the husks unusable.

Initially, Will is applying himself to getting the machinery running and producing logs. The Technical Centre helps him with some of his installation problems, and Will is proving adept at harnessing the multitude of little industries in an entrepreneurially-minded Punjabi town.

There are problems with the binding of the husks into a log without charring the husks. Slowly these are solved by trial and error.

Will has confided to me his doubts about the correctness of the huge payments for rice husks that have been made; there are literally hundreds of receipts for truck deliveries in the office. However, he looks despondently at the rice husk mountain; there's no way of checking now. There should have been someone representing UNHCR actually counting trucks coming in through the gate, watching them emptied and then going out again. He smiles ruefully. We both know that would have made things worse, for every man has his price, and who could argue with figures endorsed as correct by the customer's representative?

We look for clues in the truck receipts; the registration numbers of the trucks are recorded on each receipt. We have suspicions but not adequate proof.

I am not so sure that the rice husks themselves are uncheckable.

I worked as a surveyor on opencast coal mines in Lancashire for a while. It is not all that difficult to calculate volumes of cut and fill for road excavations or for embankments provided you can establish the initial and final basic contours of the land. Why shouldn't we survey the rice husks as though they were a land excavation or fill?

Enter our young volunteers from Seattle. They are associated with University Presbyterian Church. They have arrived in the hot perspiring days of summer. It is a good monsoon this year, and humidity is close to maximum for weeks on end.

They get one of the more unusual jobs we find for a group of volunteers. They will measure the quantity of rice husks heaped high in a field!

They have come prepared to do anything, but something like this has not crossed their minds. They have come to do something . . . well, spiritual. They are grand young men and women. First a crash course in surveying. Al has an aptitude for mathematics, so he keeps the records and does the calculations. I explain Simpson's rule for areas and volumes to him. My, he is quick to understand!

Now for the surveying itself. We have a dumpy level, and we will have to fix it on a firm spot of ground or machinery that sets the telescope higher than the top of the rice husk heap. I check and readjust the bubble of the level to eliminate error since we will not be in the center of our set of readings. I teach them how to read our European Sopwith staff. Colin will work with them, taking time out from his drafting shop duties. He has the language so can cope with any problems there.

Imagine walking on a surface of Styrofoam marbles—millions of marbles. As your foot applies pressure, so the marbles squeeze out from under your feet. You take another step forward before your feet have settled from the first step. You are getting the idea, a bit like walking on deep, loose snow. Well, it's rice husks, not snow, and you wish it was snow because the temperature is over a hundred degrees, you are covered with sweat, it is trickling into your eyes, you have been up with tummy trouble all night and what on earth are you doing here, anyway?

Several of the youngsters are working with cloth tapes, establishing on the rice husks an imaginary grid by which the levels of the various points will later be accurately located. Others are doing the actual leveling with level and staff or else setting perimeter pegs that help fix the grid. Al is writing numbers as fast as they are announced by the one at the level. It doesn't help that the staff is inverted in the telescope so they are reading upside down.

Al begins working on his figures in the evenings after each day's surveying has finished. Others assist with the slide rule calculations. Frank has a calculator; that is helpful. The field itself is virtually flat, so we can presume a straight line between the first and last readings to represent the original ground level. We have agreed on an average volume of rice husks per truck. Fortunately, the standard truck in Pakistan is the British General Motors model, the Bedford Rocket. Its size is the standard, and it can only carry husks to a certain heaped height of about eight feet before the wind will blow the husks out of the truck. We deduct the volume of the wheel boxes within the truck body. Seven hundred and sixty two cubic feet per truck.

At last, Al has his volume of rice husks in the field. About five hundred and eighty thousand cubic feet. He divides the volume by seven hundred and sixty two.

The figure that results is seven hundred and sixty trucks. That fits perfectly with what we are expecting to find.

Now it is up to the UNHCR and the project organizers to seek an explanation for the missing two hundred plus truckloads.

a boy and his lunch

I Never Promised You
a Rose Garden

November 2005

This is a story about Bob and Marina Thomlinson, retired, who live in England's Lake District. Bob had mentioned to me in an earlier letter this year that his coming to Gujranwala hinged on a chance conversation at Shafiq's wedding in Peshawar. I have forgotten such a conversation took place and have to trawl my mind for memories.

This bears on one of the themes of this book—that once we accept the premise and challenge that God works in our own day and even through us as individuals, we are constantly surprised. Things around us fall into place in a different way. Interventions appear out of nowhere. Coincidences become something more. Casual, apparently insignificant conversations acquire, for some, life-changing significance.

I have been gathering a collection of these "insignificant conversations" but in this book have mentioned but few, if any, of them. However, a letter from Bob today clarifies what perhaps is a divine principle—that He sometimes uses the oddest means, that is, us humans—you and me—to communicate His Will and Purposes for others.

Bob writes:

I first heard of God being described as the God of Abraham, Isaac and Jacob as a small boy listening to my mother's daily Bible readings. Although at the time He struck me as being a rather awesome figure, the fact that He was so closely associated with human beings made a deep impression on me.

I have many happy memories of those early days and also of a faithful Elim Sunday school teacher who sometimes took a break from her usual lessons to read an exciting account of a famous missionary. How my imagination was provoked! I would go home with my head full of these stories and I distinctly remember saying to myself, "Maybe one day I will go overseas as a missionary."

Romance came to me on a roller skating rink at Butlins Filey Holiday camp. I had traveled from Carlisle with a group of young folk from our church. Marina had also come with a group of girls from her church in Chessington. Who was that girl who always seemed to be at the head of a crocodile of giggling skaters? Although I remember saying to myself that holiday romances seldom work out, God had other ideas.

When we were planning our wedding, Marina mentioned that her dream was to move into a home where all the furniture was new and straight from the store. I could see that Marina was very much a homemaker and I sensed danger.

I asked her "If your dream comes true, would you be able to give it all up, should this be necessary?" As the answer was yes, in due course the store delivery van arrived with a houseful of new furniture.

I was enjoying my job as Office Manager of an exporting company which made Ladies Tweed. A representative soliciting donations for Save The Children Fund visited my company. I was very impressed by his enthusiasm. Although he wasn't a Christian he had seen so many starving children that his aim in life was to put food into their mouths. What a challenge to me this was! I was reminded of the thoughts my Sunday school teacher had planted in my mind so long ago.

Later that day, lying full stretch on our five-year-old settee, I discussed this with Marina. It might be time for us to move on. We talked about the possibility of writing to the Church Missionary Society (CMS).

During our short time at the CMS Training College in Birmingham we met Paul and Cathie Burgess who had already worked in Pakistan as volunteers. They were returning after training to work at the Theological Seminary at Gujranwala. We were heading for the Peshawar Mission Hospital where I would be working as the Business Manager. Although Paul and I were so different we were instant buddies. He had invited Ken Old, a missionary on furlough from Pakistan, to meet all the students who were expecting to work in Pakistan.

Ken challenged us all with the question. "How would you react if you discovered you were not wanted when you reached the place where God had called you?"

Our three years at Peshawar were probably the hardest years of our life: the very busy routine of the hospital, coping with unfamiliar aspects of the job, learning a new language and living in a culture so different from our own. The children going off to boarding school was particularly hard, as we had been told to expect local schooling possibilities.

But the hardest part was the discovery that we were not wanted at the hospital! We were determined to see our three years through. After each anniversary of our arrival we took our staff to a local restaurant to celebrate!

How prophetic Ken's words had been. They turned out to be the most valuable part of our training.

My brother-in-law sent us a music tape with the words of one of the latest hit songs:

"I beg your pardon! I never promised you a rose garden."

This became our theme song. We played it over and over to remind ourselves that the deal we had with God might bring its pain but through it we would discover His love and power in a new way.

Towards the end of our time at Peshawar we were invited to the wedding of a young local man who was expected to become the next Principal of the Christian Training Centre at Gujranwala. It was good to meet up with Ken Old again who was also a guest. We shared with him that we were coming to the end of our first tour and would not be returning to the hospital.

Ken's eyes lit up as he said, "Why don't you come down to work at the Christian Technical Training Centre? We would love to have you both!" The warmth of this invitation was like experiencing rain after three years of drought. On a previous visit to CTTC Marina had thought, "How nice it would be to live here". Maybe God knew what He was doing after all!!

I remember my first day at CTTC. The day as usual started with a service in the Chapel and then we walked a short distance to the large gates guarding the entrance to the Centre. As I walked through them, there was Ken with beaming face saying "Welcome, Bob, to the center of the universe."

For some five years this would be the place where Marina and I would live and work. This was the place where God had given Ken a vision of what could be: where so many dreams could come true for so many young Punjabi boys from poor backgrounds. It was a place where they could learn practical skills and escape the poverty of their fathers. It was an upside down school for it was dedicated to boys who would always be struggling to pass exams and to pay the full fees. In Pakistan today many thousands of men must look back and say that their time at CTTC was an important part of their life's journey.

As I look back over my three score and ten years I have mentioned but few of the people through whom God has spoken and influenced the direction of my journey. The God of Abraham, Isaac and Jacob that I discovered at my mother's knee has over the years revealed Himself through all these encounters as a most loving and gracious God whose fullness I see in Jesus. I doubt if I could have discovered Him had I not seen something of Him in the lives of the people I have met.

Doesn't this make the journey of life so exciting? We can receive and give so much to each other. This exchange is possible when we are walking along the way He has marked out for us, in spite of our failings and sometimes because of them.

Much of the way has been very ordinary and unremarkable. The last 17 years has been spent living in the beautiful English Lake District, so different from our nine years in Pakistan. The way for Marina and for me has been so varied and full of contrasts, but the God of Abraham, Isaac and Jacob has been speaking to us through each part of our journey.

a boy and his lunch

George

Gujranwala

Over the years, the volunteers coming to us from overseas, full of energy and willingness to try anything, are an inspiration and a joy. We are fortunate in Gujranwala to have opportunities where even a short visit can be made useful. Marie welcomes them all under her mothering wing. She seizes the opportunity to turn their gifts and youth to the benefit of her beloved adopted country.

Not all are young, though most of them are. Edward Balph is into his early eighties when he joins us. His challenge is building an overhead water tank in Sargodha hospital.

Then, too, there is George!

Let me tell a little about George. Perhaps it might spur some of you older readers to recognize that the wonderful, noisy, smelly, hungry, polyglot world that is the other side of the globe needs something that you have yet to give and that you are not as old as you have been thinking.

George has worked in the Atomic Energy Establishment at Harwell in England. He has been a civil servant all his working life. He has never married, and he is somewhat set in his ways. He is also, having catered for himself much of his life, a passably good cook with a gift for producing a piping hot dessert and custard before the potatoes have come to the boil. He has been a practicing Christian all his life, a member of the Anglican Church. As he approaches retirement, he feels it is too early to go out to grass like an old horse. Surely he has something yet to give, and he would like to give it. He goes to the Church Missionary Society headquarters in Waterloo Road in London.

Well, George just isn't the kind of person the overseas partners to CMS are looking for; they are looking for young people with energy and enthusiasm and adaptability. Fortunately, George, the very embodiment of an elderly English gentleman, rather vague but very charming, isn't going to be a problem.

"We're sorry but we require our overseas volunteers to have attended Bible school before we send them out." Next problem please.

This must have been an occasion of a divine appointment. How likely would it have been that George and I would both visit Waterloo Road at the same time? John Clark, the CMS Asia Secretary, asks me, when I am on furlough and visiting their office, if I would mind helping them out. A volunteer candidate for overseas service has come to them two years previously. He is over sixty; obviously, he is too old for overseas partners. So, to be gentle with him, he had been told that volunteers had to have attended Bible School. Well, ahem, he has just come back! He has now successfully completed two years Bible school at London Bible College. He has his certificates with him. He is downstairs. I was an overseas partner to CMS and, just remotely, by stretching circumstances a bit, a possible destination for George. Would I mind interviewing him? It would be kinder if a refusal came from . . . well, you know how things are.

It is easy to see the problem, and I am happy to help.

I enjoy George. He seems to come out of a different era I have long forgotten if indeed I have ever known. He is more late Victorian than Edwardian, courteous, hesitant in putting forward opinions, quickly seeing another point of view, a good listener, a good "bowler hat and furled umbrella" man. His hair is snowy white, his face cherubic and without guile. I can just imagine him in the rough and tumble of Gujranwala—Daniel amongst the lions ravening for a kill.

We chat, I ask a few questions that sound as though I am with a serious overseas organization possibly interested in his services. Oh, yes, he knows where Pakistan is and roughly where Lahore is. Aha! George is a draughtsman. That is interesting. We have a drafting section in Gujranwala that Colin is currently heading.

All the while we talk, my heart is telling me we can't let this faithful gentle man, no matter what the situation, go back out into the London streets with his hopes dashed and two years study in Bible school wasted because someone has failed to tell him he is too old. Somehow or other, we will make a place for George and, who knows, maybe God's Hand is in all this and George is merely walking faithfully in steps revealed one at a time to him and to us.

John Clark is taken by surprise by my confirmation that I think George will suit very well. When can he come out?

George is a total anomaly and a wonderful success. The time he spends in Gujranwala is simply the happiest time of his whole life. He is double the age of the other volunteers and fits in among them like a centipede amongst ants.

Colin leaves for the States, and George heads the drafting shop. We are teaching both civil and mechanical drafting. George has not trained as an engineer, so before the more technical of his lessons, I will go over the lessons with him. He teaches the boys Bowes Notation for forces in the members of space frames and roof trusses so well that one of his boys actually beats out civil engineering graduates from Lahore Engineering University for a prized job. That is a proud moment for George!

The full flowering of George is yet to come. In 1983, I hand over my job in the Technical Training Centre to Nathaniel Nawab. The new Principal needs office help if he is to cope with the ramifications of a demanding new assignment requiring hands-on management of multiple activities. It is a stroke of genius to appoint George as the English Language correspondent for the school.

Suddenly, the most extraordinary and superlative missives, always written in the passive tense and hedged with presumptions and assumptions, begin to wing between Gujranwala and Government offices in Lahore and Islamabad. They are staggering in their artistry, resplendent with 'ultimos, instts, per pros, re's and ref's' and whatnots. They are instantly recognizable as to author. George is the Van Gogh of official correspondence; one might almost mention his name on a par with Beethoven. He is a master craftsman with civil service jargon, saying nothing in a hundred or a thousand words with no one the wiser that nothing has been said. Each exemplary presentation deserves to be framed for the novices in the real use of the language to learn from and emulate. It is almost like Mordecai's declaration to Queen Esther "*Maybe it is for such a time as this . . .*" George is achieving his destiny. This alone justifies two years Bible School!

George endears himself to everyone who knows him, but no one regrets the return of George to the UK at the end of his term more than Nathaniel.

Roofs on Village Churches

Pakistan is an Islamic State. Roughly two per cent of its population is Christian, possibly three per cent. Many of those are clustered in the rural areas of the Punjab or in the crowded slums of the cities. They are not crushed and dispirited as they might very well be. They believe they, too, have rights and fight robustly for them. Their Muslim neighbors often encourage and help them, respecting each other and recognizing their need of each other. Landowners will give a piece of land for a church, brick kiln owners allow their workers bricks to help them build.

One of the problems facing these struggling communities is what to do next after a slender-walled rectangular structure, bricks laid in mud mortar, has struggled its way out of the ground and up to a potential ceiling height. The problem facing the roof provider is how to create a light roof so that a) it won't blow away in the next strong wind, and b) it will not collapse the walls on which it rests.

Here there is a lovely symbiosis. The PCUSA has sold off unneeded assets of property in Pakistan, and instead of using the proceeds to support its own stretched labors elsewhere, it has made support available to roof churches of the Presbyterian Church of Pakistan with a very simple, low-weight galvanized sheet roof supplied from Gujranwala.

Many of the congregations being helped are not only struggling, but also, like village communities everywhere, are divided into factions. There are long standing family feuds that extend right through the congregations they belong to. There is bitterness, anger and pettiness alongside kindness, sacrifice and shared struggle. It's just the way people are. Here are three stories of the ways poor Christians get roofs on their small village churches.

Mailiburji Gets a Roof

Mailiburji is the second roof this month but in the opposite direction from Manianwali and again about seventy miles distant. Pastor Mohan meets the Ford Transit as it is about to leave and joins us, but the vehicle rattles too much to permit conversation.

Had it been possible, he would have warned me and Evert and Nick, an English accountant back on holiday, that there is a problem. As the van approaches the village, some men there wave anxiously and seem to want to talk, but Evert's immediate concern is whether he can safely cross a muddy ditch, and the opportunity is lost.

Nick and I are establishing the levels of the walls, a first job, when Pastor Mohan asks me to come. Evert is sent until I am free and finds himself embroiled with a major delegation of visitors. They are all Christian villagers, and their point is simple. The church is in the wrong place, the walls are not well-made, it is not sufficiently beautiful and should be in another location where 90 percent of the forty-seven families live.

Evert listens carefully and responds, "Have not they themselves helped to get the building ready, have they not installed the electric light bulb?"

"Yes, but . . ."

They decline to stay for the short service of worship that precedes each roofing. I am working out how to overcome the six-inch difference in level between the front and back walls but promise to see them in the evening.

Within four hours, the frame for the roofing is all in place, and the boys are knocking spaces in the upper walls for the holding down blocks.

Mohan explains: It is all to do with the recent elections for local councils. This is one of the steps back to democracy at the local community level. On November 30th the Muslim community—97 percent of the population—voted in a generally well-organized and fair non-party election, and on December 12th the minorities voted for their councilors for whom certain seats were reserved.

Allah Ditta lost, and his opponent from a home near the church has won. Allah Ditta is leading the dissension.

After it becomes too dark to continue placing roofing sheets, there is a break for supper—meat curry, rice and unleavened bread.

KENNETH G. OLD   253

The meeting is in Allah Ditta's house. Eventually, about twenty men are there, sitting or squatting on the string beds.

Evert, Nick and I have chairs. Tea is brought in and served to the guests. A gentle gray-haired man starts the proceedings. He has been sick for some years and cannot work. He asks me to please pray for him. He kneels on the ground with his head almost touching the floor as I pray. It is a simple little scene that is timeless.

I ask if I might tell them a couple of stories from two other villages, Chehal Kalan and Manianwali. Evert interprets using the Punjabi the others know. They listen courteously and intently, without interruption. Now Allah Ditta, a burly man in his late thirties, in the Punjabi manner expresses his views as representing all those who are present, turning to them occasionally for murmured assent.

He says the church should be where the people live; there are only four families at that end. The distance involved is about one hundred yards, so that doesn't seem to be the reason. Others follow. The government is giving about two thousand square feet of land for dwellings to poor families, and there is an acre of government land at their end of the village. Probably this is the plank on which Allah Ditta has fought the election and lost.

An old elder, wearing cataract spectacles and huddled on a blanket, is firm. The church *must* be on their side of the village; they will not worship in the new church. Others join in, polite and firm.

I say the fault is mine, for I have seen the little mud church they have all been using and have encouraged its replacement with a new and larger building. I ask their forgiveness.

No, it is not your fault, it is Ghulam Masih's fault; he did not tell you the full position.

Evert gives a talk of his own, about their position in a Muslim community. I talk about educational programs that can benefit their children.

Bashir, the gray-haired man who probably has advanced tuberculosis, suggests they accept the church now that it has a roof and work toward getting a school for their own children where they themselves live.

It is close to nine when Allah Ditta says they will accept whatever I decide for them. I remind them of the little boys and girls who this morning carried out the brick rubble and who put rubber washers on the seam bolts. They have been asked to do these tasks so that, when they are old, they can tell their grandchildren, "I helped to build our church." I want all of those present to be able to do the same. "Come tomorrow morning, and help us complete the roof."

They agree. All is settled. Closing prayers.

Bashir accompanies me and the others as they leave. He asks us to come to his house. As we enter, he mutters, "Their lips say one thing and their hearts another. We need a school, not a second church."

Bashir's house is tiny. In the entrance, his wife is in bed with their youngest child. In the next room are two carpet looms. From behind them two boys emerge—one about sixteen and the other about thirteen. They had started work at the weaving loom at seven in the morning. It is now 9.15 p.m. The boys look tired.

Bashir asks if there is anything for them at Gujranwala. The oldest has passed fifth class, but obviously, the new sixth to tenth class boarding school will take them out of earning for the family for four years, so that won't do. Bashir himself is unable to work.

What about training them to be carpenters? That will take eighteen months, and I promise them work afterwards if there is no other work they can find. How much will it cost? If the boys bring one hundred rupees when they come, there might be scholarships for all the other expenses apart from their pocket money. I offer to take the boys with me when we leave in a day or so.

The boys want to get the training, and Bashir will try to manage without their earnings from carpet weaving.

The following morning, the only one of the dissenters who comes down is Bashir, to get the forms for his sons to be admitted to the Building Trades Centre.

By noon, the sheeting is well on its way; it will be finished tomorrow morning. I leave to get back for my court case in Lahore, and Mailiburji just about has a roof and who knows what next?

Tergha's Turn for a Roof

February, 1988

Before we get to Tergha, we call into the neighboring village to Tergha, about two miles from the Pasrur-Narowal Road.

Shahabdeke is a village very much like the others that dot the flat countryside not far from the Ravi River. Rising ground toward the center of the village is occupied by the more favored. There are peepul trees and the great open well just beside it where the church now stands. I had been there some twenty-two years earlier to build the church and have heard it is now used as a cattle shed. This is not so.

The church has weathered well. Although the red asbestos cement corrugated sheets have curled a little, and a part of the ridge is replaced with beaten-flat kerosene tins, it is in good shape. The villagers have extended a front porch, there is a concrete floor and the walls have been plastered.

Two miles beyond Shahabdeke is Tergha. Elder Channan has been the prime mover in getting the church walls built. He manages to get land assigned for a church quite close to one of the two mosques. The fields are bright with the yellow of mustard and the fresh green of the winter wheat. Rain is desperately needed. The rains failed this last year, and there have been very sparse harvests. Now all wait to see if the winter rains, already late, will arrive.

The church is relatively wide, more than thirty-two feet. We have heard rumors that as soon as old Channan was promised a roof he came back and, with some desperately urgent rebuilding and some disguising of the alterations, extended the width of the church eight feet before we arrived to measure it.

The roofing arrived yesterday, and the bottom-roofing module is badly twisted.

First, a service to give thanks for the roof and to pray for its erection to be without accidents. The boys from Gujranwala are experienced; this is their sixth roof in a little over two months. Work goes with a swing. The little children remove the bricks and rubble, scurrying like ants to clear the ground. Samuel and Nadim straighten the twisted frame while, starting at the other end, the modules are hinged together, lifted in the center and then held together with ties at their bases.

By nightfall on the first day, the roof structure is all in place, the tie bars making the roof stable are in and we go to find where we will sleep. We have each brought our own bedding. Normally in a village we will sleep in one or two rooms in which string beds are occupying all the floor space. It is so now. We have a large crew—three Youth With A Mission volunteers from abroad and eight of us others.

Channan feeds us all meals from his house, although other families would like to host us. The meals of cauliflower curry, mustard greens and unleavened bread are nourishing and tasty.

The evenings provide the opportunity to talk. There is no electricity. We hear about the interaction between the Muslims of the village and the twenty-three Christian families. On the door lintels or fascias of their houses are crosses to show who they are. We hear of opium in the village and the fermented drink brewed for carpet customers (and themselves). We hear of guns, murders and crime. This little village set far from the road has its own many iniquities.

I ask three little girls whether they attend school. The middle one attends some kind of school but the oldest, about eight or nine years old, works with others of her family weaving carpets. So many children seem to have no childhood.

I retire to bed early, but soon Channan and his son are squatted on the string bed with me, massaging my arms and legs in a centuries-old custom. To Mike's surprise, he in a few moments has one of the heavier villagers walking up and down on his body, massaging with his toes and the balls of his feet.

Channan shows his Gospels, carefully bound and yellowed with age, in Gurmukhi, the Sanskrit-type language in which Punjabi used to be recorded. He has a question we can answer for him. Turn to Hebrews 7, verses 8 and 9. What do these references to Melchizedek mean? He has no copy of Genesis to provide him the answer.

The early morning call to prayer is broadcast to the village over the battery-operated loudspeaker. After prayers, the mosque is filled with children mumbling and reciting. The Christian villagers want a school for their children, too. Wherever we go, this seems to be the desire. Whether they can spare the children from the carpets to go to school is a question they have not yet faced.

The sheeting of the roof progresses well.

Three pastors have arrived from different rural areas nearby to take me to see some of their church needs. Two miles from Tergha, a wheel slides off the narrow track into a field newly irrigated. Stuck. Nothing to lever with. No bricks in sight. I try jacking up, and an hour later am still trying, with less energy and more mud. I give up. A tractor passes nearby but does not stop.

a boy and his lunch

Channan walks into Khan Khasa, and another tractor driven by a boy comes out. So easy. So it goes.

In Khan Khasa, there is nearly half an acre of mission land around the little church. People are trying to encroach. Why doesn't the mission build a wall to protect its property? I explain to the congregation, hurriedly assembled and sitting on the floor, that the mission has handed over the land to their own church. If they would build a mud wall around the church area, there will be help for enlarging their church. Perhaps the old mission primary school can be resurrected and their children can get schooling. They are anxious about this and promise to build the boundary wall. Channan exhorts them to do as the Tergha villagers have done—get busy and trust the Lord will bring to completion whatever they are attempting.

Now for the other villages. First, to Kesowali, where Arura Mall, the pastor, lives—seven families, a dingy pastor's house and no church. Then on to Marali where Nattu had lived—a tiny church squeezed between two houses. Squatters have taken over the mission land in the village, and the school is closed down. Next comes Bhallowali where a lovingly decorated church built only recently needs urgent repair. The thinly thatched roof covered with earth has let water through in several places and should be replaced.

Finally, with Pastor Munawar, we go to Falizepur where they are hardly above floor level with their walls. It is dusty, and many of the village ponds we pass are almost dry because of the drought.

When I get back to Tergha on the fourth day, our boys are off playing volleyball against the village lads. The roof is done. The cross is set at the ridge and the scaffold stacked ready to go.

Before we leave, we gather in a circle in the church. There are prayers and promises. Tergha has become the worship center for the four or five nearby villages. Channan thinks of a school for the village elders, others of a school for their children.

Khuda Hafiz. Farewell. Come back when we dedicate the completed church. Salaam!

After we complete Tergha, we spend a day back at Shahabdeke fixing seam bolts, replacing the kerosene tins with new shiny sheeting. The villagers today will be refixing all the paper flags and decorations with which the church was lavishly adorned inside.

It is a village of Christian beginnings. In the summer of 1873, before the monsoon broke and while the dirt tracks were still good for travelers, Nattu, a Hindu of the Jat caste who had been baptized the previous year, and Ditt, a Chuhra cripple from this village, traveled together on foot towards Sialkot, thirty miles distant. They were heading for the missionaries at Hajipura.

Old Channan has remembered Ditt from his own childhood. As he talked, we recognized how close in time to the Mass Movement we are and how young the church in this land is. From this movement has emerged many of the two million people that now form Pakistan's Christian community.

We started a village school in Shahabdeke. Initially it flourished, but gradually its enrollment dropped as the children were required back at the carpet weaving looms. Eventually, we closed the school, as insufficient children were allowed by their parents to attend. The pitifully small wages these children earned made the difference. Change will come, but for these children, not soon enough.

a boy and his lunch

Badiana, Walls and Stones

Along the Pasrur Road from Sialkot

Paul Ulrickson can't quite see my advice as fitting the situation. Here is he, perched at the head of a rickety ladder, trying with the stump of his right arm and his left hand to bend hook bolts in a way they don't want to go. Down below, milling around in the church on the dirt floor, is an angry mob of people with stones and a crowbar ready to wreck the church. Over on the scaffolding, I am under the roof frame with Evert and the building boys from Gujranwala.

I call to reassure him, "Don't worry, Paul, see yourself as an observer, not a participant in the situation." As far as Paul can see, he *is* a participant and in a very vulnerable position. What is he doing here, anyway?

Paul is a pastor at Bellevue Presbyterian Church in Washington state. Just now that seems a rather attractive place to be. Was it just yesterday he arrived by air in Lahore? Within three or four hours and moving from overcrowded bus to overcrowded bus, he has found himself in a place he has never heard of, a possible candidate for a mob lynching, racing against time to get a roof on a church.

I have allowed three days to roof a church forty feet by twenty-two feet because, on Friday, kids are coming to be interviewed for scholarships for further education. That sets the deadline. As far as Paul can now see, that is a hopeless schedule.

The disturbance does not perturb me, and I am giving as good as I'm getting, at least verbally.

"Come on down or we'll wreck everything."

"Don't give me orders, you speak politely." (That seems academic, there is going to be no politeness in this situation.)

"Come on down." Stones are raised to throw.

"Who are you that stands without sin and dares to throw stones in the Lord's house?" Perched high up on the scaffolding, I pick on the most threatening and direct my attention to him. "Is this your representative, a man ready to throw bricks in the Lord's house? Shame on you all!"

Paul tries to understand the heated argument in a different language and would probably question the theology if he understood what was going on, but it seems to work. Brickbats are quietly lowered. There are still shouts to come on down, but slowly the crowd transfers its anger outside where members of the Bilal group have joined the hubbub.

Now insults and anger are being exchanged. In their arena, women are accusing each other of sexual immorality and license while the men, fists raised, get on with the drama of altercation.

They surge outside again.

More of the Bilal group have arrived. They are mostly Presbyterian while many of the Kalim group are Bhai Mission (Brethren). Numbers are more or less equal, but so far no blows have been exchanged, just words that will rankle for many a day. The women particularly are angrily dragging up the dirt of the past and throwing it at each other.

There is a history of dispute and discord. Once they had all been Presbyterian, but many have broken away. There is also division among the Presbyterians themselves, with two men claiming to be the legitimate pastor of the Badiana congregation.

Families themselves are not united. Councilor Anwar's uncle and all his family are with another group, the Jalal group. In any village community, roots of dispute go very deep.

In an eventual settlement between the two major groups over the use of the land around the well that is traditionally left for the Christians to use, decisions have been made and agreed upon. The Kalim group will build the wedding house—where visiting wedding parties are housed—and the Bilal group will build the church adjacent to it.

The wedding house has been further along than the church. An unfortunate concrete beam supported by a central column that would have been better omitted has already been cast.

Now the church is moving ahead of the wedding house and is being completed. There is a lull in the shouting, and the crowd somehow seems to disperse itself. The roofing sheets start going on again.

There is lost time to catch up.

In the afternoon, the Kalim group suddenly emerge from the village, armed with pick-axes. What now? Surprisingly, they start in, not attacking the Bilal group or the building group but digging for the foundations of a wall. They clear land and dig away like men possessed. They are never going to be able to keep up the furious pace at which they are moving dirt. Boys and women and girls bring bricks from stacks and then, when they fall short, remove bricks from the wedding house itself. That wall is going to come up, come what may.

Muslim villagers look on, curious.

The wall neatly divides the communal land into two with a common access to the deep, unshielded well around which the children play. By dark, about 6 p.m., the wall is about at ground level. By next morning, the last of

a boy and his lunch

the three days, it is about three feet high. They have worked till midnight, but the job on the wall is done.

By afternoon the ridge sheeting is in place, and the cross, fixed at one end of the ridge, marks the roofing of the first church in Badiana. A short service, with adults and children standing in a circle. Garlands of rupee notes for the Gujranwala building crew. Sweets for the children.

The Land Rover and its trailer are loaded. Farewells and promises. Evert blows the horn and pulls out beside the wall of division. The Bilal group has a stay order from the court to require removal of the wall, but this is for tomorrow. May the problems of each day look after themselves.

God bless you. Goodbye.

For Christ Himself has brought us peace.
With His own body He broke down the wall
that separated them and kept them enemies.

Ephesians 2.14

Every Little Helps

November 2005

Perhaps the purpose of this book, not as clearly seen at the beginning as now at its end, is merely to encourage us to give back more than we take. That's what LIBTYFI means—Leave it better than you found it. The story of the boy with the loaves and fishes was an encouragement to us who can do or can give only little to Him who guides us all or to the others traveling with us along our mortal Way.

If we search, there is always something more we can give, an appreciative note or card, a word of kindness or encouragement, a helping hand, even a coin or two when we have very little to spare from life's necessities. Every act of kindness helps to change our world for the better.

Patty and I live in an almost unchurched village in the southeast of England. It wasn't always so, but, like so many similar communities in Britain, it has been caught up by an aggressive pervasive secularism of commercialism and hedonism assisted by spiritual lethargy and failed parents going back several generations.

Although we would strenuously claim that we are a Christian village, barely fifty out of a community of more than thirty times that number attend any regular practice of Sunday worship. The Methodist Chapel has a regular membership of less than ten, most of them approaching or beyond retirement. When one among them is infirm and unable to join in worship, everyone is painfully aware of the drop in numbers. The sister Anglican Church, St Mary's, has an even smaller attendance, although it is a lovely old church reaching back into the twelfth century if not earlier. Even though the two congregations have a close unity and join together for worship and witness on the first Sunday of each month in the village hall, the spiritual roots of the village are steadily dropping away in the face of almost total indifference.

Yet this week, I am rejoicing.

Our local Bible Study Group, most of them elderly pensioners and averaging not more than a dozen in number, has reached a milestone. From the voluntary offering for missions that Derek organizes, they have topped £5000 given to struggling communities of need across the world. They are not interested in the big, shiny brochures showing bloated children and anxious mothers. They are interested in where the little that they can send will make a difference. They each vote their preferences from among a selection of a dozen locations and activities across the world. They are not anxious to see the little they can give eaten up in glossy administration. They want to give where what is given will be used where it will be effective.

Three of the four last gifts have gone to Fred and Margie Stock for earthquake relief in Pakistan, to George and Irmgard Boehm for the children's home they run in Pasrur, Pakistan, and to Ron Rice for tricycles for paraplegics in Nigeria.

Let me tell you about them, for each recipient is making a difference in his or her own way.

Fred and Margie Stock
Earthquake relief in Pakistan,

Fred and Margie we met off the ship when they arrived in Karachi, Pakistan, at the beginning of October in 1956. They were part of the Sialkot Mission and heading off to the technical school in Gujranwala to begin language study.

Margie, part of a glorious missionary family and heritage, we had no doubts about, but Fred . . . well, Fred was a different matter! Neither Marie nor I thought Fred would make it. He was even scared of the water we drank at the orphanage and clutched his bottle of Coca Cola as though it were a lifejacket to a mariner on a sinking ship. We were proved delightfully wrong. They have less than a year to go to complete their fifty years in Pakistan. All five of their children have also become missionaries.

Dale, their first son, lived with us when he did a course for hospital technician and hospital maintenance prior to returning to the Sindh desert in the south as a missionary. He drowned there while trying to save a child in difficulties on a swimming expedition. Dale's wife Nicky is the nurse at the missionary kid's school in Murree, and their two children are pupils there. Paul, his brother, is also working with his family in Sindh province. Ruthie and her husband are missionaries in Albania, Lois and her husband are missionaries in Bangladesh and Sarah and her husband are missionaries in some unidentified Central Asian country.

Normally, Fred and Margie work with Hindu tribal people on the plains, but currently they are helping out with earthquake relief near the epicenter in the hills.

Margie writes from the earthquake area:

> *Shad Bibi, (which means 'Happy One') always greeted*
> *me with a wide smile. The smile never left while she shared*
> *that her husband and twelve-year-old daughter were both*

a boy and his lunch

killed in the earthquake. She has one small daughter left and is six months pregnant. An ultrasound revealed the baby is dead. Her leg has multiple fractures and has been fitted with an external set of bars and screws to keep it in line.

Still she kept smiling - until yesterday.

When I started to pray for her suddenly her face crumpled and she began to sing a song of mourning for her lost ones. She sang in a beautiful high voice. The song was interrupted frequently by weeping and mentioning things remembered about her loved ones. I thanked God as I sat beside her, hugging her. At last reality has come and she is able to express her true heartbreak for those she has lost. Her healing has begun.

George and Irmgard Boehm
The Children's Home in Pasrur, Pakistan,

Pasrur is a small brick-built town a little more than twenty miles south of Sialkot. To one side of it is the Girls Boarding School where Marie Allison worked. Directly across the town and again beyond the walls is the old Maria White Dispensary and Hospital that had been long closed when it was turned over to Hans Hoster and a supportive group of German Christians to run a children's home there. This was forty years ago.

George and Irmgard, as far as I know the only white-skinned people in the town, have been there twenty-five years. Their five children, Tabea and her four brothers, have grown up there. When they are playing with the children around them, they speak Urdu and Punjabi. The family language is German, and for many others and for them, too, the language of correspondence and official communication is frequently English. Friends and family in Germany have cheerfully shared the responsibility of bringing up the four older children as one by one they return home. These young teenagers are seeking to assimilate themselves into a culture they have only known on furloughs. Irmgard has put her children through German home school in Pasrur. Sometimes, it seems to the busy mother, her youngest son, Johannes, is more interested in play than in schoolwork and its deadlines.

One of our first FITWELD primary schools with four classrooms each and only two walls was built at the Children's Home. Now they have a high school, also.

George and Irmgard have ninety children under their care—sixty boys and thirty girls. They try to retain family links for these children by closing the home for two months each hot season. The children return to their nearest family kin, and this interval also permits maintenance and repair work on the home and a break from the heat for themselves.

Ron and Sharon Rice
Tricycles for paraplegics in Nigeria.

I first met Ron and Sharon when Ron was pastoring a church in Centralia, Washington. It was clear at once that they both had an unusual heart for missions. They came out to visit us in Gujranwala.

I recall sending Ron in alone to argue our way through a police post on the outskirts of the city. They were wanting to charge us taxes for the scaffolding we had used to erect a church roof in a village beyond the town. The two parties could not understand each other at all, although Ron's English was fluent and impeccable, and he spoke slowly and patiently. In the end, the police gave up trying to communicate with this friendly smiling man trying to talk with his hands and, frustrated, sent him and us upon our way.

This is Ron's ninth visit to Nigeria where, amongst other things, he has been working on a Christian Education curriculum to be used in the State schools.

> *Driving at night is very dangerous in Nigeria and we try to avoid it as much as possible. Nigerians all have stories about themselves or friends who have encountered logs or big stones across the road in a lonely place at night, with armed robbers relieving all passing vehicles and passengers of their valuables—or worse. Equally dangerous is to break down in a dark lonely place as we did.*
>
> *We were returning from a big wheelchair presentation in Kogi State, at a leadership conference of the Christian Evangelical Fellowship of Nigeria. At least 2,000 were present in the huge church, as we presented wheelchairs to thirty disabled children and adults and folding white canes to five blind folks. The congregation had been very responsive to my talk and Ayuba's talk, as it was translated into Igala.*

a boy and his lunch

What an inspiration my partner, Ayuba Gufwan, is to all these disabled folks. He is the first university graduate in the history of his village. Affected by polio he walks on his hands. He was unable to go back to the fourth grade until he was 19, when his uncle built him his first wheelchair.

When Ayuba climbs out of his station wagon with hand controls, everything stops, because Nigerians have never seen a disabled man with his own vehicle. Together Ayuba and I have now built and donated 985 of our three-wheeled self-pedaled wheelchairs. As far as we know this is more than any other organization in this vast country.

Back at the breakdown in the dark, Ayuba and Thomas would not let me out of the jeep. "Your safety is our number one priority," Ayuba told me. "We Nigerians can always manage, but a white man is too easy a prey."

I knew it was an electrical problem but we had already checked everything we could think of that might be wrong, to no avail. Now in the dark we didn't even have a flashlight, and Ayuba's cell phone was out of range of the network. I started to pray.

Suddenly out of nowhere in the pitch dark, two young men appeared. After a brief conversation with Thomas, they left and soon returned with more people. They started to push and I jumped in the driver's seat to steer. About 35 yards down the road was a tiny break in the six-foot high grass which lined the highway.

Thomas ran ahead and motioned for me to steer into this tiny footpath, and they pushed the jeep another 35 yards into a clearing, lined with several mud-brick houses. I was incredulous. Here was a Tiv family compound, miles from nowhere, completely hidden from the busy two-lane highway. Here the jeep would be safe for the night.

I jumped out to thank the young men, told them about our wheelchair project, and that I was a pastor. "We're Deeper Life," they said. "Then I know we can trust you," I responded, for Deeper Life is probably the most conservative and strictest major denomination in Nigeria. What an amazing answer to prayer: that these angels of mercy came out of nowhere to provide us a safe refuge in a lonely and dangerous place in the middle of the African bush.

Our month-long visit to Nigeria ends this Sunday, Nov 6, when we head back to Seattle via Amsterdam. We have presented 60 wheelchairs so far this trip. We presented 85 folding white canes at the graduation of the Vocational School for the Blind outside of Jos.

The wheelchair ministry continues to grow but the needs are outstripping the supply. We have promises for well over 200 more wheelchairs in our 50/50 partnerships, but there is no money for the $10,000 that will be needed for our half. I have had to tell Ayuba there is only enough money currently available to meet our shop payroll ($500 a month for eleven employees, including Ayuba's salary) through the end of the year and no more money for supplies beyond what is currently on hand. As we get out into neighboring states, we are finding even greater needs. At every wheelchair presentation we get more names and see more disabled people who desperately need wheelchairs.

One local government official told us last week about the presentation in his area, which I missed, and how he was deeply moved by a crippled boy who showed up, but since his name was not on the list, was taken back home, heartbroken, in a wheelbarrow.

a boy and his lunch

Postscript

I hope that as you have been reading you have been glimpsing strands of mystery, a strange linkage tying some of these stories together as though there is a divine musician taking a thousand musical notes and, behind the scenes and within the apparent confusion, creating a most beautiful melody. As though the random and casual happenings even of our own day have a strange coherence.

I want you to catch the joy of that boy running down the hill towards the lake and to somehow regain the child in yourself and recognize that you, too, are running down the hill and that the boy is in you and that you, too, have something to give to the world and that He can even make it into a miracle of your own day as He did once before.

There is one final story to conclude with.

Even before the writing of these books, God had been laying upon my heart one further and surprising, almost daunting, task. It is to establish a fund for the education of the village children among whom we have worked. It is not a fund for which I shall seek money from others. Others may add to it, but I am to establish it from my own resources, and it shall be half a million dollars!

Oh yeah? And where will that come from?

Retirement has been more challenging than I could have imagined, but the journey is nearly over.

A fund has now been established called the Sialkot Mission Area Fund for Education (SMAFE). The Sialkot Mission, although no longer in effective existence, served the area of the Punjab where the proceeds of the fund will go to educate and help poor Christian children.

The Sialkot Mission was started by Andrew Gordon.

He arrives in Calcutta in 1855 with his wife and daughter and sister, charged by his small American denomination to start a mission in India. Leaving the family behind in Saharanpur, he travels alone, reaching Sialkot with only $17 in his pocket. The work develops slowly, hampered by shortage of numbers and shortage of funds from home. It seems he has been forgotten. Without the generous support of local soldiers in the British Army garrison, the mission will have soon collapsed. And then comes encouragement! He acquires the help of two remarkable Indian brothers, zealous converts from Hinduism, George Scott and Elisha Swift.

Gradually, the work expands, and the first four baptisms of new believers take place in 1857. In April 1862, a newly married couple from Pennsylvania in their early thirties, James and Mary Barr, arrives to join Gordon and his family. Five years later, the number of adult baptisms has risen to 56. After 20 years, the total is still less than 200. Thirty years after starting work alone in Sialkot, and close to the end of Gordon's own labors, there is a total of more than 2,500 adult baptisms within the mission area.

Today, there are between two and four million Christians in Pakistan, a country exceeding 150 million people.

a boy and his lunch

SMAFE - Its Getting and its Giving

November 2005

The Sialkot Mission Area Fund for Education (SMAFE) is working its way forward. It is a race against time. The initial funds, half a million dollars, are available, but how to organize their distribution and use so that they will reach the children intended?

The children I particularly want to help are the children of the Presbyterian Church of Pakistan. A century or so ago there was a mass movement of Hindu untouchables in northern India into the indigenous church. Part of them came into the church established to accommodate them by the Sialkot Mission of the United Presbyterian Church of North America. This church was known locally as the "Amreecan Mission."

Other Christian children, like Catholic and Church of Pakistan children, have their own broad donor sources to help them, but I know very well how stretched are the limited resources available to help the children who have descended from my own heroes like Kanaya and Pipo and Ditt.

This story has two parts; first, where did the money come from? And then the second part, how to ensure that it is used properly?

I will take time to tell each story, for perhaps it, too, is a story, in modern terms, that fits with our theme that every little bit helps and that we need to use the wisdom and energy we have to help that little on its way to its correct destination.

I start by needing half a million dollars. I don't need more, and I don't want less. What can I start with? None of my engineering skills have market value after I retire; they are even using different units of calculation. I could never cope in the modern engineering world.

God has given Gibbins Brook Farm in England to us as a stewardship. We are using it in that way, and we'll find a way to honor that stewardship in passing it on, but I have no feeling the sale of the property we love so much is to be part of the providing for the SMAFE fund.

I can, however, start with my pension. If I live frugally, I can spare a good part of it. I am old, I don't really need things, just enough for each day. Expensive cars and holidays and new furniture aren't really necessary; a slice of bread and butter is as nourishing as cake.

When their mother dies, I tell Colin and Tim how much they might expect for an inheritance and that I will give as much of this as I can to them while I am still alive. That has worked out well, and they have had help as they have needed it.

I will get the money I need for them and for SMAFE by investing in the stock market. How many other financial hopefuls must have started on this journey as I do?

I have little clue about the inner workings of western business and commerce, but I am accustomed to reading between the lines and taking everything with a pinch of salt. I reckon I have a reasonable amount of common sense, and I am prepared to lose my shirt without a great deal of pain since in my mind I have already given it away.

I have no profound financial principles to operate on, only those usual basics of honesty and fairness and ethical investing, and I am to learn by many errors how the market economy works.

It is surprising how many of the companies I have invested in have gone bankrupt. Actually, come to think of it, maybe it is not surprising. About 25 percent have gone under despite their initial high promise.

"Ah well, swings and roundabouts," I tell myself.

However, even so, by the time of Marie's death in 1997, my stock portfolio has moved jerkily from nothing up to $482,000 and within a further month it is $513,000.

A slide begins, and a year later we are down to $277,000. Not so good. Two years later, we are back up at $593,000, but the early signs of the sickness in the stock market are already appearing. Prices are collapsing and carrying the portfolio with them. In February of 2001, I am still over $500,000, but a year later I am at $292,000. and six months later, less than half that figure. It is a roller coaster ride, this investing business.

However, as I write, I am back well over the amount I need for the fund to get fully started, and as soon as we can get the administrative details sorted out, we shall be on our way.

I have had some help from Rachael, and this I'd like to share.

Rachael lives in Richland, she's 14 and she wants to do something nice for Gumpa who lives over in England and isn't very well. She knows Gumpa doesn't want presents, so she has an idea. She shares it with her mother who is happy to cooperate. They go down to the fabric store and buy some bolts of cloth and various other small items that will be useful. They begin cutting the cloth into large squares.

From now on, it is all Rachael. She is not only cutting and tying the throws to keep legs warm, but she makes a variety of kid-motif cushions and pillows, including some that are oversized. She is thinking of things that will especially appeal to the kids in her class at school. She is busy every spare moment making bangles and brooches and stringing beads and crocheting hot pads and potholders. Bookmarks and key chains and coin purses, bracelets and wristbands and necklaces all add to the variety. She makes scented soap in interesting shapes and packages them attractively. Slowly, the bundle of items increases. Her father wonders who on earth will buy them. He can see his office overwhelmed with scatter cushions and small colorful blankets.

Rachel takes a booth in a weekend Arts and Crafts fair at Badger Mountain.

Her notices to customers indicate all profits go to Gumpa's children in Pakistan. She displays a colorful poster showing pictures of Gumpa and the children he wants to help. One of her customers gives her money but doesn't want any goods, just wants to encourage a girl thinking beyond herself. Her tally is over $200. Kids do the loveliest things!

Now the second part of the story. The getting has been accomplished, but how about the process of giving? Can we make sure the help given will get to the children intended? It is going to be a long journey taking several years.

With the best will in the world it looks as though the first ten percent of the cash available is having to go to the cost of getting it in place to give away. That means only nine kids out of ten can be helped. Pity!

However, in November of 2005, the Society for Community Development in Gujranwala, Pakistan, passes a bylaw authorizing the establishment and management processes for the fund we are interested in. The essential parts of the bylaw permit the society to receive and administer funds and resources for others.

Our SMAFE fund will be supplied with a regular annual income from the Outreach Foundation USA. It shall have its own bank account(s) in Pakistan.

The intended beneficiaries of the Fund are the children of members of congregations of the Presbyterian Church of Pakistan deriving from specific areas of the Punjab. The fund is focused upon the early educational needs of these children and is not to be used to provide expensive academic education at undergraduate or graduate level.

Now comes the nitty-gritty of sharing out the available annual income.

It is already clear that the initial capital in the fund, which seemed in previous years such a milestone to reach, is going to be inadequate for the needs that will be placed before it. The current program of the Society for Community Development is itself in serious financial difficulties in funding its own greatly reduced number of schools and is looking anxiously for additional donors for its program. That, however, is not what SMAFE is about; its purpose is simply, with few strings attached, to give additional children in the boondocks some chance of early primary education.

We set down our priorities, and the parameters for the use of the fund, most carefully. Up to 50% of the available income may be awarded as scholarships to individual boys and girls. It will be used towards the costs of boarding school up to high school graduation level (tenth class). Or, it can be used for nursing school or graduation from the Christian Technical Training Centre in Gujranwala or the Building Trades Centre in Gujranwala or other related or successor institutions. This involves not only fees for schooling and for boarding, but may also include additional costs related to clothing and travel and books and medical care.

Furthermore, up to 30% may be used to open additional primary schools in the catchment area, and to fund their operations for a maximum of five years. Funds will not be given to support primary schools currently operating.

Finally, up to 20% may be used for additional educational initiatives to enhance the facilities available to assist the target group of children. Temporary support for operating budgets for a maximum of five years may be given to fresh educational initiatives. Projects for which no other funding sources exist shall have priority over projects for which other funding sources already exist but are inadequate.

We add a proviso to prevent the SMAFE becoming locked in to donors with continuing valid claims upon its limited resources. To avoid creating a long-term dependency which could stifle other initiatives, no one educational institution or organization or program shall receive support from SMAFE for more than five successive years without a break of two years without support funds.

We have done the best we can, and the funds are already flowing. If you wish to find out how SMAFE is doing, you can look at the website www. SMAFEpakistan.com.

It is not going to be long now before many more Punjabi children are going off to school each morning in the village or off to boarding school at the end of the holidays! Even a portion of the cost of this book you are reading is contributing to the quality of life of a Christian child in a Punjabi village. The help he or she needs is at last getting through. Hurrah!

As the ant said to the elephant, "every little helps," and the world is being changed. At last, maybe, it's time for bed!

Journey's End

What is Mission?
Mission is for you
A world that needs changing.
You start off
In a hurry,
Excited and, maybe, angry
At all that is wrong
That needs to be righted,
Or, perhaps,
At a slower pace
In company with others
You'll do it together,
Changing the world.
Your faith is so strong

And so much is wrong.
But, as you journey,
Things change,
Distances are not the same,
Speeds vary,
For it seems
You are standing still
And the world you are in
Is the same as the one
You thought you had left
And indeed perhaps
You are standing still
But wherever you are,
Near or far
From the startpoint
Your hearts are on fire
To change things for people.
To make life better
In some way for others,
To tell them of Him,
The great Changer of things,
Who changes all things

KENNETH G. OLD

And you who tell them
Are servants of Him.
But perspectives they change
And the globe is no longer
A ball in your hands
To be compassed with ease
But a place fixed in space
Where people are found
With hurts and with wounds,
Sometimes they're strangers,
Sometimes familiar,
And now, at last,
You are ready to start
Helping people for they
Have features and faces
And needs like your own
They too hunger and sicken
And strive for a land
And a life that is better
If not for them then
For those who come after.

Though your arms they don't seem
To reach out as far
As you think that they should
You find that they reach
And wrap around someone
Who's crying and hurting
And trying and failing
To change that same world
You're trying to change,
Hamm'ring on doors
That refuse to budge open.
Your journey by now
Has much smaller dimensions
It's puddles, not oceans,
You're crossing over.
By now you are finding
It's not where you're going
That matters
But what you are doing

a boy and his lunch

And who you are helping
And how you are giving,
Not what or how much
And though it's frustrating -
For those who're receiving
The help that you're giving
Don't know why you're giving
Or what you're saying
(Or even much care) -
You know there is concert
Of spirit, and contact is made.

By the end of the day
When all effort is done
And you are back home
You mumble somehow
'Mission completed'
Even though the only one
Changed by the journey
Might happen to be the one
Who started out long ago
To change the world -
Yourself -
For the world has been changed
For you are part of the world
Needing changing
And also, so strangely,
Part of the answer
And the world is better
For the journey you made.

KENNETH G. OLD

Glossary

ayah	childminder nurse
barrage	gated dam
basti	slum
bazar	narrow street of shops
caravansarai	staging point for camel caravans
chai	tea
chai lao!	"bring tea!"
chanda	church offering
chapati	flat unleavened bread cooked on hot steel plate
chela	disciple
chhappard	sewage pond on edge of village
chicks	curtains of thin, horizontal bamboo
chokhidar	watchman
dekha jaege!	we shall see!
ghee	clarified butter
guru	Hindu religious teacher
Haj, Hajj	pilgrimage to Mecca
hajji	Mecca pilgrim
huqqa	smoker's bubble pipe
jemadar	ganger, sub-foreman
lalaji	"dear friend"
lao!	"bring it!"
maulvi	Muslim priest
memsahiba	married woman missionary/married European woman
missahiba	single woman missionary
mujahideen	Afghan guerrillas
muster roll	thumbprint wagesheet
nanga pangas	the little naked ones
octroi	city boundary tax
padri	pastor
paratha	oily savory pastry
puggree cloth	turban
Punjab	land of the five rivers
Q'ran	The Holy Koran, Quran
Ramadan	Muslim month of fast
roshandan	clere-storey window
rupee	Pakistan coinage

safarish	influential intervention
sah'bji	"respected sir"
shalwarqamiz	shirt or shirtdress / baggy trousers
sharif	honorable
tabla	drum (small)
tonga	two-wheeled horse taxi

TATE PUBLISHING & *Enterprises*

Tate Publishing is committed to excellence in the publishing industry. Our staff of highly trained professionals, including editors, graphic designers, and marketing personnel, work together to produce the very finest books available. The company reflects the philosophy established by the founders, based on Psalms 68:11,

"THE LORD GAVE THE WORD AND GREAT WAS THE COMPANY OF THOSE WHO PUBLISHED IT."

If you would like further information, please call
1.888.361.9473
or visit our website
www.tatepublishing.com

TATE PUBLISHING & *Enterprises*, LLC
127 E. Trade Center Terrace
Mustang, Oklahoma 73064 USA